RETRIBUTION

The Legacy Series
Book Two

Jessica Ruddick

Cover design by Paper and Sage Design

Edited by Judy Roth

ISBN 978-1-946164-03-2

CHAPTER 1

I STARED DOWN THE SMOOTH metal of the gun and slowly squeezed the trigger, holding my arms steady. The bullet hit the black part of the bulls-eye. Not the center but close. I'd gotten so much better recently. No more spaghetti arms, no more locked elbows.

Grinning, I lowered my arms and looked over my shoulder at my teacher, also known as Cole, the guy who made me weak in the knees on a daily basis. We'd been practicing at the gun range for the last few weeks.

I was proud of me and he dang well better be, too. I removed the protective earwear that made me look like Princess Leia.

Cole hit the button and the target came speeding toward us. He yanked it off the clip. "Not bad."

I beamed at his praise, which was high coming from him. Trust me—he didn't hand it out lightly—but I'd definitely earned it. "I think I'm ready to upgrade."

He looked down at me and his grin quickly fell off his face. "Oh, you're serious?"

"Yes, I'm serious! You said once I could handle the .22 you'd let me practice with the 9mm."

He pointed to the bullet hole in the target. "You didn't hit the center. You haven't mastered the .22 yet."

Perhaps I should have referred to him as Cole, the guy

who made me want to punch him in the face on a daily basis. Because seriously?

I crossed my arms. "Close enough. Besides, I need to be ready. The 9mm barely slowed him down before. What good is a .22?"

The lightheartedness was sucked from the air as if by a vacuum, and I almost wished I could take back my words. Even though we'd had fun at the range, I'd never forgotten the reason we were here.

I could never forget I was a seeker for the Grim Reaper. Or that Xavier was out there somewhere.

Cole's eyes darkened and his hands curled into fists, crumpling my paper target.

"Do you think he's coming back?"

"I don't know," I answered honestly. "But I want to be ready for him."

My last encounter with Xavier nearly killed me, and it did kill Cole. Literally. Watching the life bleed out of him and not being able to stop it...

The air left my lungs, and taking deep breaths, I turned away from Cole. He didn't know about the nightmares that plagued me. And I didn't want him to. He felt guilty about the whole situation. Like it was *his* fault I'd given his name to Xavier. Like it was *his* fault Grim Reapers had tried to kill him as a result. Like it was his fault he'd died and I'd made the deal with an angel to bring him back to life at a cost he wasn't even aware of.

Yeah, Cole still didn't know he was now a seeker like me. That was what happened when my angel ancestor used his own blood to bring Cole back to life. So now Cole was technically part of that angel's line. Did that make us related in some weird, crazy way?

I wasn't thinking about that one too deeply.

And I wasn't spilling the beans yet, either. One day— probably soon—Cole would come into abilities, and I would have some explaining to do. Until then, ignorance was bliss.

"Hey," Cole whispered in my ear and wrapped his arms around me, pulling me against his chest. I breathed in his clean scent, leaning back against him. "Don't worry. I won't let anything happen to you."

Guilt washed over me in a tidal wave so high I felt like I was drowning. Would he feel the same way when he learned the truth?

I WATCHED COLE DRIVE AWAY in the Rustinator. I was hoping that after we'd "borrowed" some nicer, newer cars a while back, he might feel the need to upgrade, but nope. He was freakishly devoted to that heap of a car. Any day now I expected for us to come out to the parking lot and find it had disintegrated into a pile of rusty dust. But who was I to complain? I barely had my license, much less a car. And I especially wasn't going to whine about Cole's loyal nature. I more than reaped the benefits of that trait.

I trudged up the stairs to my apartment, unwinding my scarf as I went. Southeastern Virginia didn't have particularly harsh winters, but it had been especially cold recently. On the second landing, I stopped abruptly, sniffing the air.

Is that cinnamon?

Oh, shit. Oh, no.

My hearted pounded as I took the remaining steps two at a time, not stopping until I was just outside our door. I smelled again. Nothing. Cautiously, I unlocked the door as quietly as I could and paused for another sniff test. Still nothing.

I closed my eyes and took a few deep breaths. It must just be the neighbors baking something. Xavier wasn't back.

God, would I ever be able to endure the scent of cinnamon without it inducing a panic attack? I rubbed the faint scar on my wrist from where Xavier had broken it.

Although it was fading, he'd left his mark in more ways than one.

I stepped into our apartment and it was nearly as cold in our living room as it was outside.

Sighing, I hung my coat on the hook behind the door. My mom still wasn't one-hundred percent after an attack by Xavier left her unconscious and in the hospital for nearly a week. That meant she wasn't working, which meant money was tight. Ergo, keeping the thermostat at an ungodly temperature to keep the bills low. I didn't like it. It wasn't good for her health. I'd put in some job applications, but businesses were letting employees go in the post-Christmas rush, not hiring them.

I started to call out to my mom but thought better of it. I was glad I did when I found her asleep in the living room on the couch under a pile of blankets. I tiptoed toward the kitchen, leaving her to rest.

Our pantry was nearly bare. Same with our fridge, but we did have a few eggs. Scrambled eggs for dinner, then. I cracked them into a bowl and splashed a bit of milk in as well before whisking them with a fork. Then I poured the mixture into a pan on the stove.

I leaned against the counter to wait, spatula in hand. I wished we had some bread. Some toast or something would have been nice.

A letter on the counter caught my eye, so I picked it up. My eyes didn't make it past the bold red writing at the top: *Final Eviction Notice.*

My eyes bugged out of their sockets. *Final* notice? As in there had been more than one and my mom never bothered to mention it?

My gaze flickered back to the letter. We had until the end of next week to either pay up or get out.

"I didn't mean for you to see that."

I spun around to find my mom in the doorway, still wrapped in a blanket.

"Obviously. When were you going to tell me?"

She pursed her lips and I knew the answer—*never*. "I didn't want you to worry. I'll figure something out."

Her words didn't convince me, though. A few years ago, I would have believed her. But reality had slapped this seventeen-year-old around too many times for me to believe the impossible.

"How? You can't work." I peered down at the letter. "Can they do that? Can they really just kick us out?"

"If we don't pay, we can't stay." She smiled a bit at her little rhyme, but I was not in the mood. "Seriously, Ava. I'll figure it out."

I turned my attention to the eggs on the stove. It would suck to ruin them, especially now that we *really* couldn't afford anything.

Since Xavier had been out of our lives, we hadn't seen any sign of the new handler we were supposedly getting. I'd been happy about that, but now I was wondering if that was really a good thing because we needed help. Surely our handler wouldn't let us live on the streets.

I shook my head, clearing the thought. No, it was good we had no handler. No handler meant no new assignments. No new deaths on our consciences.

No telling Cole my big little secret.

This entire mess was my fault. I pasted a smile on my face for my mom's benefit. "Eggs?"

"That would be great. Thanks." She sat at the table and the little beads of sweat on her forehead didn't escape my notice. She was kidding herself if she thought she was going back to work any time soon. Just walking around our tiny apartment winded her.

It was up to me. I had to fix this somehow.

Like you fixed the last problem? the devil on my shoulder taunted me.

I tried to clear the negativity out of my mind. I didn't have time for it. Yet, it haunted me. How was I going to get us out of this mess?

I SLUNG MY BACKPACK ONTO the counter and perched atop my normal stool at Bill's Garage as I did every afternoon after school. "Hi Bill!" I called.

Bill stuck his head out of his office. "Hi." Then he closed the door.

I grinned widely at Cole. "Did you see that? He's totally warming up to me."

Cole chuckled. "I already told you he likes you." That was true, but I'd still made it my mission to break through Bill's estrogen-fearing ways. The man was unbelievably skittish around women. Or maybe it was just me. I'd never actually seen him with another female, just the patrons of the shop who all happened to be male.

Huh. I'd never stopped to consider that. Why were they all male? Did Bill project an anti-estrogen shield or something?

"Can I help with anything?" I asked the same question every day, and every day Cole's answer was the same.

"Nope."

We'd done our required internship at the shop last semester, but my participation in the actual mechanic work had been minimal at best. I made up for it in the report and presentation side of things, though. Even still, I liked to offer my services. You know, just to be polite. But we both knew I'd just slow him down. Cole was a skilled mechanic, more capable than a lot of people who'd been in the business for over twenty years. Or at least that's what Bill's letter for our project had said. From what I'd seen of his work, Cole knew what he was doing.

Then again, Cole *always* knew what he was doing.

"What time will you be free tomorrow?" he asked.

I frowned. "After school as usual."

"What about the field trip? Isn't it coming back late?"

I blinked several times before remembering. "I'm not going."

The field trip was a tour of several local college campuses. We'd gotten information about it way back at the beginning of the year, and I'd wanted to go, but when things got tight financially I decided not to spend the money. And now that I'd learned we were about to be homeless, I was especially glad I'd opted not to go.

Besides, there was no point. With all the moving around I had to do as a seeker, the best I could hope for was an online school. And that was only if I could secure some kind of scholarship or financial aid. I certainly didn't have a college fund waiting for me.

I hadn't wanted to think about it this afternoon. The whole time I was in my classes and at home, I couldn't take my mind off our situation. Did we have money for groceries? Was my mom ever going to fully recover? How would we pay the medical bills from my mom's stay in the hospital? At this time next week would we be homeless?

The few hours I spent with Cole every afternoon were my safe zone, the only time I let myself forget about everything. But it was becoming harder and harder lately, and it seemed I'd hit the tipping point. The shit storm that was the rest of my life had crash landed in the garage.

"Why aren't you going?" Cole asked.

I shrugged. "I changed my mind, that's all."

"Don't lie. Tell me why."

Damn him. He knew me too well.

"Fifty bucks is a lot of money just to be bussed around to the different campuses." I didn't bother coming up with a better excuse. He would know I was lying.

"I could have loaned you the money."

A loan implied I'd be able to pay it back. I wouldn't take his money, even if Bill did pay him well.

I looked down at my toes. "I'm probably not going to college anyway."

"Bullshit."

I sighed. I swore it was like Cole and my mother had melded minds over this. Both of them were unyielding in their insistence that college was in my future. They were obviously not living on the same plane of reality I was. I wasn't stupid and I could hack it in college no problem, but circumstances being what they were, it just wasn't in the cards. I hated it. I definitely wanted to go, but it simply wasn't going to happen. The sooner the two of them accepted it and stopped taunting me about it, the easier it would be to get over my disappointment.

Plus, I didn't think Cole realized exactly how much we moved around and that staying put for four years wasn't exactly an option for me. We hadn't discussed the possibility of me moving again because quite frankly, I didn't want to think about it. I couldn't bear the thought of leaving him. One problem at a time.

Except that wasn't really accurate. The problems were piling up. Maybe my policy should be more like deal with the problems when I had to. I wasn't about to invite more of them.

Would Cole be forced to move around as well? He was technically a seeker now, but since there was no sign of my new handler, I couldn't ask my questions. I still didn't know if Cole would be expected to take on assignments. My angel ancestor hadn't been clear on the stipulations when he'd saved Cole.

Not that it mattered. I would make the same decision again in a heartbeat.

There were just so many uncertainties. The only thing I *was* certain of was Cole. He was my rock, the one piece of sanity in my crazed world.

"I don't want to talk about it." I hopped off my stool and starting putting away the tools lying around. I didn't know if he was done with them yet, but I needed something to do.

"I just don't want you to mess up your life like I did."

Cole was too hard on himself. Sure, he'd had a rough past, but he'd turned himself around. His life was *not* messed up. He was only two years older than me, but sometimes the way he talked you'd think he was a geriatric with one foot in the grave.

"You could still go to college," I retorted. "Why aren't *you* going on the field trip?"

A snort was Cole's response. Even if he hadn't gotten behind in high school, he still wouldn't have been on the college track. I knew it and he knew it. My comment was just petty. It wasn't that he was stupid—he just wasn't interested in the sort of things that were taught in school. Luckily for him, he enjoyed working on cars and was good at it.

I decided to change the subject. Neither one of us was going to budge, anyway. "Do you think you could drive me to pick up some more job applications when you get done here?"

"Shit," he said. "Your mom's car. I swear I haven't forgotten. The shop has been so damn busy lately."

"No worries." It actually *was* a worry, but I wasn't going to put that on him. The transmission in our car had finally given up, but even if there was an empty bay for him to use to work on it, we didn't have the money to pay for the parts.

Money, money, money. It all came back to money these days. People said it wasn't the most important thing in life. I disagreed. Those people obviously weren't the ones who lacked it. Because life was a heck of a lot easier if you had an ample supply.

"I have a lot of work here," he said. "You can take my car if you don't want to wait."

My eyebrows raised. "The Rustinator?"

He pulled the keys out of his pocket and held them up, the keys rattling together.

I crossed over to him. "You'd trust me with your baby?" I reached for the keys, but when my hand got close, he moved them out of my reach.

The truth was I didn't even *want* to drive that stupid car except I was desperate to find a job. That and I knew how much the rusty pile of junk meant to him.

"This is huge," he said with a grin—one that was snarky and sexy at the same time. He needed a haircut, but his too-long hair only added to his bad boy looks. There was definitely a "bad boy" side to him—he didn't know how to break into and hot wire a car in half a minute for nothing—but his soul was pure. I would know—I'd seen it firsthand.

That was how seeking worked. We looked for pure white souls, and those people were then slated to be tested for angeldom.

That also meant they had to die first. That was the part I didn't like.

I wrapped my arms around him and rested my head on his shoulder. "I know."

He wrapped his arms around me, seeming to sense I needed it. When his lips touched my forehead, I exhaled. I wasn't going to burden him with my problems—he had enough of his own—but simply knowing he was there for me helped.

He slipped the keys in my pocket and the pressure of his fingertips on my hips made my heart race. I lifted my face and his lips captured mine, making my knees go weak. I tangled my fingers in the hair at the nape of his neck and pulled us closer together.

He groaned as our bodies aligned. "You're wicked."

"No, I'm not," I whispered. I didn't want to be wicked. Okay, maybe I did, just a little when Cole was involved. But the color of my aura was actually a huge concern of mine. I didn't like my seeker birthright, and I was worried that eventually my soul would turn black. *Evil.*

The color I was sure Xavier's was—if he even had a soul.

Cole gently pushed me away. "Go. If you don't leave now, neither one of us will have a productive afternoon."

That's okay was on the edge of my lips. Cole's apartment was actually above the shop, so we were steps away from privacy. I wouldn't have minded spending a few hours wrapped around each other.

But he was right. Unfortunately, we both had things to do.

CHAPTER 2

I TOOK MORE CARE DRIVING the Rustinator than I'd ever taken with my mom's car. Even though the pile of metal looked like a rusted out piece of junk to my eyes, if there was so much as a new scratch on it, Cole would know. I shuddered to think of his reaction.

I'd already applied to all of the stores and restaurants within walking distance from our apartment, so it was time to widen my search. Part of the trouble was it seemed most places wanted their employees to be eighteen, and I was several months shy of that. Did flipping burgers really require me to be a legal adult? I mean, seriously. Of course, I would have preferred to get a job working in a store, but at this point I couldn't be picky. Heck, I would have even donned a costume and stood on the side of the road waving people into Hilda's House of Pancakes or whatever. As long as it paid.

I wondered if Bill would consider dressing me up as a wrench or something.

I pulled into a strip mall and parked at one end, planning to hit every store on the row. The first one was a beauty salon, Nice Beauty. I almost passed it by, but in the corner of the window was a little "help wanted" sign. Might as well give it a try.

There was no one there except a woman with foil all

over her head sitting under a dryer. Her eyes were closed.

"Hello?" I called out. The woman under the dryer didn't move a muscle. She probably couldn't hear me over the air.

A tiny woman with dark skin and a no-nonsense expression appeared from a back room. She wore a black apron adorned with all sorts of hair clips sticking out of the pockets.

"Can I help you?" she asked, flipping her braids over her shoulder.

"Can I have a job application?" I asked.

She crossed her arms and looked me up and down but said nothing. Though she couldn't have even been five feet tall, she intimidated me.

I looked back at the sign in the window. "I saw the sign—"

"You're hired."

I blinked, not believing what I'd heard. "Are you serious?"

She shrugged. "Do you want the job?"

"Yes!" I cleared my throat, embarrassed by my zealousness. "I mean, yes, I want it. But what is the job exactly?"

She laughed. "You're about as desperate to get a job as I am to hire someone."

Dang, if she was desperate then this job really must suck. I didn't care, though. As long as the checks cleared, I'd do whatever.

After all, it couldn't be worse than being a seeker.

"Am I about done?" the woman under the dryer called out, her voice way too loud for the small space, kind of like when someone tried to talk with headphones on. I guessed being under the dryer had the same effect. I wouldn't know. My hair was stick straight, and my mom normally just trimmed it up when it got too long. I couldn't remember the last time I'd been to a proper salon.

"Five more minutes."

"*What?*" the woman yelled.

"FIVE...MORE...MINUTES!" She enunciated every syllable, then turned back to me. "I'm Shenice, and this is my shop. Anything beauty-related, I do. You want a blow-out, I'll do it. You want a pedicure, got you covered. You want a perm? Well, I don't know why you'd want a perm. It's not the nineties anymore, but whatever. I'll do that, too."

"What do you need me to do?" I asked tentatively.

"Whatever I say."

"Oh-*kay*." I didn't like the sound of that. I'd still do it, though. That's how desperate I was.

"I'm not talking anything crazy. Just sweeping up hair off the floor, scrubbing out the sinks, those kinds of thing. We're not busy right now, but sometimes we get slammed and I don't have time for all that."

I let out a breath, relieved. "I can do that."

"I can only pay you minimum wage."

"That's okay."

"You eighteen?"

My heart sunk. "No. Not until July."

Shenice crossed her arms and looked me over again. "That's fine. You'll do."

"Thank you," I said. "You won't regret it. I'm a hard worker."

She nodded. "I can tell that about you."

"Thanks."

"Wait here just a minute."

Shenice disappeared into the back room, and I took the opportunity to look around the shop. It was a bit run down with only one hair-washing station, two barber chairs, one pedicure chair, and one manicure station. Oh, and the hair dryer. The back half of the room was empty and the light bulbs had been removed from the ceiling, the shadows giving it an eerie vibe. There were several dark circles on the floor where some barber chairs used to be.

I wondered again why she was desperate to hire

someone. The place didn't look like it got enough customers to warrant another employee. It looked like it was about to go out of business.

She reappeared with a piece of paper. "Here. Fill this out and come back tomorrow with your ID."

"I'm still in school," I explained. "So I'll only be able to work in the afternoon and evenings."

"Works for me."

Wow. I couldn't believe how easy this was. Something was finally going my way.

"Okay. So thank you again, Ms..." I trailed off, realizing I didn't know her last name.

"Just call me Shenice."

"Thanks again," I said, walking backward toward the door. Shenice waved and turned her attention to the woman under the dryer.

It wasn't until I was outside holding the key at the car's door that I realized I never told her my name. *Shit.* Should I go back in and tell her? I stood, paralyzed for a few seconds before deciding not to. She'd get my name tomorrow when I reported for my first day of work.

I climbed into the driver's seat and smiled. "Yes, yes, yes!" I did a little drum beat with my hands on the steering wheel.

"What's the *yes*-ing all about?"

My heart jumped into my throat and I gasped.

Someone was in the backseat.

It took all the restraint I had not to turn around. Instead, I eased my hand into my purse, feeling for my pepper spray. Keys, lip balm, wallet, *got it.*

I pulled it out in one quick motion and turned, pointing it in the direction of the voice. "Who are you and why the hell are you in my car?"

It was a girl, and she looked at me curiously, her head cocked to the side in a way that reminded me of a bird.

Then she plucked the pepper spray out of my hands, like it was nothing.

And I just let her do it.

All I could do was gape at her as she climbed into the front seat.

"You won't be needing that. It really burns if it gets in your eyes, you know?"

I nodded dumbly. That was kind of the idea. Why had I waited? Why hadn't I just pressed on the trigger?

"I'm Xena, by the way. Your new handler."

OH, SHIT.

Now that she was in the front seat with me, an unmistakable citrusy scent filled my nostrils. It smelled like I was in the middle of an orange orchard. Or perhaps surrounded by lemon or lime trees. The scent vacillated between those three. I couldn't believe I had missed it before, but I'd been so excited about landing a job I hadn't been paying attention. Then again, even if I'd noticed, I wouldn't have thought anything of it. I certainly wouldn't have put two and two together that the scent belonged to my new handler.

Xavier had reeked of cinnamon. I hadn't given much thought as to what other handlers would smell like. I'd never met another one and hadn't particularly cared to. If I had thought about it though, I probably would have come to the conclusion they all smelled the same.

Wrong again. Why did it always seem I was wrong when it came to this whole seeking business?

Xena held out my pepper spray, shaking it a little when I didn't reach for it immediately.

"Take it," she said. "You might need it. There are some nefarious characters in these parts."

I looked at her incredulously. Was she making a joke? She couldn't be serious, could she? *She* was the nefarious character.

I took a moment to really look at her. She was slender

with angular cheekbones and straight silky black hair. She might be Asian, or at least part Asian. Her eyes were green, and I couldn't tell if the color was natural or if she wore colored contact lenses.

She dressed in all black, similar to Xavier's attire, except instead of a red tie for a pop of color, she wore a royal purple scarf around her slender neck.

If I'd seen her on the street, I wouldn't be intimidated in the least. Though she didn't appear particularly friendly, she didn't look strong, more like she'd be knocked over if the wind blew too hard.

But I'd seen and experienced firsthand what Xavier could do, and physical strength didn't play into it. I wasn't letting down my guard with this new handler.

"Why are you here?" I asked.

"I'm your new handler."

I waited for her to elaborate and when she didn't, I let out a breath. *Obviously* she was my new handler. She'd already said that. Did she think I was stupid?

But this wasn't my show to run. I didn't have anywhere to be at the moment, so I would just wait for her to get to the point. I'd learned my lesson when it came to trying to manipulate handlers.

Not that I was just going to roll over and become a puppet, either.

I looked at her and she looked back, unperturbed by the long awkward silence. Then she poked at the yellow cushion busting out of the seat underneath her.

She wrinkled her nose. "This car is really crappy."

My nostrils flared. I shared the same opinion, but I was offended on Cole's behalf anyway.

Shit.

Cole.

Was she going to visit him, too? Did she even know about him? I bemoaned my lack of knowledge, wishing I'd thought to ask my angel ancestor more questions, but I wasn't thinking straight at the time—Cole's blood had been all over my hands.

And he'd been dead.

"It's actually a really great car." I don't know how I managed to get that out with a straight face. If God was ever going to strike me down for telling a lie, now would have been a fitting time.

"Does the radio work?" She reached for the dial and fiddled with it, filling the car with static.

"Why are you here?" I asked again, even though I'd told myself I wasn't going to lead the conversation.

Xena looked at me like I was slow and turned off the radio. "I told you—"

"No, I mean why did you show up *here*? While I'm job hunting? How did you even know where I'd be? Wouldn't it be easier to find me at home? That's what Xavier always did."

Whoa, that was a lot of questions. But dang it, I *had* a lot of questions. And Xena wasn't scary like Xavier. Maybe I'd finally get some answers.

"I wanted to meet you. I don't know how I knew where you were. I just did."

I shook my head. "That doesn't make any sense."

She shrugged. "I just sort of know."

"So you can locate me at any time?"

"Not exactly. You have to be within a certain distance. So if you're relatively close by, I can find you. I think. I've never tested it. It's like you're a short-range homing device." She seemed pleased by her analogy.

It actually made sense. Xavier always seemed to know where my mom and I were, but then when I'd gone on the road with Cole, he hadn't found us.

So why didn't my mom just try to take me and hide from Xavier? If Xena was right, then all we would have had to do was get far enough away from him. I wondered if my mom knew about the homing device thing. I was guessing no. Xavier hadn't been very forthcoming with information, though from what my mom said, he'd been a lot nicer in the earlier years.

Even if we had tried to escape, I doubt we would have been successful. At least not permanently. Xavier would have caught up to us eventually. I would bet my life on it.

Speaking of Xavier finding us—

"Can Xavier still find us?"

She cocked her head. "I don't think so." Her tone wasn't too convincing.

"Do you know him?"

"Not really, but I've met him. He's kind of a prick."

I laughed out loud. I couldn't help it. Xena may be my handler, which meant I should hate her on principle, but there was something likable about her. At least we shared the same view of Xavier.

Although, in my book, *prick* wasn't strong enough of a word. I'd go with evil incarnate.

"Do you happen to know where he is?"

"You don't have to worry about him," she said firmly.

I looked out the driver's side window for a moment. I wanted to believe those words. My fear of Xavier consumed me from the inside out. The things he'd done to me, my mom, and Cole were the stuff nightmares were made of. In fact, I occasionally woke up, drenched in sweat, and feeling like he was there in my dream, boiling my blood. It made me start to doubt my sanity. Made me wonder if Xavier really could hurt me in my dreams.

So I couldn't simply take her word.

"How do you—" I turned and stopped mid-question. Xena was outside of the car, walking away. How the hell had she managed that? I'd only looked away for a second, and the passenger door squeaked like—well, a rusty door.

She waved to me and I quickly opened my door and hopped out. By the time I stood up and looked over the top of the car, she was gone.

CHAPTER 3

WHILE WE HAD SAT IN the car, night had fallen. I stood staring for a few moments, peering into the darkness. Half the streetlights were out and I couldn't see anything. It was like she'd never been here. So I got back in the car and drove away. What else was there to do?

Damn. I wish I'd thought to ask her how I could get in touch with her. Then again, I hadn't expected her to abruptly leave like that. It hadn't occurred to me to get Xena's number because I'd never wanted to contact Xavier—I always just wanted him to leave me alone. Even now, when he was supposedly out of my life, I still worried about him not leaving me alone.

I didn't know if Xena was an ally yet, but I felt a little better knowing she'd answer questions. My new handler was bound to show up sooner or later, and it could have been much, much worse. I knew that for a fact because I'd lived through much, much worse.

Xena hadn't mentioned any assignments, though. The whole thing was perplexing.

Figures. I'd solved the problem of a job only to have a new problem plopped in my lap seconds later. To be fair, the whole seeker thing was an existing problem, but I was content to remain on hiatus. It would have suited me just fine to never see another handler for the rest of my life.

I parked the car outside the garage and Cole showed up seconds later, like he'd been waiting for me.

He looked at the Rustinator with an intensity I reserved for triple chocolate truffle cheesecake, and I could tell he wanted to inspect it for damages. I tried not to roll my eyes and feel insulted. Because, seriously? How much damage could I honestly do to it?

He slung an arm over my shoulders as we walked into the shop. "You want to go to the gun range again soon?" he asked.

"Yeah."

"I'm surprised you haven't asked me already." Understandable because until yesterday, I'd been obsessed with it.

"I guess I've been preoccupied with the job search. Speaking of which..."

He opened the door to his upstairs apartment and leaned against the door frame, grinning at me. "You found one?"

"Yes!" I squealed. This was probably one of the only times in my life a sound that could be classified as a squeal had come out of my mouth, but in this instance it was perfectly justified. I needed that job.

Cole pulled me in for a quick kiss before we entered his apartment. "Congrats. I knew you'd find one." His easy confidence in me was staggering. I wish I had some of it.

Calling Cole's place an apartment was being generous. It had a small living area that doubled as a dining area and a tiny kitchenette space like the ones you'd find in a hotel. The ceiling sloped so that if you had any height at all, like Cole, you couldn't stand up straight unless you were in the dead center of the room. In the back was a small bedroom. And that was it.

I liked it, though. It suited Cole perfectly. He wasn't a high maintenance kind of guy. Although, if he ever managed to get his little brother to come live with him, he was going to need a bigger place. The situation with his brother was a whole other story, though.

"It's this place called Nice Beauty. Have you heard of it?" I flopped down on his couch.

Cole gave me a bland stare.

"Point taken. Stupid question. Anyway, the woman hired me on the spot. No interview or anything."

"Really?" Cole rubbed behind his neck, which I knew meant he was going to say something I wouldn't like. "That sounds kind of weird. Could she somehow be connected to Xavier?"

I shook my head immediately, but it kind of got me wondering again how Xena had found me there. Her explanation about me being a homing device was hard to believe.

But Shenice was genuine. And anyway, it didn't matter. No one else wanted to hire me, so I needed this job.

"No. It's not like that," I said. "I think she just really needs someone. She's nice."

I could tell Cole was still uneasy with it, but he let it go. There was no doubt he would check up on Nice Beauty and its owner. Cole didn't let people into his inner circle easily, but he took care of the ones there. And that was fine with me. If he wanted to do a little asking around about my new employer, he could have at it. Considering what we'd been through, I couldn't blame him for being wary.

"Anyway," I said, "I have to go back tomorrow."

"What will you be doing?"

I shrugged. "Whatever she needs. It's this rundown beauty salon and from what I can tell, she's the only one who works there, so she needs help."

Cole lifted my feet and sat, placing my feet in his lap. He absentmindedly rubbed my calves, which felt heavenly.

Anytime he touched me it was heavenly.

Now would be the ideal time to tell Cole about my *other* news from my job hunt—Xena. I probably should have told him that first, but he was going to flip out. I thought it might be easier to tell him once we'd already spent a few minutes together so he'd already know I was fine. At least then he wouldn't freak out about my well-being.

That's what I was telling myself, anyway. It had nothing to do with being a coward.

The appearance of Xena was going to change everything. Though Cole and I had only been together a short time, I liked our status quo. I'd known it couldn't last, but that didn't mean I had to like it.

"I talked to Kyle while you were out," Cole said before I could figure out how to break the news.

"How's he doing?" I asked. Kyle was Cole's younger brother who technically still lived with their deadbeat mom, but she was strung out half the time, so Kyle stayed elsewhere whenever he could. Lately Kyle had gotten mixed up with a gang. The last we knew, he hadn't actually joined yet, but Cole was eager to get his brother out of there before Kyle made a decision that couldn't be undone. Unfortunately, Cole needed to graduate first.

"He didn't say a whole lot, but he *never* calls me. So I think something's up." My heart sank because I knew what Cole was going to say next. And that meant there was no way I could tell him about Xena now. He'd feel like he needed to be in two places at once, and it would torture him.

Cole sighed. "I think I need to go up there."

Yup, I knew it. And I didn't like it one bit. Cole wasn't the only one with a protective streak. But I had no place keeping him from helping his brother.

"When are you going to go?"

"I don't like leaving you. Not with everything the way it is here. I don't suppose..."

I shook my head. "I can't leave my mom. I doubt she'd let me go, anyway." These days with her so weak, I was actually the one calling the shots, but I still liked to give her the guise of being in charge. I think we both knew it was a facade, though.

"I knew you'd say that." Cole sighed, scrubbing his hands over his face. "If he gets sucked into that gang…"

I sat up and put my hand on his cheek. "Hey. It's okay. There's been no sign of Xavier. And there's no reason to think a new handler will be a threat." I conveniently didn't mention that I knew for sure the new handler wasn't a threat. Well, as sure as I could be from a ten minute meeting.

"If you call me, I'll be hours away. I won't be able to get here fast enough," Cole said. He didn't say what he'd need to be fast enough for because we honestly didn't know.

I didn't like it, either. Not for my sake, but his. He was the anomaly in this. No one had ever been brought back from the dead by an angel to become a seeker. I didn't know what that meant for him, and it scared the shit out of me.

But if his brother needed him, what could I say?

"It'll be fine. Tell Kyle I said hi."

MY MOM WAS ALREADY IN bed when I got home, so I couldn't ask her if she'd met Xena. I was glad. She didn't need to worry about anything but getting better. With our financial situation, though, there was a fat chance of that.

I'd wait until the right time to tell her, and until then, it was better I kept my mouth shut. If Xena had approached her, surely my mom would tell me.

Just like you're telling her, the devil on my shoulder chided.

I shrugged it off. *I* wasn't the one still recovering from Xavier's attack. My wrist had healed. It was my mom who got winded just by being on her feet too long.

It worried me more than I wanted to admit. Seekers

were supposed to have advanced healing due to our angel ancestry. So why wasn't she better? Did Xavier do something that screwed with her blood or her DNA? It wasn't like we could turn to doctors for answers.

And why hadn't I thought to ask Xena about it yesterday? She'd just shown up so suddenly it hadn't even entered my mind to ask about my mom. I needed to make a list. The sheer amount of things I wanted to ask her could fill a book.

The next morning, my mom was up before I was, and she had breakfast waiting for me. It was just a bowl of cereal, but still, I was pleased to see her up and about. Her color looked better, too.

"How are you feeling?" I asked, scooping Cheerios into my mouth double time. I was running late.

"Better, I think," my mom said. "Maybe I've turned a corner."

I nodded and gave her the thumb's up since my mouth was full of cereal. While I was glad she was feeling better and optimistic about her recovery, I wasn't so sure. She looked healthier than she had in the last few weeks, but she still had a long way to go.

"Maybe I'll go to the grocery store this morning," she said. "We're out of a lot of stuff."

We were out of just about *everything*. The only things in the house were the essentials that I picked up every couple of days when Cole took me to the store. My mom must not have realized how out of it she'd been. If I hadn't started buying food, we would have starved weeks ago.

"The car still isn't working," I reminded her.

She looked confused. "What's wrong with it?"

"The transmission, remember?" It was clear from her expression she didn't. *Shit, shit, shit.* Was she losing her mental faculties now? I hoped I was jumping the gun in coming to the conclusion she had dementia, but with anything involving Xavier, I expected the worst. If I turned out to be wrong, then it was a nice surprise.

Most times, though, expecting the worst didn't begin to cover it.

I put my hand over hers. "Don't worry. Cole said he'd fix the transmission soon." Though if he went to northern Virginia to deal with his brother, it definitely wouldn't be anytime real soon. "In the meantime, make a list and text it to me. Cole can probably take me to the store this afternoon."

My mom nodded, then put her face in her hands. Her shoulders shook.

I wrapped my arms around her. "It's okay," I said.

"You shouldn't have to deal with all this," she whispered. "I'm the mother."

Now probably wasn't the best time to tell her I'd landed a job. And I was extra glad I hadn't told her about Xena. My mom always put on such a brave face. I hadn't realized our situation was getting to her so much.

I glanced at the clock on the stove. "I have to go." I hated to leave her like this, but if I missed the bus, I had no other way to get to school, not with our car out of commission.

She wiped her tears away with her fingertips. "Go. I'm fine. Really. Have a great day at school."

Filled with apprehension, I slipped on my coat and picked up my backpack. Before I went out the door, I looked back at my mom sitting at the kitchen table. Her shoulders looked so small, and the way they hunched over made her look so defeated.

I didn't like it. Not one bit.

CHAPTER 4

ON THE WALK TO THE shop that afternoon after school, I called my mom but got no answer. She still hadn't texted me a grocery list, either. I quickly texted her, wondering if I should go home and check on her. I didn't really have time to swing by the house if I was going to make it to Nice Beauty.

I stopped in my tracks, gnawing on my cuticle. She might just be napping. That was probably it, right?

God, I hoped so.

I resumed walking.

Even if it meant losing the job I didn't officially have yet, if I didn't hear back from her in the next half-hour, I was going home.

Cole was standing outside the shop leaning against the Rustinator when I turned into the parking lot. I walked directly into his arms, breathing in the light scent of motor oil from his work t-shirt. He held me for a few moments, seeming to sense I needed it.

"Is everything okay?" he asked, releasing me.

"I'm just worried about my mom." Behind him, I noticed his duffel bag on the front seat of the car. "You're leaving." It wasn't a question. He'd told me yesterday he probably needed to go. Though it hadn't seemed like a big deal then, now I wanted to wrap myself around him and keep him with me.

That was silly, though. Just like I had to take care of my family, he had to take care of his. Unfortunately for both of us, our families were both involved in some messed up situations.

"I'm sorry," he said. "I need to go."

"Don't apologize. Of course you have to go. Kyle needs you."

"Did something happen with your mom?"

"No," I lied. "Just normal stuff."

It wasn't a huge lie, more like a fib. Nothing had actually happened, really. And I didn't want Cole worrying any more than he already did.

My cell phone buzzed and I eagerly pulled it out of my pocket.

No groceries needed the text read.

I let out a sigh of relief. She was fine. She'd just missed my call. I was overreacting.

Except we actually *did* need groceries, so there was that. But at least she'd responded. I'd worry about feeding us later.

I tucked the phone back in my pocket and looked up at Cole. Sunlight glinted off his aviator glasses, and a navy beanie covered his hair. He looked like a total badass. A *delicious* badass. It still blew my mind that he chose me.

I was no one special. My skin was too pale, my features were plain, and I had these annoying freckles that kept appearing on my nose, no matter how much I lathered up with sunscreen. My idea of dressing up was wearing my nice hoodie and jeans without holes worn in the knees.

Cole, on the other hand, was tall, dark, and muscled, with that touch of badass thrown in. He could have any girl he wanted, but he chose me.

I didn't get it. But as long as he didn't change his mind, I was okay with that.

"Could you drop me off at the salon on your way out

of town?" I asked. "It might be a little out of your way." I'd have to figure out how to get home. Perhaps a bus station was nearby or if it came down to it, I could hoof it. It wouldn't be the first time.

"I can do better than that." He pulled a key out of his pocket and dangled it in front of me. "I told Bill how I'd promised to fix your mom's car but hadn't gotten around to it yet, so he offered you a loaner until I could fix it."

I snatched the key out of his hand and cradled it in my hands like the prized possession it was. "Is he sure?" He'd better be sure because I wasn't letting this little sucker go. Wasn't possession nine-tenths of the law?

He nodded. "Bill's a good guy. I keep telling you that."

"I know he is," I said, the familiar pang of guilt for ever doubting Bill hitting me. "I just hope my estrogen won't contaminate the car."

Cole rolled his eyes. "It's the maroon Honda on the side."

"Thanks. Seriously. This helps so much."

"Thank Bill, not me." He tucked his hands in his pockets. "I should get on the road. Traffic is gonna be a bitch."

"Be safe," I said simply.

"You, too."

We stood there staring at each other awkwardly for a moment, and I realized this was our first major good-bye. He was only going to be gone a few days, but I'd seen him every day for the last few months.

And besides that, there was Xavier and the new seeker—which Cole didn't know about yet—hanging over our heads.

I threw my arms around his neck. "I'll miss you."

He chuckled softly. "Yeah?"

Could that actually be a little insecurity in his voice?

"You know I will," I said.

"Call me if anything happens," he said. "I can be back in just over three hours."

"Okay."

"I mean it," he said, pulling back and looking me in the eyes. He knew me well. "If *anything* happens, you call me."

I watched the car pull out of the parking lot, and I wrapped my arms around myself, already feeling the loss. Luckily, I had a job to go to now. Otherwise, I might act like one of those pathetic girls who moped around because her boyfriend was gone.

If Bill were around, I'd pop in and personally thank him for the loaner car. He might not appreciate the gesture, though, because then he'd have to talk back to me. So perhaps it was better he wasn't there.

The Honda was parked right where Cole said it would be. It was basic—probably at least five years old with no bells and whistles. I clicked the button to unlock the doors and tossed my stuff in the backseat. Then I set off for Nice Beauty. I'd already filled out the application, which was a generic one printed from some internet site, and my ID and social security card were safely tucked in my back pocket.

When I walked into the shop, Shenice was sitting on a little stool at the pedicure station. She lifted the woman's foot out of the water, bringing out some of the most misshapen toes I had ever seen in my life. She hunted in her cart of tools and then proceeded to shave something off the woman's big toe.

Oh, my *ewww!*

"Is this a bad time?" I asked.

Shenice looked over at me and smiled. "You're back! I'll be done here in a few minutes. Can you put the load of towels in the washer? It's in the back room."

"Okay," I said. I laid my application on the front desk, which contained a computer with a big boxy screen, the kind that hadn't been used since I was in elementary school. It looked like the computer was at least that old and hadn't been turned on in a long time since there was a layer of dust on it. Next to the ancient computer was an old cash register and a spiral notebook like I used in school that appeared to be the appointment book.

Oh, boy. Even Bill had a more updated system than this. But I wasn't going to judge.

I headed back to where Shenice had indicated. The washer and dryer were even more ancient than the computer. A pile of towels lay on the floor in front of the washer. I opened the lid. There was already a load in there, so I moved that to the dryer. When I went to turn the dryer on, though, that was a little tricky. The knob was there and it worked, but there were no markings to tell what setting it was on.

I shrugged and turned it on. They were only towels.

The settings on the washer had also worn off, but there was an arrow drawn in black Sharpie on it that I assume indicated where the nozzle needed to be to start the wash cycle. I dumped in the towels along with some detergent and the machine cranked to life, sounding like it had been hibernating for the last few years instead of just having been used.

When I came back, Shenice was painting the woman's toes a bright red. They looked marginally better, but let's just say I wouldn't have called attention to those feet with such a bright color if they were attached to *my* legs.

The woman chuckled and smiled at something Shenice said. She looked happy having her feet pampered and engaging in small talk. I turned my back to them for a moment. God, I was being such a bitch. I hadn't said anything disparaging, but my thoughts...not good. When I'd been seeking souls for Xavier, I'd been concerned about the color of my aura—that it was slowing turning black. I was actually a rarity in that in addition to being a seeker, I had the ability to project my aura. My mom couldn't, and she said she'd never heard of anyone else doing it, but then again, we didn't know any other seekers. And it wasn't like we were going to advertise this skill to

Xavier. It was very difficult to do, and I didn't have strong control over it. Sometimes it happened while I slept without my even knowing it. But I was always petrified that one day I'd project it and be met with a black veil.

Since I hadn't had any assignments lately, it'd been on my mind less and less. But this was a good reminder that there was more than one way to a black soul and being a judgmental bitch was one of them.

"Hey—" Shenice broke off, frowning. "I don't even know your name."

I turned around. "Ava."

"Ava, come over here and meet Miss Bernie. She's been letting me paint her nails since I was a kid."

I crossed over to the two women, hoping the shame of my catty thoughts wasn't evident on my cheeks.

"So, do you want to be a beautician like Miss Shenice here?" Miss Bernie asked.

"No, ma'am," I said. I didn't consider myself a disrespectful teenager, but I didn't usually bust out the "sirs" and "ma'ams" either. I must have been assuaging my guilt.

"Oh, I just thought since you got a job in a salon you might have an interest in it."

"I do," I said hastily, lest my lack of interest in the beauty field lose me the job I didn't even officially have yet. My application was still sitting untouched on the desk.

Shenice laughed. "No, you don't. Not with cuticles like that."

I immediately spread my fingers in front of me to inspect my cuticles. Okay, so one or two—*maybe* five or six of them—had been chewed. But dang it, I'd been under a lot of stress lately. Chewing my cuticles was better than taking up smoking or something like that.

I tucked my hands behind my back. "They may need a little work."

"Relax," Shenice said. "I don't care if you eat your cuticles for breakfast. Although I wouldn't recommend it."

She made a face. "Germs, ugh."

I grimaced. "Yeah, I guess it is kind of gross. It's a stress thing."

"Why are you stressed, baby girl?" Miss Bernie said.

I ran my toe along the line of the linoleum while I figured out what to say.

Oh, you know how it is. Sentencing good people to death in my free time really takes its toll. And did I mention I'm about to be homeless?

"My mom can't work because she's sick, so we need money." Short, simple, and *true*. The closer I could stick to the truth, the better. Less lies to get caught up in.

Not that I was a huge liar, but these days, sometimes it was necessary. If the situation with Xavier had taught me nothing else, I learned that right and wrong weren't always so clear cut.

"You're a good daughter." Miss Bernie pointed her finger at me. "I can tell how much you want to help your mama, but don't let your schoolwork go. I dropped out of high school and didn't finish until twenty years later. Biggest mistake of my life."

"Don't worry," I said. "I'm on top of it."

"You going to college?"

What was it with people lately and the college questions? Geez, I was still a junior. As the guidance counselors at school were quick to tell us, it was never too early to think about college, but for me, kind of, yeah, it was. I had no idea what the state of my life would be like a week from now, much less a *year* from now.

"I'm not sure yet." I averted my eyes as I spewed the blatant lie. I wasn't going. How could I?

"Don't pressure her," Shenice said. "Leave the girl alone."

"Is there anything else you want me to do?" I asked.

"It's pretty slow today, so I'll probably close early. Maybe just straighten and clean. Supplies are in the back."

"On it," I said.

I hoped business picked up. I didn't want to be out of a job when I'd barely even started.

CHAPTER 5

I PARKED WAY FARTHER AWAY from my apartment than I needed to, just to make sure no one else parked next to the loaner car and banged their doors into it. I wasn't taking Bill's gesture for granted, and I wanted to return the car in the same condition I'd received it.

I walked past the apartment management office and sighed. Closed. Again. Now that I had a job, I needed to talk to the manager to explain our situation and see if we could work something out. By the time I got home every night, though, he'd already left. They were supposed to stay open until nine, but most nights the closed sign was posted by seven. I'd never met the manager, but I hoped that once he talked to me, he'd see we weren't deadbeats— just good people in a bind.

Sure, we could move to another apartment, but I knew for a fact these were the cheapest in town. If we couldn't afford to live here, then where else could we go? And I didn't want to put my mom through a move. She needed to lay low.

I pulled my phone out and stared at it as I walked, willing it to ring. Cole promised he'd let me know when he got there, and I hoped he'd call instead of text. I wanted to hear his voice.

I was so focused on my phone I didn't notice our front door was wide open until I was nearly up to it.

"Oh, shit!" I bounded up the last few steps and burst into the room. I didn't know what I expected to find, but it wasn't my mom and *Bill*, of all people, packing boxes.

"Language, young lady," my mom said, using valuable energy to give me the mom glare. I tried not to roll my eyes. Seriously? With everything else going on, she was worried about my use of a curse word?

"What's going on?" I asked, my eyes wide and my feet rooted to the floor. Half of our belongings were packed up in old motor oil boxes. Bill was up to his elbows in our things. That was a sight I never thought I'd see.

"Packing," my mom said.

I wanted to say *no shit*, but I didn't need a lecture about nice girls and bad language.

"I can see that," I said, using all my will power to keep the sarcasm at bay. "I thought we had until next week."

"We don't have the money," my mom said quietly, looking down at her hands. I knew that was hard for her to admit. The last we talked about it, she'd confidently said she'd handle it.

"But I got a job!" I exclaimed, wishing I'd gone against my instinct and told her. "I was taking care of it."

She shook her head. "A part-time job isn't enough to keep us afloat. Bill called—"

"*Bill called?*"

"Yes," my mom snapped. Bill ducked his head down and disappeared into her bedroom. I immediately felt bad.

"Sorry," I said. "I'm just surprised. I didn't realize you and Bill talked."

"He calls to check up on me every couple of days. He caught me at a bad time today, and I told him about the eviction."

I was a little bitter about her willingness to talk to him about our problems when she hadn't even planned on confiding in me.

I looked around at all the boxes and put my hands on my hips. "So where are we going?"

"Bill's house."

"*Bill's house?*" I screeched, not able to contain my shock.

"Is there an echo in here?" My mom's eyes fired up for a second, then she sighed. "Sorry. I know this is hard for you. Bill offered to let us move in with him until I get back on my feet. I couldn't say no."

"But..." I trailed off, trying to comprehend this new turn of events. First of all, I had *no idea* my mom and Bill had kept in touch after everything that had happened last fall. Second of all, *we were moving in with Bill?* Wouldn't our estrogen be bad for his health?

"Once I agreed," my mom explained, "Bill showed up an hour later with his truck full of empty boxes. He said there's plenty of room and a bedroom for each of us."

I looked at the pile of empty boxes stacked by the front door. There was no way we'd need them all. Since we moved so often, we traveled light. Plus we'd never had a lot of money for anything beyond the essentials.

My mom closed the distance between us and put a hand on my arm. Her eyes were clear and lucid, not cloudy and confused like they were this morning. But there were huge dark circles and she looked wobbly, like she'd fall over at any moment.

"We didn't touch your room," she said. "I figured you'd want to do it."

I nodded. "You should rest. I'll take care of the rest of it."

"Bill's done almost everything. He made me sit on the couch while he packed."

Thank goodness for that. Good old Bill.

It didn't take long to pack up my stuff. My clothes fit in the one big ratty suitcase we had, and all of my other stuff fit in two medium size boxes. I quickly packed up my mom's room while she and Bill finished with the kitchen.

An hour later, I followed Bill's pick-up truck out to a part of town I'd never been to. Once we passed Walmart, the busyness of the city died away, leaving fields on either side of the road that narrowed to two lanes. Bill turned onto another curvy two lane road. I scrambled to keep up with him, my knuckles whitening on the steering wheel. There were deep ditches on both sides of the road, and I was petrified a deer was going to dart out of the trees at any moment.

After about two miles, he turned left onto a gravel drive and I followed him. When he stopped in front of the house, motion lights came on, lighting up the exterior.

The house was huge. Well, not huge *huge*, but huge considering only Bill lived there. Unless he had a family stashed away somewhere I didn't know about?

There was a two-car garage and a huge wraparound porch. The shutters were a cheery red against white vinyl siding. White lace curtains hung in the windows.

I got out of the car and stood next to it, my hands shoved in my pockets. I didn't know what to make of this. It was so *domestic*. I'm not sure where I pictured Bill living, but this wasn't it.

Bill helped my mom out of the truck and went around to drop the lift gate. He hefted the largest box, and I ran over to help unload. We'd only brought stuff—no furniture. I didn't know if the plan was to go back for that later when there was someone to help or what. It would be no big loss if we left it there.

I grabbed two of my mom's bags and hauled them up the front steps.

"Upstairs. First door on the left," Bill said gruffly, passing me on his way out the front door.

"Okay," I said, staring after him. The stairs were right inside the front door so I went straight up instead of looking around downstairs like I wanted to.

The door was shut, so I dropped one of the bags to

open it. I was greeted by a slightly musty smell. Not strong like an attic, but just enough to know this room wasn't used much, if at all. It was homey, with a worn patchwork quilt on a double bed and a small matching dresser and nightstand. An old wooden rocking chair sat in the corner, and there were cobwebs connecting the bottom curving pieces to the hardwood floor. It looked like the rest of the room had hastily been dusted, but he missed a spot on the dresser. I wiped it with my thumb and smeared the dirt on my jeans.

Bill still hadn't come back in, so I gave into my curiosity, leaving my mom's bags there and wandering down the hall. I paused at another door that was shut, suddenly petrified I was going to find myself in Bill's room.

That would just be too weird.

My curiosity got the better of me, and I opened the door with one hand near my eyes, in case I needed to suddenly shield myself. It was a girl's room. I could tell by the pink bedspread and ruffly curtains. An *outdated* girl's room, judging by the poster of 'N Sync hanging on the wall. I only knew who they were because Justin Timberlake managed to make it through boy band purgatory and come out successful.

I wandered over to the mirror, which had gobs of pictures stuck in the frame. A girl with hair similar to mine was in most of them. Some of them showed groups of teens, mostly girls, and a much younger Bill was in a few of them. One in particular caught my attention—the girl wore a pink prom dress and Bill stood next to her in jeans and his trademark Bill's Auto Repair t-shirt, a shy smile on his face. His gaze was directed at her, though, and it was one of pure love.

A scuffling sound at the door caught my attention and I turned around to find Bill standing there, his hands shoved in his pockets.

I blushed. "Sorry." Although we were apparently

going to be living here now, I still felt like I was snooping, which I technically was. The ground rules hadn't been set yet.

"Your mother can take the first room, and you can sleep here," Bill said. "I hope the room suits you."

"No, this is great," I said. "Who's the girl in the pictures?"

Bill kicked at a floorboard with the toe of his boot, his eyes trained on the floor, and guilt struck me. There was much more to Bill than I gave him credit for.

"You don't have to answer," I said. "I'm sorry for prying."

"My daughter," he said. "My daughter, Jill."

CHAPTER 6

MY MOUTH FELL OPEN A little. *"Your daughter?"*

Bill nodded and stepped into the room, fingering the curtains. "She liked pink."

I noticed his use of past tense, so I hesitated but I had to know. "Where is she now?"

"She passed away some years ago." Though he said it was years ago, the pain in his voice was raw, like it was recent.

Or perhaps it was a wound that never healed.

"I'm sorry," I said.

"It's okay," he said. "You can take down the pictures if you want to. I didn't have time."

It seemed Bill wasn't good at lying, either.

"No," I said. "I'll leave them up."

He nodded, then left the room.

I dropped onto the edge of the bed. Deep down, I'd known there had to be more to Bill than met the eye, but I didn't expect this. I didn't know why not—having a family was totally normal, one of the most normal things in the world.

I immediately wondered about the girl's mother. I assumed she was no longer in the picture. Bill didn't wear a wedding ring, not that that necessarily was a guaranteed indicator of marital status. He was rough around the edges, so I doubted he had a woman looking after him.

No, Bill was definitely a bachelor.

But obviously, he hadn't always been. The evidence was covering the mirror, staring at me.

My phone chimed and I pulled it out of my pocket.

Sorry it's late. Got caught up with Kyle. But I made it.

I was actually a little glad Cole had texted instead of called, which made me feel guilty. All day I'd wanted nothing but to hear his voice, but I wasn't ready to discuss my new living arrangements with him. Not yet.

I fired off a quick text, then gathered my hair in a ponytail and trotted downstairs to help carry the rest of our stuff in.

BILL WAS GONE BY THE time I came downstairs the next morning. Last night after carrying in all our stuff, which now sat in neat stacks in the middle of his living room, he'd made himself scarce. My mom and I had gotten ready for bed immediately. And though it'd been a long day, I lay awake for hours in Bill's daughter's bed. It somehow felt wrong to sleep in the bed, like I was contaminating it or something. The drawers and closet were empty, but it didn't look like much else had changed. Was it a shrine to his late daughter? The thought disturbed me.

Eventually my tossing and turning gave way to sleep, and my alarm went off too soon. My world might have been completely turned on its axis, but the rest of the world was still moving along as usual, which meant school.

My mom sat at the kitchen table with a mug of coffee in her hands. "Good morning."

"Hey," I said, giving her a quick once-over like I'd grown accustomed to doing. She seemed no worse for wear, like the move hadn't affected her. We were used to moving, but this one was different than the others.

"Bill said there's not much but to help yourself to whatever you can find."

I nodded and opened a few cabinets at random. His kitchen was fairly well outfitted. There was even a bread machine, though I couldn't picture Bill baking fresh bread.

I found some bran cereal in the pantry and luckily there was some milk in the refrigerator. It tasted like tree bark, but at least I would get my daily fiber allotment.

"I can go to the store and pick up some stuff," I said between bites. "So we don't eat all of Bill's food."

"That's a good idea," my mom said and her eyes met mine. "I know you're mad at me."

I put my spoon down. I hadn't planned to bring it up because I didn't want to cause her any more stress, but since she mentioned it—

"I can't believe you made this decision without talking to me first," I said. Part of me said to let it go, but I didn't want my feelings to fester and damage our relationship. We'd only recently gotten back on track after the fallout of my sweet sixteen birthday present—coming into my birthright of being a seeker.

"I didn't have much of a choice," she said quietly. "I'd just started researching women's shelters."

My spoon fell out of my hand and clattered in the bowl. I didn't realize she'd done that. But realistically, what choice did we have? If I was honest with myself, my part-time job and trying to work things out with the apartment manager was a hail Mary.

"This is definitely the better option," I said, suddenly wanting to reassure her and feeling like a sullen brat for complaining. "It just took me by surprise. I didn't even realize you and Bill talked."

"He's really a nice man. He had a family once. He doesn't talk about it much, but a few little things he's said clued me in."

"I'm staying in his daughter's room."

My mom nodded.

I hesitated for a moment. "It feels weird. It looks like he hasn't changed anything in there."

"I think he's had a hard time letting go."

"I shouldn't be staying in her room. It's not right."

"He wouldn't have put you there if he didn't want you to stay there. I think it's a big step for him. In a good way."

I thought about that for a moment. Cole was always telling me Bill liked me. Given how Bill seemed to avoid me, I never really believed him. But maybe Cole was right. And maybe his avoidance of women was part of a larger story.

"Do you know what happened to her?" I asked. I'd known Bill as long as I'd known Cole, but I knew so little about him. I still couldn't believe he'd been a father.

She shook her head. "Not really. He doesn't talk about her and I don't press. I know she was young when she died."

"What about the girl's...Jill's mother?" It felt weird saying her name.

"I don't know. And if I did, I don't think I would tell you." She put her hand up at my disgruntled expression. "It's not my story to tell. Bill is a private person and if he confides in me, then I'll keep his confidence. He's got a good heart. That's enough for me."

I STARTED THE CAR AND flipped the heat on high, thankful it worked better than the heat in our car. The car was in the shade and the windshield was iced over, so I adjusted the setting to include defrost. If there was an ice scraper, I hadn't seen it. Of course, I hadn't looked very hard, either. That would require me standing in the cold and rooting through the trunk. I'd much rather sit in the toasty driver's seat and wait for the defrost to do its job.

The passenger door opened suddenly, and I jumped,

flattening my back against the driver's side door, my hand at my throat.

I relaxed—just a bit—when I saw it was Xena. I needed to work on my reaction. What if it hadn't been her? What if it had been Xavier?

Damn. This was twice now she'd snuck up on me. And in two different cars. I hoped she wasn't planning to make this a habit. If she was, I wouldn't have to worry about Xavier because I'd end up having a heart attack.

Dead at seventeen from a heart attack. That would be just my luck.

"Jesus," Xena said. "It's cold out there."

I cocked my head. "Are you allowed to say that?"

"What? That it's cold?"

I shook my head. "Never mind."

"This car is definitely an upgrade over the other one."

"Thanks." I didn't know why I said that. Neither one was my car, and anyway, it didn't matter. I glanced over my shoulder at the house where I'd left my mom sitting with her coffee at the kitchen table. *Shit, shit, shit.* Was Xena going to approach my mom? I wanted to keep the handler away from her for as long as possible. She didn't need to be seeking anytime soon.

Then a thought occurred to me. With my mom in her weakened state, would she even be able to seek? Looking at auras sucked up energy—perhaps that was why I'd always been able to eat like a linebacker and not gain any weight.

Hurry up, I urged the defrost. There was a small spot of visibility, but it was still too dangerous to drive yet.

"Can you tell me more about Xavier?" I asked. There were so many other things I wanted to know but most pertained to my mom and Cole, and I didn't want to remind her of either of them. So maybe I could keep her distracted and get some valuable information.

"What do you want to know?"

I shrugged. "He was around my whole life, but I don't

know much about him. Like, for instance, what is he?"

Xena looked at me for a moment, seeming startled by the question. I realized then that it might pertain to her as well, so oops. Perhaps that was a bit rude. But I deserved to know more about the person—or people—who ruled so much of my life.

"A fallen angel, of course," she said. "And before you ask, yes, I'm a fallen angel, too. All handlers are."

That surprised me. Although I'd only met one angel, I could safely say that Xavier had no angelic qualities.

The jury was still out on Xena.

"How does one get to be a fallen angel?" I asked. "I know the story about one..." I trailed off, not sure if I should advertise I'd met my angel ancestor. He wasn't supposed to have any contact with me, and besides that, the story concerning why I met him revolved around Cole, so I'd best keep my mouth shut.

"Different ways." She shrugged. "Some do bad things and get forced into it. Others volunteer."

"They volunteer? Really?"

"Being a fallen angel isn't necessarily a bad thing. I realize it has negative connotations, but it's not like fallen angels are demons. They're just...fallen."

Well, that explained it.

"I actually know the story about Xavier," she continued. "He and another angel came to Earth for a while, and each of them developed relationships with mortal women. I don't know the exact details, but eventually they both wanted to return to heaven. Xavier's friend was allowed, but he wasn't. And he's been a handler ever since."

That story sounded a little too familiar for comfort. Exactly how many angels had left heaven to be with women? Had that been a trend at one time? I hoped it was. I hoped there were scores of angels who did just that because I did not want to consider that my angel ancestor and Xavier had been friends once upon a time.

The windshield was finally clear enough for me to drive, so I clicked my seatbelt. "Do you mind if we continue this conversation on the drive to school? I don't want to be late."

And I wanted to get Xena away from my mom. It was silly, though. If Xena just appeared out of thing air anytime she wanted to see me, she could probably do the same thing for my mom, but I had to try.

She shrugged, which I had learned was one of her signature moves. "Sure. I don't have anywhere to be."

I peeled out of the driveway.

"Do all fallen angels have abilities?" I asked, keeping both eyes on the narrow road and cringing when a big truck approached.

"Sure. Don't people all have some sort of abilities?"

"No. I mean, yes, but...that's not what I mean."

"I know." She grinned. "I'm just messing with you. But to answer your question, yes, we do. The abilities differ depending on the angel."

I was betting hers had something to do with stealth movement or "Beam me up, Scotty" travel abilities or something like that. All in all, that wouldn't be a bad ability.

"Xavier could do some freaky things," I commented, not wanting to go into detail. The very thought of what he could do sent chills to my soul.

"Yes, I'd heard about that. It's rather unfortunate."

Unfortunate. She didn't know the half of it.

"You're telling me," I muttered, pulling to a stop at a traffic light. "So if a handler, let's say, *does* something to a person, is it permanent?"

I didn't know how to ask that without mentioning my mom.

"Are you referring to your mom?"

So much for my attempt at covertness. Was there anything these handlers didn't know about us?

"Yes," I admitted. I squeezed my eyes shut for a

moment, willing the visions of Xavier suffocating my mom to exit my brain. That had been the least of what he'd done. I hadn't been there to witness the real damage that had caused her current plight.

But I could imagine.

"Handlers aren't supposed to do things like that." Xena sounded troubled.

"But *he did*. So how do we fix it?" The desperation in my voice was thick, but I couldn't help it. I *was* desperate.

"I don't know."

That wasn't the answer I wanted. I wanted Xena to tell me she could wave her hand and invoke her own fallen angel voodoo and undo the damage Xavier had inflicted. Or at the very least, I wanted her to provide more information. But it seemed she was as clueless as I was.

Why couldn't anything be easy?

I pulled into the parking lot and stopped, earning a honk from the car behind me. I hadn't thought about where to park. I didn't have a parking permit. Dang. I'd have to find street parking in the nearby neighborhood.

"Is this your school?" Xena asked. "It's nice."

"I guess." I tapped my steering wheel impatiently. People were taking their sweet old time to walk across the parking lot, and they thought nothing of stepping right in front of my car. And now that I had to get back out of the lot, find street parking, and hoof it back to school, I was pressed for time. And that was assuming I could manage to parallel park on the second or third try.

"You don't have to worry about your mom," Xena said, and I couldn't tell if my whiplash was from her yet again abrupt shift of conversation or my slamming on the brakes when a punk freshman ran into the aisle without even looking.

"How can you say that? She's sick, no one knows what's wrong with her, and she's not getting better."

"I mean, I'm not going to bother her. Not while she's unwell."

Well, that was something at least.

A block and a half away from the parking lot I found a space that was wide enough for a bus, so I was confident I could get the car in there. I turned my head so I could see to start backing in, and Xena stood on the curb.

How did she do that?

I shook my head and added it to my list of questions.

CHAPTER 7

NOT THIRTY SECONDS AFTER THE final bell sounded, my phone rang. I answered it with a big smile on my face.

"Cole, hi. How's it going?"

Even with everything else going on, I still missed him like crazy. I was so ready to hear his voice.

"Why didn't you tell me you were being evicted?"

Or maybe I could have stood to wait a few more minutes...or days. This wasn't a conversation I wanted to have right now. I grabbed the last book I needed from my locker and slammed it shut.

"Um..."

"Ava, that's so messed up. I heard from Bill. *From Bill*, who you never even talk to!"

"I didn't want you to worry." A lame but true excuse.

"That's beside the point." The frustration was evident in his voice, and I could almost see him pacing while he gripped the phone.

"No, that *is* the point," I said. "You've got enough stuff to worry about. My mom and I were handling it."

"Obviously not if you had to move in with Bill."

I took the phone away from my face for a minute to stare at it. Then I put it back up to my ear, my jaw clenched. "That's not helpful, Cole. In fact, it's downright hurtful."

"Goddammit, Ava, I shouldn't learn stuff about my girlfriend from my boss."

"So he's just your boss, now? How convenient." Bill was more than just Cole's boss. It was almost like Bill was Cole's patron or something—he'd given him both a job and a place to live. Cole had never defined their relationship, but it wasn't as simple as boss and employee.

"You know what I mean. Look, I don't want to fight with you over the phone."

But you do want to fight with me in person? I bit back the thought.

"Me, neither." I paused, forcing myself to swallow my anger. "How's Kyle?"

Cole sighed. "Not good. He borrowed some money and then gambled it away in a poker match. Now he can't pay it back. If it's not one thing with that kid, it's another."

"So he wanted money? That's why he called you?"

"Yeah."

"What about the gang?"

"He's still hanging out with them, but he assures me he's not planning to join, for what that's worth."

Not much. I'd only met Kyle once and he didn't seem like a bad kid, but he was definitely impressionable and aimless.

I noticed Cole didn't mention his mom, so I didn't ask, though I did wonder if he'd gone to see her. But if he wasn't going to bring it up, then neither would I.

"You can only do so much," I said.

"I know." He sounded defeated, and I knew he felt like he was failing his brother. "I should go."

I hated ending the conversation like this, both with him feeling down and being at odds with one another. It was unfamiliar territory and it left my stomach in knots.

"When will you be home?" I asked.

"Probably tomorrow. The more time I spend with Kyle, the more I can steer him in the right direction, but I can't miss much more school if I want to graduate."

Guilt hit me with a pang. He'd missed a lot of days in the fall because of the shenanigans with Xavier. Cole had defeated the odds stacked against him and was getting his life on track. His biggest motivation was saving his brother from making the same mistakes. I hated that Cole's involvement with me may jeopardize that.

But things had already been set into motion that I couldn't change. It was only going to get worse.

"I miss you," I said quietly.

"I miss you, too. So," he paused, "is there anything else I need to know?"

His tone was joking, but the question rang true. But there was no way I was going to tell him about Xena on the phone. His response would be to jump in the car and break every speed limit on the way home. Kyle needed to be his sole focus right now. I could handle Xena on my own. Besides, there was nothing to handle. Not really. So far she just showed up at random times and wanted to chitchat. I had the chitchat thing locked down. I *was* a teenage girl.

"Same old," I said. *Liar.*

Shenice told me to come by after school, so I trudged out to my car—stopping briefly to admire my awesome parallel parking skills—and headed to the salon. When I'd asked her about a schedule, she'd kind of shrugged and changed the subject. I wasn't wild about that, but she was the boss. Maybe after I'd been there for a while, we could agree on something more regular.

At a red light, I flipped through the radio stations, looking for one that didn't play commercials every three seconds. When I looked back up, the light was green.

And Xavier was standing on the corner.

I blinked and peered closer, but the car behind me honked, causing me to jump and look away. By the time I looked again, he was gone. I cut over and took an illegal left, going down the street he may have disappeared on. My hands were sweaty on the vinyl steering wheel, and my heart tried to pound its way out of my chest.

What was I doing? Shouldn't I be running away from Xavier and not trying to follow him?

If that really was him. I had only seen him for a second, and he'd been on my mind so much lately. Maybe it was just a manifestation of my fear. Yes, that's probably what it was.

But I had to know for sure.

It was difficult to keep my eyes on the road and search for Xavier. I nearly ran the next red light. There was no sign of him. And now I was late for work.

Well, not exactly, but I told Shenice I'd be there right after school.

Shit. Had I really seen Xavier? Or was my mind playing tricks on me?

WHEN I ARRIVED AT THE shop, I stopped at the front desk and flipped the appointment notebook to the back to note the time. Big shock, but there was no formal time clock, so I was keeping track of my hours there.

The door clanged behind me, and I jumped, a little shriek also escaping. I spun, my fists in the air.

It was a delivery man. I dropped my hands. I don't know what I was going to do with them, anyway. I wasn't trained in hand-to-hand combat.

Although I probably should be. I'd focused on learning to use a gun because I figured that would be the only thing that might stop Xavier, but what if Xavier really was on the street? And he'd followed me here? I had no gun. So what good would it be to know how to use one?

I wished I was eighteen so I could get my own gun and apply for my concealed carry permit. My mom wouldn't like it, but what she didn't know wouldn't hurt her. It might even save her life.

Until then, I would have to get Cole to teach me some hand-to-hand skills.

"Delivery for Shenice Watkins," the man said. "Sign here."

"Oh, um, okay." I took the stylus he offered and scribbled on the pad. I hoped I was allowed to sign for stuff for her.

I set the box on the desk.

"Shenice?" I called out. The shop wasn't that big and there was no one else here. Wouldn't she have heard me come in?

She stuck her head out of the back room. "I'm here! This stupid washing machine is so loud I didn't hear you." She ducked back into the room.

So how would she hear any customers who might come in? There was a huge sign in the window inviting walk-ins. She might want to think about a bell or something. I walked to the back room.

"That's a lot of towels," I commented.

There were piles and piles of them. I didn't get it. I just did a load the other day, and there was no way she could have used this many towels since I was here last, not with the scarcity of customers.

Shenice looked at them, unperturbed by my observation. "It never hurts to be prepared."

I shrugged. As I picked one up to start folding, Shenice perked up, turning her head so her ear was closer to the door.

"That must be my next appointment." She left, but I stayed behind to finish folding. I'd cleaned the whole shop last time, so I didn't know what else she'd need me to do considering the lack of customers.

How the heck was she managing to keep the business afloat? Did she at least make enough money to pay me? Maybe most of her business occurred while I was at school. I hoped so.

Once I was done, I went to find Shenice to see what I should do next.

Instead, I found Xena sitting in the barber chair with

foil all over her head.

My tongue nearly fell out of my face with how far my jaw dropped.

Shenice walked past me on the way to the back room. "I need more color."

I rushed to Xena. "What are you doing here?" I hissed.

"Getting my hair colored. I'm going with purple streaks." Her brow furrowed. "I hope they don't come out too dark."

"That's not what I mean and you know it." I crossed my arms. "Out of all the salons you had to come into this one?"

Xena shrugged. "I heard good things about Shenice."

"From who?" I threw my hands up. "The shop is empty most of the time."

Xena's eyes focused behind me, which meant Shenice was coming. *Shit.* I shot Xena a look that meant *You better behave.* She just scrunched up her eyes and shook her head like she didn't understand, but she knew damn well what I meant.

I hovered while Shenice went back to work on Xena's hair.

"So are you still in school?" Shenice asked.

"No," Xena said, her eyes slanting over toward me. "I'm a lot older than I look."

"Girl." Shenice laughed. "I won't ask you how old you are, but you don't look any older than Ava here. Is this amount of color okay?"

Xena nodded. "Looks great."

"So what do you do for a living then?"

Shenice was just making small talk like all good beauticians do. I swear they must be required to take Small Talk 101 in beauty school.

Xena glanced at me again and opened her mouth to answer. Before she could get any words out, I started coughing, working so hard to make it convincing that I forced myself into an actual coughing fit.

Shenice pounded me on the back. "Are you sick? You could've taken a sick day, you know. I wouldn't hold it against you. It's all that cuticle chewing. Germs. I told you."

"No, I'm fine." I gasped for breath. "I just choked on some...spit."

"Why don't you go in the back and get yourself a drink of water or something."

"No, it's okay. I'm fine."

"I got this, Ava," Shenice insisted. "Go on."

I reluctantly shuffled toward the back room. What was I going to do—tell my new boss no? In the thirty seconds I was gone, I think I had twenty-seven almost heart attacks. When I got back, though, Shenice and Xena were talking about the latest season of *The Bachelor* and which girls were more likely to end up in a cat fight by the end of the season. Apparently, Danielle, because she had shifty eyes and an attitude.

For all intents and purposes, it looked like Xena really was here to get her hair done. Maybe I should be grateful to her for giving the salon some business, but I couldn't shake the sneaking suspicion she was up to something.

I couldn't figure out her deal. Three times now she'd shown up randomly and none of the visits seemed to have a purpose. She just wanted to chitchat. It was so weird, and I couldn't tell yet if that was weird in a good way or in a bad way.

An hour later, Xena was admiring the royal purple streaks in her hair, which matched perfectly with the scarf she had tied around her arm. "I love it, Shenice. Thank you."

"You're welcome," Shenice said. "Come back when you're ready for a touch-up."

Xena handed over a wad of cash, which Shenice stuck in her bra. Then Xena left.

She...could...not...keep...doing...this!

Like I had any authority over it anyway.

I picked up the broom and started sweeping the stray hairs.

"After you're done with that, you can go on home. I'm closing up early tonight," Shenice said. "And I think I'll close for the next few days. I don't have any appointments."

I didn't have a business degree or anything, but if she wanted people to come to her salon, shouldn't she adhere to her posted hours? How was she making enough money to stay in business? Maybe that was why she had trouble keeping an employee. Maybe they saw the writing on the wall and flew the coop before the business went belly up.

I wondered if I should spend the next few days looking for another job.

"Okay," I said, leaning down to guide the broom into the dustpan. "When do you want me back?"

"I'll call you," Shenice said. "I'm not sure what my plans are yet."

"Okay," I said again, this time through clenched teeth.

AT LUNCH THE NEXT DAY, my friend Kaley squinted at my trig homework. "No, you've got this one wrong. You did cosine, but it was supposed to be sine. See?" She pointed to my error.

I peered at it, and the numbers and words all swam together. "Okay."

She sighed. "You still don't get it, do you?"

No, I didn't. And the trouble was I didn't really care. Kaley was a saint for trying to tutor me, despite my surly attitude.

I meant that almost literally. She was one shade away from having a completely white aura. Unless I was actively seeking, I kept my guards in place. Life was easier if I wasn't constantly distracted by everyone's auras. Well, not everyone's. I could only see auras from those near my age, which basically meant everyone I went to school with.

Anyway, I still checked her aura from time to time, just to make sure she hadn't gone completely saint on me. Though I'd never met another seeker other than my mom, they had to be out there. And I didn't want to take any chances with my friend.

I didn't know what I would do if the Reapers came after her. Seriously—I didn't know. Try to save her somehow, but that was what I'd done with Cole and it hadn't panned out so well.

I wondered if I should try to corrupt her as a preventive measure. If her aura was darker, she'd be safe. But that raised another bevy of concerns. Like should I really try to corrupt one of the few truly good people in the world? What would that mean for the greater good of humanity?

I was way too young to have to worry about this crap.

"Sorry, Kaley," I said. "I'm having trouble focusing."

"Is everything okay?" Her eyes were kind and concerned.

I started to chew on my cuticle, but Shenice's warning about germs rang in my mind, so I fiddled with my pencil instead. "My mom and I had to move. She's still sick and can't work."

"I'm sorry about your mom."

Kaley hadn't met my mom until after she became sick, but the two of them liked each other. My mom was simply thrilled that I had a girlfriend.

It wasn't like I was a social leper or anything, but once I learned about my duties as a seeker, I cut myself off from other people. It was a matter of self-preservation really. I didn't want to have to turn in someone I cared about. My plan had worked, too. Until Cole.

"You know Bill?" I asked. At her blank stare, I elaborated. "He owns the garage where I did the internship with Cole?"

"Oh, yeah. Sure." Kaley hadn't met him, but she knew

who he was.

"We moved in with him."

"Huh."

Yeah, huh.

Kaley didn't say much else about it, though. She was probably the least judgmental person I'd ever known. I didn't know why I thought we deserved to be judged. I guess I wasn't used to taking handouts, and that was what this felt like—one Bill-sized handout. My mom and I had always taken care of ourselves—we'd had to with all the moving we did and no family to speak of. So leaning on Bill like this was going to take some getting used to.

And even though he claimed it wasn't an imposition, it had to be. He'd been living alone for almost two decades and then two women moved in with almost no notice. That would drive even the saintliest person batty.

By the end of lunch, I was still nowhere closer to understanding the Trig concepts Kaley had tried to teach me. I tried to care. Honestly and truly, I did. But I just couldn't.

When the final bell rang, I found myself shuffling to my car at a snail's pace. I was at a loss for what to do. Normally, I'd hang out at the shop with Cole, but he was still out of town. Shenice had closed the shop, so I didn't need to go to work. I couldn't go to the gun range by myself since I wasn't eighteen.

I had nowhere to go but Bill's house.

I got into the car and waited for the endless stream of traffic to pass by on the street so I could pull out. Just as a gap was opening, my passenger door flung open and Xena jumped in. Her hair was a mess and she had a long cut on one cheek. She cradled her left wrist.

"Drive," she said through gritted teeth.

"What the—"

"*Drive.*"

I turned back to look at the traffic, but I'd missed my window of opportunity.

"Go!" she yelled.

"I can't! There's too much traffic."

"Oh, for cripe's sake." Xena stretched her leg out and pressed on the gas pedal.

I turned the wheel and missed the car parked in front of me by inches. Horns blared and tires squealed.

"Shit, shit, shit!" I yelled, frantically trying to keep from crashing into the car passing by at that moment. The car swerved and we came so close to hitting it I could smell the passenger's peppermint gum.

But Xena still didn't let up on the gas. I tried to kick her foot away, but she held it firm.

"Stop!" I yelled. "You're going to get us killed."

"Keep driving," she said through clenched teeth. Once she saw my affirmative nod, she removed her foot from the pedal.

I slowed down just a hair, but I continued to weave through traffic, going as fast as I could manage.

"Where are we going?" I asked, desperately trying to maintain a speed that would keep Xena's foot away from the gas pedal.

"Away. Just keep driving."

I spared a glance at her. She'd closed her eyes and rested her head back against the seat. Her skin was normally creamy white, but she looked even paler.

Fear filled me, starting in my brain and working its way down my entire body. What did handlers have to be afraid of?

"What happened?" I asked, scared to know the answer. Deep down, though, I already knew.

"Xavier."

CHAPTER 8

"WHAT DO YOU MEAN 'XAVIER'?" I shrieked. "That's a who, not a what!" I was being irrational. Given what I knew about Xavier, I shouldn't need to have it spelled out for me. And now was not the time to be nitpicky about word choice.

"Damn," Xena said, adjusting the rearview mirror so she could see. I wanted to slap her hand away. With as fast as I was driving, I needed all the visibility I could get.

"We didn't get away in time," she said, the panic in her voice setting me on edge. "He's behind us."

"*What?*"

Xena moved the mirror back so I could see. Several car lengths back, a black motorcycle was zipping and zagging through traffic and gaining on us.

Since when did Xavier drive a motorcycle?

I stomped on the gas, riding the bumper of the car in front of us. A delivery truck was beside us, so I couldn't pass. "Hurry up, hurry up!" I looked in the mirror again and there was only one car separating us. "Xena, what do I do? He's almost behind us."

"Turn up there," she said. "See that road?" She pointed to a small two-lane road between two buildings.

"Yeah." I gripped the steering wheel tighter and eased up on the gas in preparation for the turn.

"Don't slow down!"

"I have to! I can't make that turn this fast."

I spared a glance at Xena and her eyes narrowed at me. I shifted my body to try to block her from pressing on the gas pedal again. She was freaking crazy and suicidal on top of that. It wouldn't matter if we escaped from Xavier if I rolled the car. We'd be dead anyway.

Sure, Reapers had saved me from death before and Xavier had given me the whole "you can't die until we're ready for you to die" speech, but I still wanted to avoid any and all near death experiences if at all possible.

I made the turn at three times the speed I normally would, and I swear the car rode on two wheels. I held onto the steering wheel for dear life and said a silent prayer of thanks when the car righted itself.

But Xavier was right behind us. His front tire was nearly rubbing our bumper and the loud whirring of the motorcycle vibrated in my ears.

"Go," Xena commanded.

She didn't have to tell me twice. I stomped on the gas and we took off, flying past houses. Thank God they were set off from the street and there were sidewalks. Less likely to have people on the street that way. Less chance of collateral damage.

Without warning, Xena kicked my leg off the pedal and slammed her foot down on the brakes. My chest slammed into the seatbelt and my neck snapped back.

There was a loud crunch as the motorcycle crashed into the back of the car, followed by the thud of Xavier as he landed on the roof. His body rolled off and fell right outside my window.

My gut reaction was to unbuckle my seatbelt and put my hand on the door handle, preparing to get out and see if he was okay. But Xena snapped my seatbelt back into place.

"Go," she said.

Wide-eyed, I looked at her dumbly but did as she

directed. I stomped on the gas before I even had my hands back on the steering wheel. In the rearview mirror, I could see Xavier still lying on the road. A few seconds later, two people ran over to him.

Xena settled back into her seat, leaning her head back and closing her eyes. "Good."

"STOP HERE."

I'd driven for what seemed like hours, but in actuality, it had only been fifteen minutes since we'd left Xavier behind. I'd been on autopilot, obeying all the rules of the road and driving at a safe speed, which seemed incredibly slow compared to how fast I had just been going.

My hands shook as I turned into the Wendy's parking lot and shifted the car into park. As soon as I turned the car off, my brain turned on.

My God, what did I do? Did I kill him?

My next thought scared me a little—*good*.

Sure, I'd thought about killing Xavier constantly since the last time I'd seen him, but it turned out the thought of doing something and actually doing it? Totally different. *Way* different.

I would never forget the sound his body made as it hit the roof. Or the sight of him falling to the ground right outside my window.

"He's not dead," Xena said.

I looked over at her, surprised.

"I could see it on your face. You're worried you killed him."

"Well, yes. I mean, no. I mean...I don't know what I mean."

"Handlers can't be killed like that."

"Like what?"

"By Hondas. It would take a lot more than that."

"How much more?"

Xena's eyes slanted over to me, but she ignored my question. I didn't ask again because after all, she was a handler herself. She probably didn't want to advertise her Achilles' heel, and I couldn't blame her.

Her color had returned and the cut on her face was almost unnoticeable. She also was no longer cradling her wrist.

I guessed fallen angels could heal even faster than seekers could, which made sense. Seekers got their healing powers from our angel blood, and we only had a tiny amount of it. Fallen angels were full of it. Obviously.

I felt like an idiot. How had I not thought of that before? I'd been practicing at the gun range, but how many bullets would it take to kill Xavier? Or cause permanent damage? Was that even possible? I was way out of my league, yet again.

This wasn't the first time I'd been in a high speed chase, and now that I knew I hadn't killed anyone, I was surprisingly calm, unlike last time when I'd nearly gone into shock. I was oddly proud of myself. My mind turned to practical matters.

"What about the car? Someone might have gotten the license plate."

If I hadn't killed Xavier, and he couldn't be killed anyway, then I didn't want to go down for a hit-and-run, especially since it was a defensive maneuver. Xavier hadn't been chasing us down just to say hello.

"No one saw."

"How do you know? How can you *possibly* know that?"

"Trust me. No one saw. I wouldn't risk the cops coming after you. I can't protect you if you're in jail."

"*Protect* me?"

Is that what she thought she was going by jumping into my car and forcing me to drive like I was a NASCAR driver? And not even a good one, at that!

Xena's expression remained neutral. "You should

probably go home now."

"No. Uh-unh. No way you're getting out of this. I want some answers. Since when do handlers protect seekers?"

"It's complicated."

"No shit!" I banged my fists on the steering wheel. "I am so sick and tired of *not knowing anything*! I spent most of my life not knowing what I really am, and the secrets just keep coming."

"Hey," Xena snapped, her expression stern and bordering on angry. "You need to check yourself. This is about more than just *you*. Have you ever thought of that? You're just one tiny piece in a giant ass puzzle."

That was the first time Xena had been anything but chill and laid back so it should have signaled that something important was up, that maybe she was really good and pissed off, but I didn't care. My life was just in danger and to top that off, the back of the car was probably smashed all to hell. I didn't even want to look at it.

So no, I wasn't going to *check myself*. I hadn't asked for any of this. It wasn't my *choice* to be born a seeker. I was doing my best to play the hand I'd been dealt, but hell would freeze over before I *checked myself*.

"No, you need to *check yourself*. You get to *exist* for I don't know how long, maybe for-freaking-ever, but I only get *one* life. That's eighty years if I'm lucky. That's it. So excuse me if I freak out a little at the big cluster it's become."

Xena narrowed her eyes at me, waiting a beat. "Are you done with your little hissy fit?"

"No, as a matter of fact, I'm not," I shot back. "Maybe if someone explained some things to me then I would know I'm a small piece in a big puzzle or whatever."

The silence in the car stretched on between us as I breathed deeply.

"How about now?" Xena asked finally. "Are you done now?"

I crossed my arms and slouched down. "Yes."

"Good. I need to go away for a little while."

"What? Why? Where?"

She *had* to be kidding me! Xavier just tried to kill me, but she told me not to worry because she was my protector. And now she was leaving? How the hell was she going to protect me if she *wasn't here*?

I felt another tantrum coming on. But dang it, my outrage was justified.

"And while I'm gone," she continued as if I hadn't asked any questions at all. I supposed her telling me she was leaving instead of just disappearing like she normally did was her version of explaining things to me. "You need to tell Cole the truth."

I gulped and my anger turned into nausea. "What do you mean? He knows what happened."

"You know what I'm talking about."

Shit. I knew *exactly* what she was talking about. Cole knew my angel ancestor brought him back to life, but he didn't know that by the angel giving him a drop of his blood, it made him a seeker. He also didn't know why his aura was unnaturally white.

"He's going to hate me," I whispered.

Xena cocked her head. "Don't you think it's a little hypocritical for you to bitch about no one telling you anything and then you—"

"Stop," I said, dropping my forehead to the steering wheel. If I hadn't already forgiven my mom for keeping me in the dark all those years, I certainly would now. I totally understood.

Once Cole learned how seeking worked, he'd figure out I was the reason the Reapers were after him in the first place. I'd given his name. It was my fault he'd died and the only way to bring him back to life was to curse him with the existence of being a seeker.

Basically, I was about to rain down a shit storm on his life, and every bit of it was completely my fault.

"He needs to be trained," Xena said. "I haven't

approached him because I know you haven't told him yet, and I thought you might want to be the one to do it. But now that I have to leave—"

"*Why* do you have to leave?" I asked, hoping if I limited my questions to one she might actually answer.

No dice. She continued like I hadn't even interrupted her.

"You'll have to train him. He needs to know how to find white auras."

"But he hasn't come into his abilities yet. He still doesn't see them."

"He will. It's only a matter of days."

How could she know that? As far as I knew, Cole was the only person who'd been brought back to life by way of angel blood. But then again, I didn't know shit about shit, so maybe he wasn't the first.

I closed my eyes. I'd been dreading this day since my angel ancestor brought him back.

"You need to decide if you want to tell him before or after he starts seeing auras," Xena said. "Either way, he's got to be trained. You had your entire life to learn the trade. He only has weeks."

"Why?" I was nearly begging. Any crumb of information would be welcome. "Why does he have to be trained?"

"Just trust me on this. He needs to be trained."

"I find it hard to trust you when you don't confide in me and ignore all my questions."

"Have I ever given you reason to distrust me?" She almost sounded hurt. I wanted to roll my eyes. With everything going on, that was what she decided to be upset about?

"No," I replied begrudgingly. "But trust has to be earned."

"I just saved your life."

It hadn't needed saving until she jumped in the car with me. Who knew? I might have been A-okay if she hadn't done that. Maybe she was the reason Xavier was chasing us.

"How do I know you didn't lead Xavier to me?" I asked slowly, coming to a realization. "He didn't start showing up until you came around."

Despite my voiced skepticism, I still trusted her. If she did lead Xavier to me, it was probably unknowingly.

"You have to ask yourself which is the cause and which is the effect." Good Lord. Now Xena was starting to sound like Morpheus from *The Matrix*. I didn't want the red *or* the blue pill, thank you very much.

Yet she had a valid point. If her purpose was to protect me, then I wouldn't need her unless Xavier was around. But if that was her purpose, then what about seeking? Would I still need to find auras? This circled back around the question of why Cole needed to know how to find auras.

I just wanted answers. I didn't think it was too much to ask.

"If you're supposed to protect me," I said, "then why are you leaving just when we know Xavier is after me?"

"Don't worry. I doubt he'll bother you for a while."

"*How   do   you   know?*"   Ugh. This...was...so...frustrating. We kept coming back to the same points.

"Remember—"

I jumped.

Xena was no longer in the car. She was now standing outside the driver's side window, true to her normal exit strategy. "Train Cole."

CHAPTER 9

I BACKED INTO MY NORMAL parking space at Bill's so my bumper was obscured by the bushes. I felt horrible about the damage to his car, but I didn't know how to explain what happened yet.

Should I tell my mom? I hadn't wanted to stress her out, but now that I knew for sure Xavier was a threat, she needed to be on guard. Of course, his quarrel was with me.

I sighed. That didn't mean anything. Xavier didn't care who he hurt. He'd gladly hurt my mom to teach me a lesson once, and I was sure he wasn't above doing it again. To him, the ends definitely justified the means.

Or perhaps he was simply a sadistic slimebucket who liked causing people pain. That was a definite possibility.

Before I started causing trouble, he and my mom had practically been chums. Obviously, it still burned my butt she'd been so cowed under to him. She'd come around and stood up to him at the end, but by then it was too late.

I circled the car one more time to make sure the damage was hidden. There was a huge v-shaped dent in the bumper and trunk. There were scratches all over the top and I couldn't tell if it was slightly caved in, but there was nothing I could do to hide that. I just hoped it was fixable. I didn't know how I would pay for it, but I'd make it right with Bill. Somehow.

For now, though, what he didn't know wouldn't hurt him.

My mom sat at the kitchen table holding a mug of tea. She blinked several times when I came in, like she was coming out of a daze.

"How was school?" she asked.

"Fine." That wasn't a lie at least. It was after school that things went to hell in a handbasket. "How was your day?"

"Good." She smiled, and it was then I noticed she was still wearing her pajamas and her hair had that just-got-out-of-bed nappy look.

"What did you do today?" I asked cautiously, slowly approaching the table.

"I'm still deciding what I want to do." She frowned. "Did school get out early or something? Why are you home already?"

I glanced at the clock on the wall. It was after five and school let out at three. Exactly what time did my mom think it was?

"No early release today," I said.

She cocked her head, looking at me with a confused expression. Then she stared down into the mug. I gently took it from her. It was cold, and when I dumped it out in the sink, I realized it wasn't tea—it was her morning coffee. I stared at the black liquid with bits of coffee grinds in horror.

How long had she been sitting at this table?

"Have you eaten breakfast?" I asked.

"No, but I was about to fry some eggs. Do you want some?"

I gaped at her. She'd sat right across from me while I'd choked down a bowl of some kind of super fiber cereal Bill kept in his pantry.

"No, I'm not hungry."

"But you should have a good breakfast before you go to school. It'll help you focus."

"I'll grab something on the way," I said slowly. I'd read somewhere that when dealing with Alzheimer's patients, you shouldn't contradict them. It just made them more agitated. I figured the same might be true with my mom.

I dropped into the chair across from her and rested my forehead in my hands. How far gone was she? Just yesterday she'd seemed so much better, and now this.

I didn't know what to do. It seemed like she was getting her strength back, but it was at the cost of her mental faculties.

"You'd better get going so you're not late," she said, looking at me with the *mom* look, the one that expected me to do as I was told.

"Okay," I mumbled, shuffling out of the kitchen. I glanced over my shoulder one last time to see her still sitting at the table, staring into space again. The sight made my heart hurt.

I LAY IN MY ROOM—well, Bill's late daughter's room—for the rest of the evening, staring at the ceiling. I didn't eat dinner, didn't touch my homework, didn't do anything the least bit productive.

I'd like to say the break was refreshing, but I wasn't taking a break because I was tired or lazy—I simply didn't know what to do next. I was at a complete loss.

My mom was getting worse, Xavier was most definitely an active threat, and I had to train Cole, which meant I had to confess some things to him that would surely make him hate me.

And I was on my own. In just a short time, I'd come to think of Xena as my ally, but she'd left me. I felt totally abandoned. Funny how much of a one-eighty I'd done regarding my handler.

A knock sounded at my door.

"Yes?" I asked, not bothering to remove the arm I had flung over my face. I couldn't bear it if my mom showed up wearing a bikini and ready to go to the beach or something even though it was the middle of winter.

My door opened with a squeak and my overhead light flicked on. "Are you okay?"

"Cole!" I sat up straight and blinked, my eyes adjusting to the light. God, he was a sight for sore eyes.

He wore his usual jeans and t-shirt and he had that rumpled just-finished-a-road-trip look. But the warmth in his eyes when he looked at me touched my soul and was exactly what I needed.

"Are you okay?" he asked again, coming in and swinging the door shut behind him. "Why are you lying in—"

I launched myself at him, wrapping my arms around his neck and burying my face in his shoulder. No motor oil smell since he hadn't been working on cars—just good, clean Cole scent.

"Whoa," he said softly, taking a step back and folding his arms around me. "What's going on?"

"I just missed you," I whispered, wiping the tears out of my eyes before he could see them.

Then I kissed him, tangling my fingers in the hair at the nape of his neck. I kissed him hard, furiously trying to show him how much I loved him and convince myself that love would be enough when I told him the truth.

He kicked the door all the way closed with his foot and guided me to the bed. We lay down next to each other, chest to chest, our limbs intertwined.

His mouth tasted like peppermint, as usual, a result of his addiction to mints. It was an addiction I couldn't say I minded.

His tongue swirled with mine and I used his shirt to pull him closer. Then I snuck my hands up the back of his shirt so I could feel his bare skin.

He yanked my shirt up and when his fingers ran

across my stomach, goose bumps formed and tingles shivered down my spine. He moved his hand up, brushing the undersides of my breasts. My back arched and I pressed against him.

He groaned and pulled away. "Ava, we need to stop."

"Why?" I said, my lips swollen and my entire body tingling.

"You know why." He gave me a pointed look. We'd had this conversation before.

I was a virgin. He wasn't. Add that to the fact that he was nineteen and I was only seventeen, and he felt this insane need to protect my virtue.

I'm not saying I was ready to go all the way, but we could take things a little farther. I wasn't going to argue this point with him today, though. So instead, I snuggled close to him. He wrapped his arms around me and pressed his lips to the top of my head.

"Besides," he said, "this is Bill's house, and I just don't feel right about that."

"Okay," I said, not wanting to fight with him. He could say whatever he wanted as long as he continued to hold me.

"Now tell me why you're in here in the dark?"

I sighed and told him about coming home to find my mom thinking it was still morning. I didn't tell him about the other stuff, though. I needed to build up to that. One disaster at a time.

"I'm sorry," he said. "We'll figure something out."

"I hope so," I said, but I didn't really have much hope in us. We had no resources to figure this out. We had no idea what we were even dealing with. I hated to say it, but I was relying solely on Xena. She was my mom's only hope.

"I'm starving," Cole said abruptly. "Have you had dinner?"

"Nope."

Twenty minutes later we sat at Wendy's. Cole had an array of food in front of him: a burger, a chicken sandwich, fries. I don't know how he managed to eat that much on a regular basis and not puke.

I poked at my salad. I'd been ravenous when we first got here, but now that we were sitting here and I had no excuse not to tell him what had been going on, my appetite had gone MIA.

"How did you leave things with Kyle?" I asked.

Cole swallowed and took a sip of soda. "Okay, I think. I'm sure he'll manage to get himself in more trouble between now and June. At least this time when I talked to him about moving down here, he seemed more receptive to it."

"Will your mom sign the papers?" Since Kyle was still a minor, Cole would need to become his guardian, which required his mom's consent.

Cole snorted. "If she doesn't agree, I'll just wait until she's whacked out and stick the paper in front of her. She won't even know what the hell she's signing."

"Do you think it will come to that?"

"No. He's not even there half the time and she doesn't notice. She doesn't give a shit about him. She'll probably be glad to get him out of her hair. At least the truancy officers will stop bothering her."

I grimaced. *Ouch.* It made me sad that Cole had come from such a rough background. Despite the many, many problems in my life, I had no doubt my mom loved me. I didn't know what I'd do without her.

It was a shame Cole couldn't say the same.

"He's still skipping school, then?" I asked.

"Yeah." Cole sighed. "He's making the same dumb mistakes I did. It kills me."

"Sorry." I shifted uncomfortably in my chair. Cole was already dealing with problems, and soon I was going to make things much, much worse for him.

I hated myself for it. I wanted to shrink to nothing and hide under the table. But I couldn't. Even if he did end up hating me—*please God, no, but I didn't see a way around it*—he needed me. Xena was gone, so I was the only one who could train him. She'd said he needed to know how to use his abilities and though she didn't tell me why, I believed her.

Something was coming and we needed to be prepared.

"It's not your fault."

No, but the shit storm that's about to be unleashed on you is.

"So..." I swallowed, sucking in air. "I met the new handler."

Cole paused with his burger midway to his mouth. "When?"

"Well, I saw her today, actually."

He put his food down and narrowed his eyes at me. "You *saw* her today?"

Damn. Figured he'd get to the bottom of my evasive language right away. Cole might have dropped out of school for a while, but he was no idiot.

"Yes." I focused on winding the straw wrapper around my finger. "I met her a few days ago."

"Dammit, Ava. Was this before or after I left?"

"She showed up right before you left. I was going to tell you, but before I could, you said you needed to go see Kyle."

Cole closed his eyes for a moment, and I could tell he was thinking back to the conversation we had about him leaving.

"That's bullshit and you know it. You had plenty of time to say something before I brought up Kyle."

"If I told you, would you have gone?"

"Hell no."

"Exactly. Kyle needed you. And I knew if I said something, you'd feel compelled to stay. Then what would have happened to Kyle?"

Cole leaned back in his seat with a scowl on his face.

"Besides," I said gently, "this one is nothing like

Xavier. She's not a threat. I wouldn't have kept it from you otherwise."

He sighed. "Tell me about—it's a her, right?"

I nearly grinned. I'd won this round and that almost *never* happened. I was glad that at least Cole could see my intentions were in the right place.

"Her name is Xena and she's about the exact opposite of Xavier."

"What do you mean?" He didn't seem convinced, but more than that, he didn't seem open to that idea at all. I couldn't say I blamed him. Our only frame of reference for handlers was Xavier, and Xavier had killed Cole and tortured me and my mom.

"For starters, she'll answer questions. Well, if she knows the answers, anyway." I didn't tell him about the way she also ignored questions she didn't want to answer, especially lately. I wanted to focus on the positives because like me, I believed Xena had good intentions. "And she's not scary. She's like...*friendly*."

"Friendly?"

"Yeah. It was a little weird at first. She just kept showing up—"

"How many times have you seen her?" His tone was incredulous, and I could tell he was getting irritated again that I hadn't told him about her sooner.

"Um, four times."

I paused, waiting for Cole to get angry. Instead, he just shook his head and said, "Go on."

Color me surprised. It wasn't that Cole didn't trust me or my judgment. He did. It was that his protective streak wasn't really a streak—it was more the size of a football field.

"Okay, so she has a habit of showing up in random places. I think her superpower must be teleportation or something."

Which I much preferred to Xavier's freaky ability to cause pain by boiling and freezing people's blood. And whatever he'd done to my mom.

"Teleportation?" He made an are-you-sure-you-didn't-hit-your-head face.

I didn't blame him for being skeptical. I wouldn't have believed it either if I hadn't witnessed it several times. Teleportation might not even be right—she could just be super fast like a superhero or something—but I didn't know how else to explain it.

"She shows up like that." I snapped my fingers. "One minute you're alone and then, bam! She's there. She's even more in stealth mode when she leaves. She'll be sitting in the car next to you and in as long as it takes to blink, she's outside walking twenty feet away from the car. I don't know how she does it."

"Hopefully that's her only power," Cole said mildly.

"She..." I stopped as some people walked by, not wanting them to overhear us. Then I thought, you know what? Screw that. Even if someone overheard, it wasn't like they would think we were talking seriously. I had to put a gun to my head for Cole to believe me, and he already knew me. "Anyway, she's nice."

"Your mom used to think Xavier was nice."

"That's not exactly true." I stopped to consider. When I was really young, Xavier had seemed almost like an uncle—the kind of honorary uncle role that male friends of the family took on. It wasn't until I was a teenager that he started getting noticeably creepy. I didn't know if he hid his true nature all those years or if he changed somehow.

"Either way," Cole said, "I don't trust her."

"You haven't met her. She's nothing like Xavier."

"She's a handler. That makes her *exactly* like Xavier."

I shook my head vehemently. "Not true. She *saved* me from Xavier."

Cole leaned forward on his forearms. "*What?*"

Shit. So much for breaking it to him gently. And this wasn't even the part I was dreading telling him.

"So Xavier's alive and well," I said brightly with a fake

smile. "And he chased us. Apparently he has a motorcycle now, so that's neat, I guess."

"Goddammit!" Cole pounded his fist on the table. "I *knew* something like this would happen as soon as I left. Tell me *exactly* what happened. And don't sugarcoat it or leave anything out."

I sighed. He was not going to like this. "Xena and I were in the car Bill lent me when Xavier started chasing us. We tried to get away, but we couldn't shake him. To make a long story short, he ended up rear-ending the car with his motorcycle and we finally got away."

Cole said nothing at first, just clenched and unclenched his fists. He had an insane need for revenge on Xavier, easily rivaling mine. I couldn't blame him. Xavier had literally killed him. I didn't know if that was what angered Cole the most, though. Sometimes I thought he was angrier about what Xavier had done to me. He'd boiled and frozen my blood a few times and broken my wrist, so nothing as serious as what he'd done to Cole and my mom. But still that was what Cole focused on. He rarely mentioned what had happened to him.

And soon I would have to bring it up.

"Say something," I whispered, reaching across to hold his hand.

He stared at my hand in his for a moment before speaking. "I should have been there."

"Cole," I said gently. "You can't be with me all the time. And it was fine. Xena protected me."

"How do you know she isn't part of it? She's a *handler*." His voice was laced with animosity.

I'd wondered the same thing at first, but just like I could read auras to determine if a person was good, I felt like I could *read* Xena. Though she was a handler, she cared about me. She wanted me safe. I knew it.

"You'll have to trust me until you meet her. She said she had to go away for a while, but she'll be back eventually."

"Where did she go?"

I shrugged. "Don't know."

"It seems like there's a lot she isn't telling you."

I felt the same way and in fact had given Xena a hard time about the same thing, so it was difficult to reconcile the fact that I was defending her so valiantly. But I *knew* she was on our side. I didn't know how I knew, but I did. I had to trust my gut on this one.

"I don't think she knows everything, either," I said. "But I trust her. She's not like Xavier. I can't explain it to you. You'll just have to decide for yourself when you meet her."

Cole looked down at the rest of his uneaten burger. This was tough for him—all the unknowns and uncertainty. It was in his nature to protect the ones he loved, but he couldn't protect me if he didn't know what I needed protection from.

He wrapped the burger paper around the sandwich and tossed it into the bag. Uh-oh. Cole not finishing his food wasn't a good sign. This news was hitting him harder than I'd expected.

And I hadn't even gotten to the really bad stuff yet.

"Ready to go?" he asked.

I nodded and gathered up my trash.

He needed time to process. That was all this was. I'd give him a few minutes before diving into disclosing the next round of secrets.

I'd been granted a temporary stay of execution.

As we walked out of the restaurant, I clutched his hand and laid my head on his shoulder, fearing it would be the last time.

CHAPTER 10

COLE KILLED THE ENGINE IN front of Bill's house. The porch light was on, and so was a lamp in the living room. I peered out of the window, half-expecting a curtain to move and reveal my mom spying on us, just like in sitcoms or commercials.

I would have welcomed it because that would mean she was at least somewhat in control of her mind.

When I walked through the front door, would I find her still sitting at the kitchen table? I should have called Bill to let him know what was up, but with Cole back, I got a little distracted. And I didn't like talking about it. The less I talked about it, the more I could pretend it wasn't real.

I wasn't ready for it to be real. I'd be ready for it to be real when we had a solution for it, when we could start to put the nightmare behind us.

Unfortunately, it was just one of many.

I glanced over at Cole then down at my hands. I didn't know if he'd had enough time to process everything I'd told him about Xena, but I couldn't put it off any longer.

I shouldn't have even waited this long.

"There's more you need to know," I said in a rush before I lost my nerve. I would rather do anything than have this conversation. Ask me to walk over broken glass?

Sure thing—my skin would heal. Ask me to eat a live tarantula? I might gag, but I'd get it down. Ask me to destroy Cole's trust in me? I'd rather die.

But that wasn't an option. Both my mom and Cole were depending on me.

Cole looked at me expectantly, not saying anything. I usually loved that about him—that he didn't waste his breath on useless words, but tonight, the silence was unnerving.

"It's about the night you..." I almost said *died*, but I choked on the word. I couldn't say it. "The night Xavier attacked us," I said instead. That made it sound so much less severe.

The memory of feeling the warmth of Cole's blood while he breathed his last breath was still so vivid, even now, months later. If I closed my eyes, I could still feel the sticky liquid on my hands, could still smell the stench of cinnamon and gun powder, could still feel the anguish as Cole died.

He'd died.

I'd lost him that night, but it hadn't been forever. Now I feared that with what I was about to tell him, I *would* lose him forever.

I choked back a sob, looking away from Cole to hide it. If he saw, he would try to comfort me, and I couldn't take that. Not now. I didn't deserve it.

But he deserved to know and I'd already put it off too long.

"There's a reason the Reapers were after you."

"Because my aura was white, right? That's what you told me." His tone was disbelieving. He'd never fully believed he had a white aura.

He had good reason to doubt—his aura wasn't natural. He was definitely a good person, but he wasn't saintly. His aura shouldn't have been white.

And that was my fault, too. But I would get to that later.

"Cole—" I took a deep breath. "I gave your name to Xavier. I set the Reapers after you."

Cole stilled as he took in what I was telling him. He didn't react and I was dying for him to say something. *Anything.*

When I'd explained to him I was a seeker, I'd told him my job was to find auras. I'd never told him I'd given his name, though, and I'd always wondered if he'd figured that part out on his own.

"Why?" he asked quietly, staring straight ahead. In that second my suspicions were confirmed—he'd already known. But like me and my refusal to admit and accept what was happening to my mom, maybe he'd refused to acknowledge it.

But he couldn't ignore it anymore.

"Xavier was torturing my mom. He was killing her." Tears streamed down my cheeks as I relived another painful memory. "I said what I had to to save her."

Cole nodded. "I wondered." His voice sounded detached somehow.

"Cole, I'm so sorry. If I could take it back, I would. I regretted it the second the words were out of my mouth."

"Ava, I'd pretty much figured something like this had happened, but I didn't ask." He gently wiped the tears from my cheeks with his fingertips, and I grabbed hold of his hand. "I get it—you had to save your mom. But then you saved me, too. I figure that makes up for it."

I closed my eyes, letting his words sink in. *He'd already known.* He'd already known and he never said anything. Because he'd already forgiven me.

I didn't deserve him.

I didn't tell him about how I'd given other names. At first, I hadn't realized what I was doing. My mom kept the true nature of why I was finding white auras a secret. But even after I found out, I still turned in a name.

And I didn't save her. Didn't even try.

"There's more."

Cole was silent again, waiting for me to speak.

"When Xavier—" *killed you* "—shot you, and the angel came, do you remember any of it?"

"No."

"You were dead. I watched you die. My angel ancestor—"

"He's your ancestor?"

"Please let me explain," I pleaded. Cole was prone to interrupting which irritated me under normal circumstances, but I couldn't handle it now. "This is hard for me to get out. I'm a seeker because I have angel blood. My angel ancestor fathered a child and I'm a descendant of that line. When he brought you back, he gave you some of his blood. That technically makes you part of his line."

Cole looked at me, his brow furrowed. "What are you telling me?" he asked slowly.

Oh, God, he was making me spell it out for him.

"You're a seeker, now."

CHAPTER 11

I WATCHED COLE AS HE processed what I'd just told him—he was a seeker.

My eyes searched his face, looking for any kind of reaction, but Cole was a master at keeping his feelings to himself. His face was a blank slate.

The seconds ticked by and the atmosphere in the car grew thick. I had so much more to tell him, but still I waited.

"But I don't see auras," he said finally. It was a logical reaction—the defining characteristic of being a seeker was the ability to see auras.

"Not yet. But you will soon."

"How do you know this?"

"Xena told me."

More silence.

"Okay." His voice was detached. It was almost as if I were telling him about someone else. It was like he hadn't grasped the effect this would have on his life.

I hated to ask, but I needed to know. "Do you understand what that means?"

He looked at me, and I could tell he didn't. Or at least, he was in denial.

"You'll have to start collecting names. For reaping."

He stared straight ahead. "I'll have to kill people.

Good people. People who deserve to live."

I cringed at the bluntness of his statements. My heart bled for the hollowness in his voice.

But I'd be lying if I said I didn't have the same thoughts.

"Not exactly," I said anyway.

"Pretty fucking close!"

There. There was the reaction I'd been expecting. I didn't know if it made this better or worse, the fact that his emotions were kicking in.

Worse. Definitely worse. I'd only seen Cole lose his cool a few times—once when a gang member friend of Kyle's put his hands on me. Another time after Xavier had broken my wrist.

And now when he'd learned I ruined his life. I had to go on and finish telling him everything.

"Xena wants me to train you."

He clenched his fists in his lap and his jaw muscle worked as his nostrils flared slightly. "What if I don't want to be trained?"

"You don't have a choice."

"Bullshit."

I laughed bitterly, wishing I had better news for him. "That's what I thought, too, and you see where that got me." I looked down at my lap, my fingers playing with the drawstring at the waist of my hoodie. "I'm sorry, Cole. I wouldn't have wanted this for you, but it was the only way to bring you back."

"What you're saying is I don't have a choice because you already made that choice for me."

If he had sliced open my chest with a shredded piece of metal, it would have hurt less. The venom in his voice was thick, harsh. It struck me in the heart like a poisoned arrow.

"You died. Right there in front of me." My voice was heavy with emotion and I squeezed my eyes shut as visions filled my mind. If I thought about it hard enough, I could still smell his blood, feel it on my hands. It was the hardest thing I'd ever gone through. "It was the only way to bring you back."

He turned to look me in the eyes, and his were dark and furious. I'd seen that look before but never directed at me and never as intense. "So you chose a life for me that you yourself hate."

"It wasn't like that," I begged for him to understand. "I chose for you to live."

"No matter what the cost."

"Yes."

He gripped the steering wheel and gazed out the window. "How can I take care of Kyle if I'm a seeker now?" The despair in his voice was evident.

I didn't have an answer for him. Actually, I did have an answer—he couldn't. If Cole would be expected to live the kind of life my mom and I did, there was no way he could drag Kyle along.

He looked over at me. Except he wasn't looking *at* me. More like *through* me.

"Ava, I think we need to call it a night."

I gripped the door handle, closing my eyes momentarily and praying for the courage to go on. "There's more."

"What the hell else could there be?

"Your aura is different," I said. "It's not naturally white."

"I knew it." He slammed his open palm on the steering wheel.

"My angel ancestor adjusted it," I explained. Why hadn't Cole ever asked me about these things? This wasn't the first time tonight he'd said he already knew what I told him. Was he scared of the answer he'd get if he asked?

Smart. He should have been. But he had no choice but to listen to the answers now.

"Why would he do that?"

"He saw how you protected and looked out for me and

thought you'd make a good guardian angel."

"For you." It wasn't a question—it was a matter-of-fact statement spoken in a dull tone laced with anger. The thing about this particular part of my confession was that this was only indirectly my fault. I'd never asked for this, just as I'd never asked to be a seeker.

Yet there was one constant in everything I was telling him—*me*. I couldn't deny that I was the cause of all of this, whether because of my own decisions and actions or someone else's.

"Yes," I confirmed.

"So as soon as I started to care about you, I became a dead man." Another matter-of-fact statement with the same tone.

I stared straight ahead, not able to answer him. He was right, but I was emotionally drained. I just couldn't. Not anymore, even though I deserved it.

"When you're ready to talk, call me." I opened the door with one hand and wiped the tears out of my eyes with the other. I hesitated a moment. "I still love you, Cole."

Then I got out of the car and went inside to the sound of his squealing tires.

MY MOM WASN'T WAITING UP for me, but Bill was.

He sat in an ancient wooden rocking chair in the living room right next to the lamp I'd seen in the window.

"Where's my mom?" I asked, keeping my hair in my face so he wouldn't see I'd been crying.

"In bed."

"How was she?"

Seeming to contemplate the question, Bill rocked back and forth for a moment before answering. "She's been better."

I put my face in my hands, but I didn't have any tears

left. "I'm sorry."

"It's not your fault. You're not the one who hurt your mama."

Not directly, but it was still mostly my fault. If I hadn't tried to buck the system, if I'd just gone along with Xavier like I'd always done, then none of us would be in this mess.

My mom wouldn't be sick. Cole wouldn't be a seeker. And I wouldn't be losing the two people who meant the most in the world to me.

But other innocent people would be dead because of me. There was that. It looked like I'd be back to doing that anyway, so how many lives did my shenanigans actually save? One? Maybe two?

Was it worth it?

I didn't know. All I knew was this was an entirely messed up situation.

And I should have at least given Bill a heads up so he'd know what he was walking into when he came home. I wondered if her state startled him as much as it did me. Probably not. Not much got to Bill.

As I removed my hands from my face, I noticed I'd tracked mud in on my boots.

Perfect. Just perfect.

"I'm sorry," I said to Bill, sitting on the bench by the door to pull them off. "I'll clean up the mud tomorrow. I promise."

I *should* do it now, but I simply didn't have it in me.

"I don't mind," Bill said. "Was that Cole you were with?"

Cole. Hearing his name made my heart hurt. He actually hadn't taken everything as bad as I'd feared, but it hadn't been good, either. He was like Bill in that way—not much shook him.

Still the question remained—would he ever forgive me?

If the roles were reversed, would I forgive him?

I'd like to think I would, but I honestly didn't know. It

had taken me a long time to forgive my mom and she was my *mom*. And that was after I'd completely messed up.

Cole and I hadn't known each other that long. Who was to say he wouldn't wash his hands of me and be done?

Except, he couldn't. Xena needed me to train him. I couldn't do that until he started seeing auras, though. Hopefully that ability wouldn't kick in for at least a few days. That would give him time to come to terms with everything.

Normally, I hated being away from him. Those days when he went up to help his brother had been tough—I'd missed him so much. Yet here I was hoping for time apart, right after I'd gotten him back.

Would it be better to at least see him even if he hated me? Or would it be better to stay away? The thing was it wasn't up to me. I'd contact him in a day or two to see when he wanted to start training. I couldn't force him one way or the other. The ball was in his court, and Xena would have to pick up the slack if I couldn't complete my mission.

I realized Bill was still waiting for me to respond.

"Yes, that was Cole." Who else would it be? I didn't really have any friends other than Kaley—the seeker lifestyle wasn't conducive to BFFs—and she didn't drive.

"Huh," Bill commented, leaving me to interpret what that meant. I was about to tell him goodnight when he spoke again.

"You remind me of her."

"Who?" I had no idea who he was talking about.

"Jill. She was about your age when she..." he trailed off but I could easily fill in that blank. "Anyway, that's why I'm not so friendly sometimes."

"I understand." And I did. It couldn't be easy having a living, breathing reminder of his dead daughter hanging around. I felt bad now for all the unflattering thoughts I'd had about him in the last few months. "How long ago did she pass away?"

"Seventeen years ago this past summer." The pain was freshly etched on his face, like it was seventeen days ago instead of seventeen years ago. Did parents ever get over that kind of loss? Judging from Bill's expression, I'd say no.

"I'm sorry. I know it must be hard to lose a child." My heart ached for him, just like it ached for the parents of the teens who'd died because I submitted their names to Xavier. It all around sucked, and I hated that I'd contributed to causing that kind of pain for other families.

If I hadn't already cursed the system I was unwillingly a part of, I would do it now. I didn't understand it. Maybe if I knew I was somehow contributing to the greater good of the universe, I could come to terms with my role.

But I didn't know that.

Seeing Bill made me realize I'd done the right thing. Despite what had happened to my mom, despite the rift between me and Cole, what I'd been doing as a seeker was wrong. I'd been right to stand up for myself.

I only wished I'd been better at it.

CHAPTER 12

AT SCHOOL THE NEXT DAY, I looked everywhere for Cole, even being late for a couple of my classes so I could wait near his. He didn't show. By lunchtime I'd given up.

I hid in a bathroom stall instead of eating in the cafeteria so I could text Bill to ask about my mom. He'd promised to go home and check on her.

How is she?

His response was almost immediate: *same.*

Damn. I was hoping she'd snap out of it today, that perhaps it was just a one-time thing. She was still in bed when I left this morning, and I didn't wake her. I didn't know if extra sleep would help, but it sure as heck wouldn't hurt.

Next I called Shenice, but there was no answer. She hadn't told me when she planned to go back to work and when she wanted me to come in. I hadn't been paid for my first few days yet, either. That didn't bother me so much, though. What bothered me was I had nowhere to go after school but straight home to Bill's. I dreaded what awaited me there—a mother who was slowly losing her mind and the ghost of a dead daughter.

I hated that my presence caused Bill pain. He'd done so much for me and my mom, and all this time I'd unknowingly been hurting him.

That was quickly becoming the story of my life.

I texted Shenice, hoping for a miracle—that she'd reply in the next few hours and want me to come in. If she didn't, maybe I'd swing by the shop anyway, just in case. I could do that since I still had Bill's car.

Which was another issue. I still hadn't told him about the accident. Was it really less than twenty-four hours since that happened? A lifetime and a half had passed since then.

When school finally ended, I took my time walking out to my car and then once there, I sat behind the wheel for at least ten minutes, gathering the motivation to get moving. The good thing about school was that for the most part, things were normal. Same old classes, same old teachers, same old stuff. For minutes at a time I could pretend everything was okay. As soon as I set foot outside those cinder block walls, though, that became impossible.

I headed toward Nice Beauty, my gaze darting to the rearview every few seconds. Xena had told me Xavier wouldn't bother me while she was gone, but I didn't trust that. Besides, Xena could pop up any second using her wacko teleportation or super speed or whatever it was and then BAM! Xavier could be right behind her.

It did not make for a relaxing drive.

The lights in the shop were off. I parked the car anyway and got out to peer in the windows. It looked even more uninhabited than usual. Maybe I should spend my afternoon putting in more job applications. There was no way this job would last longer than a few weeks. And that was *if* Shenice ever got in touch with me.

I had no choice left but to head home. It was probably better that this job wasn't going to work out. I'd need to spend all my free time training Cole, anyway. And now that Bill had come to our rescue, our need for money wasn't quite as urgent. Though I did want to make it up to him somehow. Perhaps I could work off what we owed him in the shop. I could turn myself into an indentured servant.

Coward that I was, I backed the car in again so the damage to the back wasn't noticeable. Then I headed straight to the kitchen to forage. I had no appetite and hadn't eaten breakfast or lunch, but I knew I needed to eat. With both Cole and my mom depending on me, I couldn't afford to make myself sick.

I opened the refrigerator and frowned. That was weird—the milk was on its side on the middle shelf, right between a head of lettuce and a bottle of mustard. I pulled it out, careful not to accidentally pop the lid off and put it on the top shelf where it belonged. Then I moved the lettuce to the crisper drawer where it should be. I poked around for a few more minutes, contemplating the yogurt on the bottom—which I almost didn't notice because yesterday it was on the top shelf—but decided against it.

I opened the pantry, staring for a few seconds before slowly closing the door again. Everything in there had been rearranged as well. All the cereal was normally on the top shelf, but the raisin bran had been shoved on the next to the bottom shelf next to some packages of rice.

Something wasn't right.

"Mom?" I called, walking with trepidation toward the stairs. I hadn't heard her downstairs, so she had to be up there somewhere.

By the time I got to the stairs, I took them two at a time. I was so scared of learning what state she'd be in that I hadn't checked on her immediately. *Stupid, stupid, stupid.* It was selfish, pure and simple, and now I was really scared of what I'd find.

"In here, Ava!" Her voice, bright and cheery, came from the guest room she'd been staying in.

I raced in. She stood in front of the bookcase. Half the shelves were empty and books were stacked on the bed.

"Hi, Mom," I said cautiously, trying to gauge just by looking at her how she was. She was dressed in jeans and long sleeve flannel shirt, no socks. It looked like she'd showered and blown her hair dry—it was light and fluffy instead of limp and oily. So, in other words—she looked normal. Like the *old* normal. Before Xavier normal. "How are you?"

"I'm good. Just doing some straightening." She sounded fine—almost like her regular self. But she'd fooled me yesterday.

I stepped closer and realized she wasn't straightening—she was rearranging by putting the books in alphabetical order. I thought back to the state of the fridge—lettuce, milk, mustard. The pantry was similar—raisin bran, rice.

She was alphabetizing things.

I looked away, needing to gather my thoughts.

The clothes hanging in the closet had also been organized, though by color. *Pink, purple, red*...Nope. These were *alphabetized* by color.

What the heck was going on inside my mom's brain that made her obsessively alphabetize everything? Putting the books in order that way made sense, but everything else? Not so much.

I turned back to her. "Did Bill ask you to straighten?"

"No. But I noticed this morning that everything was a complete mess. It's the least I can do to pitch in while we're staying here."

I nodded, like it made total sense to me.

It didn't.

Bill's house was spotless. The only mess was the little bit I'd made in my room, and I'd been making a concerted effort to keep things neat.

I wanted to ask her what was going on in her mind, but she didn't seem aware her behavior was out of the ordinary, and I didn't want to bring that to her attention.

"Did you have a good day?" I asked instead.

"Yes, just a lot of cleaning." She glanced at the clock on the wall. "You're home late, aren't you? Didn't school get out an hour ago? Speaking of that, you need to leave me your work schedule so I know where you are."

I waited a beat, gaping at her. "Sure thing."

Yesterday she didn't have any sense of the time, yet today she was berating me about my schedule. Still, though, I'd say this was an improvement. OCD tendencies sure beat yesterday's lack of awareness.

She continued to place the books on the shelves, humming a little bit as she went. When she noticed me watching her, she shooed me away. "Go do your homework. You've got to keep those grades up so you can get into college."

I backed out of the room slowly, but she didn't look at me again. In my room, I took out a spiral notebook—not for homework but to start a record. If I ever found someone who could help my mom, I wanted to be able to provide all the necessary information. I jotted down what I could recall about her symptoms since she'd first gotten sick with approximate dates. Then I started a new page for today, writing down every little thing I could think of. It was actually kind of therapeutic.

Almost an hour later, I flipped the notebook closed and shoved it under the mattress. If my mom got around to organizing my room, I didn't want her to see I was keeping notes on her. As soon as it was out of sight, the good feeling I'd gotten from writing faded.

I could fool myself into feeling like I was confiding in someone as long as I was actively writing, but pen and paper didn't come close to talking to a flesh and blood person.

I missed Cole.

I curled up on my bed and stayed there until it was time to brush my teeth and put on my pajamas.

MY PHONE RANG AT 3 A.M. In my groggy state, I slammed my hand on the ignore button, knocking it off the nightstand and onto the floor in the process. About a minute later, it rang again. This time, I managed to gain some coherency as it rang, realizing that few people had my number and none of them would call at this hour unless it was important. I leaned over the side of the bed, but I couldn't see the light of the screen, so it must have landed facedown. I fumbled around for the phone in the dark, using the ringing sound as my guide.

It was Cole.

My palms immediately slicked and my heartbeat ratcheted up a notch. I clutched the phone for a few seconds before answering, picking up just before it went to voicemail again.

"Hello?" I said tentatively. I could think of no good reason he'd call me in the middle of the night, and my first thought was that he was drunk or something and wanted to yell at me. Cole wasn't a big drinker, but why else would he call at 3 am? Drunk dialing seemed like the logical explanation.

And the only one that didn't mean something very, very bad.

"Ava," he rasped out. I could barely hear him, but it was enough to set my nerves on edge.

I sat up straight. "Cole? What's wrong?"

"Oh, God, Ava, I'm dying."

My pulse hammered against my throat. "What happened?" I was already slipping off my pajama bottoms and grabbing for my jeans.

Had Xavier found him? I would kill that devil creature. And this time when I saw his limp body, I'd have no regrets. I would kill him and I would make it hurt.

"I don't know. I'm so sick. I—"

The phone clattered like he'd dropped it, and there was a retching sound in the background.

Shit. It wasn't Xavier after all, which I guessed was good, but I didn't like this either. I waited for him to come back on the phone while I tied my shoes. I put the phone down for a second so I could change my shirt, and he still hadn't picked up. I paced and with each step, my fear amplified.

"Cole!" I spoke loudly, wanting to yell, but not wanting to wake anyone else up. My mom couldn't stop me from going to him, but it'd be a lot easier if I didn't have to deal with her interference. And Bill? I didn't know if he'd try to stop me or wake my mom so *she* could stop me. It would put him in an awkward position, which I didn't want.

"Cole!" I said again, louder this time. I pulled my bedroom door shut behind me and raced down the stairs as quietly as I could.

"Ava." His voice was so weak, and if I didn't know how strong he was, I might have been afraid he was actually dying.

I refused to consider that Xavier had somehow done his voodoo magic hex and made Cole sick without him realizing it. He would be fine. He *had* to be.

"I'm coming. Just stay there." As I disconnected, I realized what a stupid command that was. What was he going to do in his condition? Run a marathon?

I couldn't think straight. I scratched out a brief note for my mom and put my coat on as I ran out the door. I fastened my seatbelt as I turned the key in the ignition.

My hands shook on the steering wheel and my breathing was erratic. I stopped at the end of the driveway to close my eyes and take several deep breaths. *Get yourself under control, Ava.*

I had the ten minute drive to pull myself together, and I would need every second of it.

I shoved a piece of gum in my mouth, wishing I'd brushed my teeth. I hadn't wanted to take the extra minute, though, not when Cole needed me.

Driving faster than I probably should have, I slammed my foot on the brakes at a red light. There was no other freaking car in sight. *Dammit!* There was a little camera attached to the light, though, so if I ran it, I'd get a ticket in the mail in seven to ten business days. No, thank you.

I shot off as soon as the light turned green and made it to the shop in record time.

The door was locked. *Shit*. I called Cole's cell but got no answer. I waited exactly one minute, then called again. Still nothing.

One time I forgot my phone in the shop and climbed in through an unlocked window to retrieve it. Cole had pulled a gun on me and I almost peed my pants.

I could guarantee that wouldn't be a problem tonight.

I checked the windows, but no such luck this time— they were all locked. And they didn't keep an extra key out here anymore. Great for keeping out Xavier, but—

You know what? On second thought, no, it wouldn't have done any good against Xavier anyway. So Cole might as well have left the damn key out here.

I circled around front and kicked at a brick that lined the pathetic flower beds. It came loose relatively easily, and I carried it to the back door with me.

I looked at the brick, then at the window and winced. "Sorry, Bill."

Then I threw the brick at the window as hard as I could. The piercing sound of the breaking glass made me jump. The brick didn't go through to the inside and landed at my feet right where they had been moments earlier. I mentally thanked my skittishness for saving me from crushed toes.

I reached through the broken window pane, sucking in air when a shard of glass caught my hand. Damn. I was in such a hurry I wasn't careful. But I still managed to flip the lock and get the door open.

I started toward the stairs that led to Cole's apartment but thought better of it. First I needed to secure the door. Xavier might be able to get in no matter what, but this wasn't the safest neighborhood, so he wasn't the only one we needed to keep out.

I looked around the shop in search of a chair to wedge under the doorknob. The only chair was in Bill's office, and it was on wheels. *Damn.* I was going to have to get creative.

I found a thick chain and laced it through the broken window pane, then around a pipe that ran up the wall next to the door frame. That could work, but how to secure it? The chain was no good just hanging there.

I had a combination lock in my gym bag in the car, so I undid the chain and flung the door open to race out to the car to retrieve it.

This was taking entirely too long. Probably less than twenty minutes had passed since Cole called, but it felt like so much longer.

Finally, I secured the door, tugging on the lock to make sure it would hold. The door hung open a few inches, but no one should be able to slip through and they'd need industrial strength bolt cutters to slice through the chain. It was as safe as I could make it. Hell, it was probably safer. I'd gotten in with little difficulty.

Then again, Cole had probably heard the breaking glass. Under normal circumstances, he'd be all over it, probably with a loaded gun, but he was in no condition to check things out.

I charged up the stairs and pounded on Cole's front door before trying the knob. It was unlocked. That wasn't good. He would never leave it open if he was in his right mind.

Stepping inside, I stripped off my coat, not even caring that blood from the cut on my hand rubbed against it and stained the inside lining. "Cole?"

"Here." His voice was weak and I couldn't tell where it was coming from. "In here."

His apartment was so small it didn't take long to find him. He lay on the bathroom floor, flat on his back with his eyes closed. He wore nothing but jeans, and those were unbuttoned and hanging low on his hips, showing the waistband of his boxers. His skin was pale and glistened with sweat.

With a groan, he rolled to his side and curled up in the fetal position, shivering uncontrollably.

"Oh, Cole." I knelt next to him, putting my hand on his forehead. It was burning up. I didn't need a thermometer to tell me he had a fever—and a high one at that.

"Ava." He reached up and grabbed my hand, but the pressure he used to squeeze it was so weak my heart broke.

Please don't let him be sick like my mom.

His body lying limp on the ground reminded me of when he'd died, and a horrid feeling washed over me.

Cole was always so strong. The only time I'd seen him weak—well, not *weak*, exactly. He'd been shot in the chest, so I wouldn't consider that weak. But that was the only time I'd seen him down.

He peeled his eyes open, and it seemed to take all his strength. When his eyes turned toward me, he immediately squeezed them shut, wincing.

"Fuck, God, fuck, the light. Turn it off."

"What light, Cole?"

"You," he rasped out. "You're glowing."

I sat back on my heels, finally realizing what was happening. Right on the schedule Xena predicted, Cole was getting his abilities.

CHAPTER 13

I SMOOTHED COLE'S HAIR OFF his forehead, not sure what to do. I was born with my abilities, and I couldn't remember ever not having them. As I got older, the auras got stronger, more difficult to block out. But by then, my mom had trained me how to guard myself.

It seemed that Cole was being blindsided by the full force of the auras with no way to protect himself.

"When did this start?" I asked. I felt wetness on my hand and looked down to see I was wringing my hands and getting blood from my cut all over the place. I grabbed a tissue and blotted the blood. I'd have to find a Band-Aid later.

Cole groaned and mumbled incoherently. Then he began retching and with shaking arms, he pulled himself up to the toilet to hang his head over it. There was nothing left though. I wrapped my arms around his shoulders as he dry heaved, rubbing his back like my mom used to do to me when I was sick.

Poor Cole. There was nothing I could do for him. Even if there was some miracle medicine, I doubted he could keep it down.

I moistened a washcloth and wiped the clammy skin on his face and neck before he collapsed on the floor again, his elbow banging the bottom of the toilet. *Damn.* That was probably going to bruise.

"Cole, you should move to the bedroom," I said. "You'll be more comfortable." That and there was a window in there. The air in the bathroom was stale and rank, the putrid odor no doubt from his being sick. Some fresh air might make him feel better.

He groaned and shook his head, clutching his stomach.

"Can you stand?"

He shifted like he was going to climb to his knees but shook his head again. "No," he said through cracked, dry lips. It seemed to take all his energy to get that one word out.

Then mercifully, he passed out.

I sat back against the wall, resting my elbow on my knee and my chin in my hand, watching him. How long had he been like this? Cole wasn't one to ask for help. And considering how angry at me he'd been when I saw him last, he must have been desperate.

I couldn't blame him. He looked like hell. I reached out and put my hand on his forehead again. Still hot, but slightly less so. Or maybe that was wishful thinking.

In his delirious state, did he realize what was happening? I was sure if he didn't feel like death, he'd understand. After all, I'd projected my aura once to prove to him I was a seeker, so he knew what they looked like. It hadn't bothered him like my aura did now, though. I guessed my projection wasn't as strong as his seeing it with his newly formed abilities.

If he'd been alone in his apartment this whole time, he wouldn't have seen any auras yet. Mine would have been the first. I just didn't know and until he woke up and could talk to me, I was clueless.

The only person I knew who might be able to help us was off God knew where doing God knew what. I never did get Xena's cell phone number. How much of an idiot did that make me? Because I definitely felt like one. Maybe if she didn't disappear like Houdini or maybe if we weren't being chased by a psychopath I could have made it more of a priority.

What good was having a handler if she wasn't around when I needed her? Of course, her job wasn't to serve me—it was the other way around.

As far as I knew—which wasn't saying much—no one had ever died from seeing auras. I'd just have to treat the symptoms as they came, which right now were that of the worst stomach bug known to man.

"Cole," I whispered. I smoothed his hair back from his forehead and pressed my lips there. Yesterday I'd wondered if I'd ever get to kiss him again. And today here I was. I hadn't wanted it to be like this, though.

"I'm sorry," I told him, even though he couldn't hear me. "I'll take care of you."

The first order of business was getting him off this nasty bathroom floor. Cole's place was cleaner than most guys'—yet again, what did I know since I wasn't a frequent visitor to guys' bathrooms—but he was still lying on aged, cracked linoleum.

Maybe I could move him into the bedroom myself. I put my hands under his arms and tugged. He didn't budge—total dead weight.

Shit. *Guess we'll both be spending the rest of the night in the bathroom, then.*

I went to the kitchen and filled a glass of water. He had to be dehydrated. As soon as he could hold his head up, I'd make him take small sips of water. On my way through the living room, I picked up a blanket and two throw pillows. Once back in the bathroom, I grabbed a bath towel and shimmied it under him, so that at least his bare skin wouldn't be touching on the nasty linoleum. I tucked a pillow under his head and draped the blanket over him. Then I sent Bill a text with the combination of the lock so he'd be able to remove the chain when he came to work in a few hours.

Finally I lay down behind Cole and wrapped my body around his.

COLE'S STIRRING WOKE ME. IT had taken me a long time to drift off and when I finally did, it was a fitful sleep. Every time his breathing hitched or he let out a moan in his sleep, I went on high alert. Eventually, his forehead did cool, and he slept more soundly.

Until now. His body jerked like it wanted to be awake, but his mind fought it. I sat up and felt his head. Normal.

My shoulders slumped in relief. *Thank God.* One of the things that put my mother in the hospital for so long was a fever—Xavier had boiled her blood and the fever went on and on. Nothing the doctors did affected it. So even though I knew fevers were a normal part of getting sick and the body's way of fighting infection, I feared them.

His eyes cracked open. They were unfocused. I sat off to the side so he wouldn't be blinded by my aura.

"Cole," I said.

He turned his head and immediately shut his eyes. "Damn, that's bright."

I scooted behind him. "Try now."

"Okay."

"You should try to sit up."

He shook his head.

"You're dehydrated," I explained patiently. "You need to drink."

I put my hands under his arms to help him sit up, but though he was weak, he didn't need the help. Knowing he wouldn't want it, I let go. I took the glass of water off the counter and reached my arm around his body to give it to him, trying to keep myself out of view. "Take small sips."

His fingers wrapped around the glass and the water shook as his hand quivered. He sat perfectly still, breathing heavily. Finally, he brought the glass to his lips and took two small sips.

"Enough," he said, holding the glass up for me to take.

He'd barely swallowed any liquid, but I wouldn't press it on him right now. We needed to be sure he could keep it down first.

"Can you stand?"

"Probably." But he didn't move. He leaned back against the cabinet and closed his eyes. I closed the lid on the toilet and sat on it, still out of his line of sight.

"What happened?"

"Migraine. At least that's what it felt like."

"I didn't know you got those."

"I don't. But my mom does, so I know the symptoms. Light sensitivity, nausea, pain above the eyes. I had all of that." He paused. "And then some."

"Did you go anywhere?"

"No. It started yesterday morning, so I stayed home from school. I figured a few Advil and some sleep would knock it out."

Unfortunately, over-the-counter meds wouldn't change his new genetic makeup.

"Turn your head slowly and look at me," I said.

Cole hesitated but did as I commanded. As soon as his gaze landed on me, he clamped his eyes shut and whipped his head back around, tucking his face into his shoulder.

"Fuck. It's like looking right at the sun."

I blew out a breath. If it was that bad just looking at me, he had no idea what he was in for when he went out in public. Or worse—back to school. In public, he'd only be able to see select auras. At school, he'd see almost all of them since the students were close to his age. Maybe it would be a little better for him since he was nineteen—the freshman class might be too young. I'd never been able to figure out exactly where the cut-off was for my age bracket as far as aura visibility went.

"It's my aura. You've seen it before, remember?"

"It wasn't that bright."

I couldn't explain it. My mom was the only other seeker I knew, and she wasn't able to project her aura. It was just some freaky ability I had.

"I'll have to help you learn to block them."

"Shit," Cole muttered. "I'm not going to be able to go to school, am I?"

"No. Not until you get this under control."

He sighed and cradled his head in his hands. "I've already missed a lot of days. If I miss many more, I won't graduate."

I didn't know what to say to that, other than "I'm sorry." Some of the days were due to him dealing with Kyle, but a lot of them were because of my seeker mess.

He climbed to his feet, using the vanity to pull himself up. When he reached his full height, he wobbled and I quickly stepped forward to steady him.

"Whoa," I said, putting my hands around his ribcage.

He jerked away from my touch, instead leaning on the wall to stay upright. My hands recoiled and I tucked them in my pockets, tears blurring my vision.

Of course. He was still pissed. His being sick and calling me changed nothing. If anything, he was probably even more pissed at me. And rightly so. It was my fault he felt like death.

I hastily wiped away my tears as they fell—not that he would see them anyway since it blinded him to look at me—and followed him as he teetered toward the bedroom. It was close—maybe fifteen feet, but it took him a long time. When he collapsed on the bed, sweat glistened on his brow.

"Can I get you anything?" I asked.

"Water."

I quickly returned with a fresh glass of ice water and placed it on his nightstand. I had also grabbed a pack of crackers for when his appetite returned. Then I moved his trash can next to his bed, just in case.

"Anything else?"

"No."

I hovered in the doorway. He didn't want me here, but I didn't want to leave him, not like this. But he was too sick to start training.

"I guess I'll go," I said. "Unless you want me to stay." I hated how pathetic I sounded, begging him to want me to stay.

His silence was my answer.

I ducked my head as my chin started to quiver. Then I sucked in a breath and leaned my head back so the tears wouldn't fall. *Suck it up, Ava.*

This wasn't about our relationship. This was about helping Cole learn to manage his abilities so he could function in society like a normal human being.

Except he wasn't a *normal* human being, not anymore.

My fault, my fault, my fault.

I righted my head and threw back my shoulders. I didn't have the luxury of giving in to a self-pity—or self-loathing—party. Not now.

I plugged in his cell phone since it was almost dead. "Call me if you need me. I'll come back this afternoon to check on you."

Still nothing. It shattered my heart.

CHAPTER 14

I MANAGED TO MAKE IT through the shop without running into Bill, who was in his office. As I passed through the door with the broken window pane and the chain lying on the floor next to it, I looked at my hand and flexed it. The only sign of my injury was the dried blood on my sleeve. My skin was smooth, like I had never been cut. Our healing ability was probably the only perk of being a seeker. But a fat lot of good it was doing my mom. And Cole right now, for that matter.

As I sat in the car in the parking lot waiting for the windshield to defrost, I texted Bill to let him know Cole was sick. It made me feel a little better to know Bill was right downstairs if Cole needed something. Bill would be a better caretaker since Cole wouldn't be able to see his aura. His presence wouldn't hurt him, not like mine did.

Sure. Keep telling yourself that's why he wanted you gone.

By the time I made it home, it was ten a.m. I should be in second period, but there was no way I was making it to school today. I was exhausted—emotionally, physically, spiritually, basically every *ally* there was.

I would take a nap and then return to Cole's apartment later this afternoon to begin training him. The sooner he learned to deal with auras, the sooner his life could get back to normal.

Sort of. He'd have to find a new normal.

The note I'd left for my mom was still sitting on the table. I wondered if she'd seen it. Shrugging, I threw it in the trash.

I poured myself a bowl of Cheerios—found in the way top of the pantry in the C section. What did Bill think about the new organization of all his things? Thank God he was patient and easy going. At some point, though, that patience would wear thin. Or he'd get curious at the very least.

He could get in line. I was more than curious about my mom's strange behavior, and I knew the origin of it. I wouldn't curse Bill with that enlightenment, though. He probably wouldn't believe me, anyway. It had taken a lot to convince Cole.

I gripped the spoon tighter, remembering the crazy trip I'd taken to northern Virginia with Cole when the Reapers had been after him. I'd been trying to save his life while he thought he was protecting me from some gang members who were after us—he hadn't realized the gang members were simply pawns of the Grim Reaper.

Despite the messed up nature of the ordeal, it was kind of a fond memory, too. That was when I realized Cole cared about me.

I pulled a piece of notebook paper out of my binder along with a pen. I needed to make a lesson plan. As I shoveled cereal in my mouth, my hand remained poised above the paper. I didn't know where to begin.

Why had Xena tasked me with this? I'd never taught anyone how to deal with auras. Sure, I'd had to learn myself, but I didn't remember my mom teaching me. She must have, though. Perhaps she could help me.

I loaded my bowl in the dishwasher and went upstairs. My whole body tensed by the time I'd made it to the second floor. What would I find today? Maybe she'd decided alphabetizing wasn't the way to go. Maybe she'd be organizing by color. Or size. Or shape.

It was anybody's guess.

I knocked lightly on her door.

"Come in," she called. So far, so good. She sounded normal. But she had yesterday, too.

Filled with trepidation, I swung the door open. She was still in bed, reading one of the books she'd so painstakingly organized yesterday. It was an old hardback with yellowed pages, the kind that had that fantastic musty old book smell.

"What are you reading?" I asked.

"*Rebecca*." She put the book on her lap, open with pages down to mark her spot. "I read it a long time ago, probably when I was your age. I forgot how much I liked it."

She'd forgotten a lot of things lately.

I nodded, sticking my hands in my back pockets. I used to read a lot, too, before I started spending all my free time with Cole. It was always nice to escape into someone else's problems for a while. Unfortunately, lately my problems were too big to forget, even for a little while.

"I need to talk to you about Cole."

She moved her book to the nightstand and sat up straight, a seriously concerned expression on her face. "Oh, honey. I should have talked to you about this a long time ago. Have you..." she trailed off, her lips pursed and her brow furrowed as she tried to find the right words.

Horrified, I gasped as I realized what she was getting at. I could feel my face turning thirty-seven shades of red. "Oh, God, Mom, no." I shook my head vehemently and put my hands up to ward her off. "We don't need to have *the talk*."

"You're seventeen, so I know you already know everything, but if there's something specific going on with you and Cole—"

"No. I mean, there is something going on, but it's not about *that*."

I wished that was what this was about—that awkward conversation when I told my mom I wanted to go on birth control. But nope. That time wasn't coming any time soon. Not with Cole protecting my virtue.

And especially not now that he hated me. Couldn't forget that.

"Cole's abilities are kicking in." I sat on the edge of her bed.

"Ah," she said with a knowing nod. She put her hand over mine and squeezed. I glanced over at her and really looked—other than her pale complexion and the circles under her eyes, she looked normal and seemed alert and mentally stable. Just like good old Mom.

Thank God today was a good day for her, a day when I really needed her. I wished she could fix it for me, like when she'd kiss a boo-boo when I was young and the pain would magically disappear.

But unlike then, this pain was real and there was no easy fix—not even an imaginary one.

"I told him everything. He hates me." I wiped a tear from my eye and she passed me a tissue. "Understandably so."

"He's just angry right now," she said. "He'll understand, and if he doesn't, then he's not the guy you thought he was." Such a mom thing to say. It was nice to hear, even if it wasn't true. Cole was *exactly* the guy I thought he was. It would be easier for me if he weren't.

"I guess." I sniffed, wiping my face clean with the tissue. I would have liked to curl up next to my mom and cry like I did after we watched *The Notebook*, but I didn't have time for such a self indulgence. "I'm more worried about him, though, not just our relationship. Like, his health, I mean. He's really sick. Fever, vomiting, chills. And he can't stand to look at me—because of my aura."

And because I was the one who caused all this, but that went without saying.

"Hmm..." She tapped her finger on her lips. "It could

be because he came into his abilities later in life. Since we were born with them, they got more powerful gradually. He's getting slammed with them all at once. I imagine it's a lot for his body—and brain—to handle."

"That's what I figured," I said. "And Xe—" I broke off. *Shit*. I forgot I hadn't told my mom about Xena yet. I closed my eyes for a moment, then decided I wouldn't get into that right now. "I need to train him to handle the auras, but I don't know how to start."

"I used to play peek-a-boo with you."

"Okay?" What did that have to do with anything?

"So that's how I taught you the concept of blocking the auras. It was silly, but you were three and you understood playing peek-a-boo with them. You made them disappear that way."

I frowned. That wasn't as helpful as I'd hoped. "You didn't explain it to me?"

"You were three," she repeated. "Toddlers pick up on things easily, so it wasn't hard. You taught yourself."

In other words, she couldn't help me. She must have read the despair on my face. "You'll figure it out. It's a mental thing, and I'm honestly not sure everyone blocks them the same way."

"Yeah, I guess so."

For not the first time, I wished I knew other seekers. They were out there, but for whatever reason, my mom and I had never tried reaching out to them. I really wished I had the extra resources right now. When—if—Xena ever came back, I was going to ask her to put me in touch with other seekers.

"Are you going to train him to pick out the white fated auras?" my mom asked.

I'd have to, wouldn't I? Xena had said he would need to know. She might not have told me everything, but I believed what she did tell me. If Xena said he needed to know, then I'd have to figure out a way to teach him.

"I think so. He should be ready..." I trailed off, not

explaining what he needed to be ready for.

Her lips pressed into a thin line. "I wonder when we'll get another handler."

Now was the perfect time to tell her about Xena. She'd all but asked me. But instead I said, "I don't know."

I was such a liar.

THE NEXT MORNING I GOT up when my alarm went off, like I did every school day. Except I wasn't going to school. I'd made arrangements to meet Cole at a park up the street from his apartment.

It might have been better to meet at his place, since it would be private and we wouldn't risk him being blindsided by the auras of people walking by, but I had the feeling he didn't want me there.

It made me sad.

At least he was taking me up on my offer to help him. That was a result of his desperation—he didn't want to fail due to attendance—so he needed to learn to deal with these auras and learn it quick. I think he was clinging to the hope he'd still be able to take Kyle in, despite his new status as a seeker.

I didn't know if his hope was fruitless or not. Based on my life experience, I would say there was no chance he'd have enough stability to take on Kyle, but now that Xavier was out of the picture...well, the game had changed.

And I still didn't know the rules.

Unlike Cole, I wasn't worried I'd fail due to attendance. The administration at school knew about my mom's illness, and every week, a counselor would check in with me to make sure I was coping okay. So I'd tell them some sob story about how my mom had a relapse and needed me. That was sort-of true but not my reason for missing school. Not today, at least. And honestly, my school performance was so low on my list of priorities it had fallen off. College wasn't in my future, so what did I care? If it came down to it, I'd get a GED or something.

I quickly showered, dressed, and headed downstairs. I'd heard my mom up early, which was surprising considering how much she'd been sleeping lately. She was downstairs before it was even light out, doing Lord knew what.

I opened the pantry, somewhat pleased to find the Raisin Bran back on the top shelf where it belonged. Good—that meant my mom had let go of her OCD "organizing." That was the only cereal up there, though. I needed to pull together what little money we had and do some grocery shopping. We'd eaten up most of Bill's food. It was nice enough that he'd taken us in and made himself scarce, basically giving us run of the whole house. He shouldn't have to feed us, too.

As I was pouring milk on the cereal, my mom walked into the kitchen carrying two baskets of laundry stacked on top of one another. She couldn't even see over them, so I rushed over to take the top one.

"Whoa," I said. "Take two trips next time, will you?"

Geez, I sounded like a mother. I was not totally comfortable with this role reversal. But dang it, we had enough problems without her tripping and breaking her leg or something.

She blew the stray strands out of her face. "Laundry is all clean! That basket you have is Bill's. Can you go put the clothes away in his room?"

I paused, and I'm sure a look of horror, worthy of any Wes Craven movie, crossed my face. I glanced down at the neatly folded clothes and sure enough, right on top, was a pair of Bill's underwear. I averted my eyes.

"No way, Mom."

I was just saying how we needed to pay Bill back for everything he was doing for us. We didn't have money, but here my mom had found a way to help him out that didn't cost anything.

But I didn't want to paw through Bill's clothes. That just seemed too *intimate*. I shuddered at my word choice. *Yikes. Bill* and *intimate* in the same sentence. *Not cool, brain, not cool at all.*

She gave me the "mom" look. "*Yes* way. Hurry and do it now so you don't miss the bus."

My heart sank and my shoulders slumped. She *knew* I'd been driving to school since we'd been living here. She was having a bad day again. *Damn.*

I opened my mouth to protest, but one look at her, and I didn't have the heart. So I dutifully went off in the direction of Bill's bedroom.

I stood outside the door for a moment, feeling very much like a creeper. Bill usually kept the door shut, and I respected his need for privacy. Usually. Apparently my need not to rock my mom's boat took precedence.

And maybe this was okay, anyway. No one *liked* doing laundry. Bill would probably appreciate coming home and finding his drawers replenished with clean clothes.

I took a deep breath and knocked, just in case he'd changed his schedule and stayed home today. Not likely. Bill was more predictable than the weather.

Swinging open the door, I stepped inside. I was surprised to find the room tastefully decorated in sage green. It had a little bit of a feminine touch to it, and I realized that must have been a woman's doing. Perhaps Jill's mother. Or maybe Jill herself.

I set the basket on the bed and pulled out the first stack, cringing and trying hard not to touch more of Bill's underwear than was absolutely necessary to get the job done. I pulled open the top drawer and got lucky. I shoved the underwear in and pushed it closed, hoping to erase the memory from my mind.

My gaze landed on a framed picture on his dresser. It was of a woman with light brown hair. She wore a sundress and had her hands on her hips and a take-the-picture-already smile on her face. She was gorgeous.

This must be Jill's mother. There was enough of a resemblance. I didn't even know her name.

I reached for the picture to pick it up and examine it closer, but I yanked my hands away at the last second. It was bad enough I was invading his privacy by being in here. I wasn't going to touch what looked to be an important memento.

I picked up a stack of socks and pulled open the other top dresser drawer. Right again! Bill was so predictable, even with how he organized his clothes. As I pushed the socks in the drawer back to make room for the ones in my hand, my fingers brushed up against something metal. I put the socks down and pulled out the other ones so I could see what it was.

Just what I thought—a gun.

I hadn't yet learned enough about guns to know exactly what kind it was, but it was similar to the ones I'd been firing with Cole. Some kind of semi-automatic. I popped the clip out. Full. I spied a cardboard box way in the back and pulled that out—9mm bullets.

I held the gun in my shaking hand, my thoughts heavy.

Would Bill notice if it were missing?

If I was faced with Xavier again, would I be able to pull the trigger?

I closed my eyes for a moment, and in the background, I could hear my mom humming in the kitchen, a song I didn't even recognize. She never used to do that. It was like I didn't know her anymore. Where was the mom I knew and loved?

I opened my eyes, my resolve hardened.

Yes. I most definitely would be able to pull the trigger.

And I hoped I'd have the opportunity.

CHAPTER 15

ON THE DRIVE TO MEET Cole, I kept one eye on the glove compartment where I'd stowed the gun and extra rounds. There was a lock, and I'd used it, but part of me thought it might be better to leave it open. If I needed to get to the weapon quickly, I wouldn't want to waste time fumbling with the key. And what if I needed it while the car was in motion?

I chewed on my lip. *Damn.* On the other hand, basic safety called for it to be locked away. But it was not like I was going to have any toddlers in the car. Or anyone else other than Xena or maybe Cole, for that matter.

It was a conundrum.

In the end, I kept it locked. Besides, if Cole looked in there for some reason, he would be pissed I'd taken Bill's gun. I could hear him now—*You stole from Bill? You can't handle a gun like that! Ava, go put it back where you found it or I will.*

I didn't need to give him any more reasons to be pissed at me.

And anyway, I was just borrowing it, not stealing it. This summer when I turned eighteen, I'd buy my own gun—with what money, I had no idea. I'd have to figure that part out. Until then, I had this one. I wouldn't use it unless it was life-and-death.

I turned right into the park's lot and pulled into a space next to the Rustinator. Cole had beaten me here—naturally—and he sat on the top of a bench, his feet on the seat and his elbows on his knees. I peered at his profile, trying to determine what his hatred level would be today.

On a scale of one to ten, one being you won't pause to tell me the time and ten being you want to see me six feet under—and maybe even put me there—how do you feel about me today, Cole?

I would wager an eleven.

Okay, that wasn't fair. Cole had never wished any ill-will upon me, at least not out loud. He just didn't want anything to do with me anymore.

To me, it was the same thing.

I stared at him for another moment before pulling myself out of the car. The cold smacked me in the face, and I zipped my coat all the way up, ducking my chin down. Shoving my hands in my pockets, I came up with one tattered glove and groaned.

Screw it. I was wearing that one glove, even if it did make me look like a retro Michael Jackson. At least one hand wouldn't be at risk for frostbite.

Cole turned his head and when his eyes locked on mine, I slowed my pace, nearly stumbling over a pronounced tree root.

His eyes were blank, his expression neutral. He might as well have been waiting for a perfect stranger. He held my gaze for a few seconds before turning away.

I picked up my pace and stopped several feet away from him. "Are you ready?"

He shrugged and hopped down off the bench. "Do I have a choice?"

Nope, not really.

"The first thing you need to learn is how to block out auras. How does mine look today?"

He looked at me again, and I held my breath, hoping to see some spark in his eyes when he looked at me.

Something, anything indicating he'd forgive me. Not today, but someday.

Nothing. Only the slight curl of his lip before he looked away. "It's not as bright."

My heart shattered and the fragments pierced my insides. It hurt so bad to be near him and feel the waves of indifference roll off him.

I swallowed. "That's good." My voice sounded hollow and distant, like it wasn't even me talking. That's what I would have to do to get through this—keep myself distant. Pretend Cole was just a stranger, that he was nothing to me.

As if I ever could.

His face haunted my daydreams and my nightmares. He was there when my subconscious daydreamed about my future. He was there in my nightmares when I relived Xavier killing him. I'd wake in a cold sweat, and always, always, always with the feel of his blood on my hands.

My eyes open or shut, he was always there.

I hugged my stomach, suddenly finding it hard to breathe the frosty air. I doubled over, sucking in oxygen.

"Are you okay?" he asked. Again, his voice was neutral. His comment was the kind you'd say to a stranger who slipped on an icy sidewalk, laced with detached concern.

"I'm fine. I just need a minute." I turned away so he wouldn't see the tears gathering in my eyes.

This was harder than I thought it would be. Not the actual teaching him part because I hadn't even started that, but coming to terms with the fact I was inducting him into a life I hated. *Nobody* wanted this.

There were no winners here. In this game, we were all losers.

I walked to the car and got in for a moment, pretending to look for something. I ducked my head down below the level of the windshield and wiped my eyes. A quick look in the rearview told me my skin was blotchy and my eyes red, but that couldn't be fixed. I would blame it on the cold.

But he wouldn't ask, anyway.

He would not see me cry.

I got out of the car (again) and walked over to Cole (again). This time, my own face wore the guise of indifference, a mirror of his. The only difference was he wasn't faking. But Cole needed to learn these things, and if I was going to keep myself together enough to help him, I needed to stay detached.

Once I learned I was a seeker, that became my new policy—no friends, no attachments. It was easier that way. I'd made an exception for Cole—and Kaley, I guess—but perhaps it was time to get back to my old way of doing things. If I could.

"Okay," I said, all business. "The first thing you need to learn is to block auras so they don't overwhelm you."

"Okay." He looked at me expectantly, like he was waiting for me to say more. "How do I do that?"

This was where things got dicey. I still didn't know how to teach him. I cursed Xena for the billionth time.

"Visualize a curtain. Or a door. Or a wall. Anything that blocks light will work."

He waited a beat. "Are you serious?"

I scowled at him. "Yes. I'm not standing out here in the cold to mess around. Let's get this done so we can get back inside."

That's right, Ava. Find your attitude. Maybe if I stayed just on the edge of irritated, I wouldn't succumb to my heartache.

Cole was good at irritating me. I just needed to let him.

His nostrils flared slightly and he assumed an annoyed posture—his hands tucked in his pockets, one hip cocked, one shoulder lower than the other. "Fine." He stared off into the distance.

"It might help if you close your eyes."

"If I close my eyes, then I don't see the auras, anyway. So why do I need the wall if my eyes are closed?"

Logically, his point made sense, which annoyed me. I *hated* feeling stupid, even more so when Cole was the one who made me feel that way.

I narrowed my eyes at him, a snappy retort on the tip of my tongue, but I swallowed it. *Just get through this. Stay detached. Do not engage.*

"It's just to help you get the hang of the concept," I said. "You have to crawl before you can walk."

Totally lame explanation, but I wasn't backing down. It was like learning to play a sport, when players would close their eyes and "*be* the ball." Same idea, or so I hoped.

He huffed but closed his eyes.

"I personally picture a huge door that closes in from top to bottom. It's metal with teeth that interlock when they come together."

I felt silly explaining this out loud but that was really how it worked for me. When I blocked out the auras, I would slam the barrier in place, and the auras would disappear from the top and bottom, the void making its way into the middle until they were totally blocked.

"Okay."

"Can you see it?"

"Sure."

He wasn't giving me much feedback to work with. I couldn't tell from his tone if he was being sarcastic or serious. I was going with serious because I wanted to move past this.

I steeled myself for this next part, making myself like my metal door—impervious to emotion.

"Now open your eyes and look at me."

He opened his eyes and looked directly into mine. I couldn't help it—my breath hitched and my gut tightened.

I was so bad at my new door incarnation.

"Can you see my aura?" I whispered.

"Yes."

I wanted him to see so much more than my aura. I wanted him to see *me*, the girl he cared about, the girl he was willing to risk his life for, the girl he'd once said he loved.

Our eyes stayed locked, and I swallowed.

Next step, Ava. Get to it.

"Okay, now mentally try to put that wall in place while your eyes are open."

He squinted at me for a moment, breaking the spell, then threw his hands up. "This is pointless. It's never going to work."

"This is all I've got," I said quietly, trying to keep my chin from quivering. "I'm trying to help you, but if this is going to work you need to take it seriously."

"I *am* taking it seriously. I closed my eyes and did as you asked. What more do you want from me?"

I stared at him, my heart pounding in my chest and my breaths coming long and hard.

There was no easy answer to that question. Everything and nothing all at the same time. I wanted him to forgive me and love me again, but I didn't feel I was worth it.

I was no one special, just a girl with a life so messed up, it'd spilled into his.

So what I wanted right now was for him to accept this last gift I was offering—lessons on how to live as normal a life as possible with this curse—my birthright and his inheritance.

It was my retribution.

He cursed under his breath and shoved his hands in his pockets, then walked a few feet away. "I didn't ask for this."

Neither did I was on the tip of my tongue, but that would only be partially true. I didn't ask for it either, not for myself anyway.

But I did ask for it for him. And I couldn't take it back. I didn't want to. Because then he'd be dead.

"Just practice visualizing," I spat. "If you feel up to it, go find some people to try this out on. As long as they're close to your age, you should be able to see their auras."

Cole jerked his head in the other direction, not bothering to respond.

I stalked to the car and yanked the door open. My eyes blurred with tears as I buckled the seatbelt. I wiped them away, no longer caring if he saw. But I doubted he did, anyway. He didn't even want to look at me.

I put the car in reverse and backed out of the space. I pulled into traffic, not looking back.

What a stellar first lesson.

I COULD HAVE GONE TO school. It was just past ten, so I'd only missed two classes. But I went back to Bill's. My lesson with Cole wasn't long—or successful—but it had taken a lot out of me. I was exhausted and depleted and empty. My aura was probably all kinds of gray.

My soul felt bare.

I parked at Bill's—still backing in, coward that I was—and sat in the car for a while, putting myself back together, mentally piecing together the shards of my broken heart. Next was my mind, though there was not much I could do about that. It was torn in so many different directions, stretched so far I feared it would snap at any moment. I couldn't go on like that. Something had to give.

As I pulled my backpack out of the backseat, I tried to come up with some excuse to give my mom for being home so early. Though depending on how she was today, I might not need to worry about an excuse. I'd give anything for her to try to ground me for skipping school. I slung my backpack over my shoulder and trudged up the steps.

Silence permeated the house—the kind that made the hair on the back of my neck stand up. I didn't know how I knew, but something wasn't right. Something was wrong.

Really wrong.

"Mom?" I called up the stairs. I dropped my backpack on the ground and took them two at a time. "Mom?"

I pushed open the door to her room. She was there in bed, a big lump beneath the quilt.

I exhaled, putting my hand on my chest to still my racing heart.

She was fine, just sleeping, which wasn't unusual lately. Nothing to worry about. I was totally overreacting.

At least I didn't have to explain my presence here at the house and my absence from school.

I tiptoed closer to the bed and pulled the quilt up around her. As I did this, I nudged her shoulder and she flopped onto her back.

Still asleep.

Wow, she was really out of it.

Then something at her mouth caught my attention—a white liquid.

Oh, shit. She was foaming at the mouth.

I grabbed her shoulder and shook, gently at first and then harder when I got no response. Her head lolled back and her arm fell limply off the bed.

"Oh no, oh no, oh no. Mom, please wake up."

More white liquid bubbled at her mouth and I tilted her onto her side. I pulled my phone out and called Bill.

He answered on the second ring.

"Bill, my mom won't wake up."

"Call 911. I'm leaving now."

I hung up and tried to dial the three digits with my shaking hands. I was an idiot. Why did I call Bill first? Those seconds could make the difference between—

No, not going there.

"911, what is your emergency?"

I babbled some kind of incoherent mess of words. I didn't know what the heck I said, but it must have worked because the operator told me what I wanted to hear—the paramedics were on their way.

Well, what I really wanted to hear was that my mom was going to be fine, but that would be an empty promise. I knew now, beyond a shadow of a doubt, that my mom wasn't going to get completely better. Not without a miracle.

But I feared I'd used my only one on Cole. And he hated me for it.

I sat on the edge of the bed and stroked her hair while I waited for the ambulance. The 911 operator wanted me to stay on the line in case something changed so I kept the phone propped on my shoulder.

"It's going to be okay," I said to my mom, even though she couldn't hear me. "Help is coming. Just hang on."

Her skin was pale, her breaths shallow, her skin cool to the touch. No fever this time.

Why weren't the Reapers saving her? What was it Xavier had told me—seekers couldn't die until they were done with us? Did this mean they were done with my mom? Were they throwing her away?

I choked on a sob.

The sound of sirens blaring in the distance, getting closer with every second, were comforting. *Help is coming. Help is almost here.*

"Hang on, Mom. They're only seconds away. I can hear them."

"The paramedics are in your driveway," the operator said, "so I'm going to hang up now. If the door isn't unlocked, go down and open it."

"Okay." Numbly, I disconnected, trying to remember if I'd locked the door behind me. I didn't think so.

I squeezed my mom's hand. "I'm so sorry, Mom. This is my fault. I'm so sorry. I'll make Xavier pay."

Those words were on my lips as the paramedics streaked through the doorway. I stepped back to let them work and after a minute, Bill arrived. He didn't say a word to me—just opened his arms. I walked into them, and he held me as we silently watched them work on my mom. He held me as I watched my mom's heart stop, watched them bring her back with CPR. He continued to hold me as they strapped her to a board, carried her down the stairs, and out the front door.

He was still holding me when I broke, knees collapsing and sobs wracking my body.

CHAPTER 16

MOMENTS AFTER THE AMBULANCE PULLED out of the driveway, Bill hustled me into his truck so we could follow. It wasn't until we were almost there that I realized I'd left my phone on my mom's nightstand. Oh, well. It didn't matter.

At the hospital, I followed Bill around like a zombie while he asked where we needed to go. Straight to ICU.

It was like deja vu. Hadn't I just done this a few months ago?

The doctors were examining her, so they didn't let us in. I wanted to tell them not to waste their time. They wouldn't be able to figure out what was wrong with her. One day, some doctor could write an article about this or appear on one of those "strangest medical mysteries" shows because it truly was a mystery. Even if I told them about Xavier, it still wouldn't do them any good, and that was *if* they believed me. A big *if*.

I sat in a hard plastic chair in the waiting room, staring at the white wall and counting my breaths as I inhaled the antiseptic-smelling air. I told myself that by the time I got to a thousand, we'd get some news. Then it turned into two-thousand. Then five-thousand.

Finally I stopped.

I wanted to quit. I wanted to quit everything—school,

being a seeker, life. Most of all, life. What did I have left?

I thought back to when Cole pulled me out of traffic. My angel ancestor had saved me from death—or at least some serious disfigurement. Maybe it would have been better if he hadn't. Maybe it would have been better for everyone if I'd just kicked the bucket. Sure, my mom would be sad, but she'd be healthy right now. Cole would be living a normal life. Bill wouldn't have gotten pulled into our mess.

We'd never be able to repay Bill for the kindness he'd showed us.

He sat next to me with his arms crossed and every once in a while, he reached over and patted my knee. It was oddly comforting. Just enough contact to let me know he was there but not enough to set me into tears again.

Lunchtime came and went. Bill bought me a sandwich from the cafeteria, and I choked down a few bites for his sake. Then when he got up to use the restroom, I tossed the rest in the trash.

Every hour on the hour, he would go up to the nurse's station, only to return to his seat moments later. No news.

His phone rang and he answered it. After a second, he held it out to me. "It's for you."

I frowned and stared at it for a moment. Who would want to talk to me? The only person who unequivocally cared about me was hooked up to God knew what machines while doctors poked and prodded at her.

"Hello?"

"Ava."

I closed my eyes. *Cole.* I waited for the pang of longing to strike, but I felt nothing. I was hollow inside.

"What?"

"How are you?"

"How do you think I am?"

There was a pause.

"I'm sorry about your mom. Bill texted me."

I didn't say anything. There was nothing to say.

"I would come to the hospital, but I can't block the auras yet." He sounded apologetic.

"Thanks," I said. I didn't mean it. In order to mean it, you had to feel something. I felt nothing.

Inside, I was hollow. Bare. Broken.

"I know things are...weird between us, but if you need anything—"

"I have Bill," I said. "I need to go."

"Okay." Cole sounded unsure, very unusual for him. But I didn't care. I couldn't worry about him right now.

"Bye." I hung up and handed the phone back to Bill, then fixed my gaze on a water stain on the ceiling.

It was funny how quickly priorities could change. Yesterday, I would have killed for Cole to reach out to me.

Today, though...today, the only thing I could focus on—the only thing that helped to block the pain—was how much I wanted to kill Xavier.

WE FINALLY WERE ALLOWED IN to see my mom. She looked skeletal and her skin matched the white hospital blanket someone had tucked around her frail body. Tubes were stuck in her arms and sensors were pasted to her temples.

Bill listened to what the doctor was saying, but I tuned her out. Nothing she said mattered. Modern medicine couldn't fix this.

Maybe nothing could.

I held my mom's hand, running my fingers over her skin. The feel of her pulse in her wrist was comforting. As long as her heart continued beating, there was a chance. Right now, that was all I had.

"Ava," Bill said. I looked up. The doctor had left and I hadn't even noticed. "We should go. You need rest. There's nothing we can do here."

I nodded then looked back down at my mom.

"I'll step out for a moment to let you, *ahem*..." Bill

shuffled out of the room.

I smoothed her hair back and tucked it behind her ears like she liked and for the first time, noticed strands of gray streaking through the auburn.

I couldn't say what I wanted—that everything would be okay—because that was a lie. Between the two of us, we'd had enough lies. So instead, I told her something else.

"I'm going to avenge you," I said, my voice sounding like a stranger's. "I promise you Xavier will pay for this."

I tucked her arm under the blanket and left the room without looking back.

Bill was waiting just outside the door. When I came out, he didn't say anything, just fell into step beside me. The drive home was also quiet.

I'd never appreciated Bill's silence more.

At the house, he heated up two microwave meals, handed me one, then left me to my own devices.

The food went straight into the trash.

In my bedroom, I paced. With every step, something snapped within me. My insides fractured and rearranged until I was filled with nothing but rage.

I grabbed my keys and slipped out the front door. Keeping the headlights off, I pulled out of the driveway and onto the road. Then I flipped on lights and pounded on the gas.

I didn't know where I was going—I just drove. I found myself heading toward the street I'd been parked on when Xavier started following me. I slowed down, peering out the window for any sign of him.

It was stupid, so stupid. Not because I was hunting Xavier—no, I was ready for him. I'd pulled the gun out of the glove box and it sat on my lap. No, it was stupid because what were the odds I'd find him on a random street?

I needed to be smarter. I drove toward Nice Beauty. I'd seen him near there once. Besides that, if he was looking for me, he might know I worked there by now.

I almost laughed at my own accidental joke. *Worked there.* Ha! How funny. Shenice hadn't called again. I probably wouldn't even get paid for the hours I put in. It was just my luck to land a job that ended just as it'd barely begun.

I pulled into the parking lot and cut off the engine. It was past nine, so the strip mall was deserted. I got out of the car and strode over to the shop's windows, cupping my hands around the glass so I could peer in. There was no sign of activity.

I dropped my hands to my sides and took a step back.

Then arms wrapped around me, pinning my arms to my sides. My heart went into overdrive and my adrenaline pumped. As I opened my mouth to scream, a hand clamped over it. I twisted my neck, gnashing my teeth against the hand. I managed to get a little bite in, but the hand only clamped down harder.

Shit. This wasn't good. And I'd left the goddamn gun in the car.

Be calm, be calm. Think.

I inhaled, but there was no cinnamon smell, just the weak smell of rot from the trashcan to my right. It wasn't Xavier.

The door to the shop opened, but I couldn't see who was holding it wide. I struggled against my captor, leaning backwards and planting my feet firm. It did no good—I was dragged through the door.

My mind raced. What should I do? I stopped thrashing around, wanting to conserve my energy. If I couldn't free myself while I was being dragged, I certainly wouldn't be able to do it when my captor was standing still. Maybe if they thought I was cooperating, they'd let go, and then I could make a break for it. Or somehow fight my way out.

I mentally inventoried the things I knew to be in the shop, trying to figure out what I could use as a weapon.

Scissors. The salon had cutting shears.

And chemicals. If I could get my hands on some perm or dye chemicals, I could use them to blind someone.

Because I wasn't going down, not like this.

Hours earlier, I'd been thinking it would be better if I'd died, but now that I faced a deadly situation, I realized something. Something important.

I wanted to live.

If for nothing else than to make sure Xavier got what was coming to him and so that if my mom woke up, she wouldn't be faced with the pain of losing her only daughter.

So I would fight.

The door slammed closed and locks turned. Then I was dragged to the back room, all the while my captors staying behind me and out of my line of sight. Once there, they shut and locked that door. Then I was let go.

"What the hell! She bit me!"

I *knew* that voice. It *couldn't* be. I whirled around. "*Xena?*"

CHAPTER 17

XENA STOOD BEFORE ME, A disgruntled expression on her face as she examined her hand. "Don't worry," she said. "You didn't break the skin."

"I wish I had!" I shot back. I was utterly flabbergasted. Why in the hell had Xena grabbed me like a damn rapist?

Now that we were away from the trashcan, I could smell the faint scent of citrus. I had missed it before, but her scent wasn't as strong as Xavier's.

"Hey, be nice."

I whirled around to the second person in the room, the one who'd opened the door. "Shenice! *What...the...hell?*"

She looked at me and shrugged, like it was no big thing. But it was a *very big thing.*

"What the hell is right," Xena said. "What the hell were you doing out there? Anyone could have grabbed you!"

"Anyone *didn't* grab me! You did!" I closed my eyes and pinched the bridge of my nose. "Can someone please tell me what is going on?"

"What were you doing?" Xena peered at me, her eyes squinted. I couldn't help it—I fidgeted under her scrutiny. I wouldn't be able to lie to her. Or at least she would know I was lying.

"Nothing," I said anyway, wincing as her eyes narrowed. Then I stood up straight and squared my shoulders. *I* wasn't the one who should be questioned here. I should be the questioner, not the questionee. "Where have you been? My mom's in the hospital again. I needed you." My voice turned small for that last sentence, and I hated how vulnerable and needy I sounded.

Xena's eyes softened. "I'm sorry." With those two words, some of my anger faded away.

"Did you learn anything?" A tiny bud of hope bloomed within me, rising from the rubble. "Can you save her?"

Her forlorn expression told me the answer and the hope died a bitter death, short lived that it was.

"I'm sorry," Xena said again.

I wanted to cry—sympathy made me do that, especially sympathy from people like Xena. Because if Xena was being sympathetic, then you knew things were bad.

Instead, I swallowed it down. "Where have you been? And why did you grab me? And wait—do you two know each other?" I waved my finger back and forth between them.

Shenice and Xena exchanged a look at that last question.

"You were in danger," Xena said simply. "So I grabbed you to keep you safe." She paused. "And maybe to scare some sense into you," she added as an afterthought.

She'd accomplished half her task anyway. I'd definitely been scared, but I didn't know what this *sense* was that she spoke of.

"How was I in danger? Is Xavier here?" My senses heightened, thinking maybe this wasn't a worthless trip after all. Maybe I could avenge my mom tonight. It would be so much easier with Xena's help. Excitement coursed through me.

"No, he's not here," she said, "but you were being reckless."

I jutted my chin out, not bothering to deny it. Even if I weren't looking for Xavier, it still wasn't smart to run around after dark by myself in this part of town.

A normal person would sit me down and try to talk sense into me, not enact a faux kidnapping. Although this was Xena, so I'd be more surprised if she actually acted like a normal person.

"So what?" I retorted. "You told me I was safe from Xavier. And I can't die, remember? The Reapers will save me if I'm in danger."

"You'd be surprised what a person can withstand and not die, especially a seeker," Xena said.

My blood ran cold, starting at my heart and flowing out to my extremities. "You sound just like Xavier."

He'd said almost the same exact thing to me. I'd never forget it. I could almost smell the cinnamon as his creepy voice echoed in my mind: *Do you have any idea how much pain can be inflicted on someone who can't die?*

Xena blinked, my statement seeming to surprise and trouble her, but she recovered quickly. "It's true. And you're not exactly in the good graces of the Reapers right now. You've caused quite a bit of trouble and then on top of that, you haven't provided any names in a while."

"*I've* caused trouble?" I threw my hands up. "You've got to be kidding me! And as for the assignments, *I had no handler*. How was I supposed to turn in names? Not that I even want to." I muttered that last part. Refusing to turn in the names of pure souls was what had started this epic ball of disaster rolling.

"I'm not saying you *should* turn in names, just that you haven't."

Huh. That was certainly interesting. I wanted to know more about that, but not now, not tonight, not after everything I'd already been through today.

"Xena, I've had a really bad day and I really can't deal with your word games and semantic tricks tonight." I turned to Shenice. "And now that you're here, since you won't return any of my calls, do you ever want me to come work again?"

Yes, I was being disrespectful to my employer, but I didn't care. She probably wouldn't be my employer much longer anyway.

Shenice exchanged a look with Xena, and I ground my teeth.

"Do you care to tell me what's going on between the two of you?"

"I thought you might have figured it out by now," Xena said, cocking her head. "We're all related."

CHAPTER 18

"WE'RE RELATED?" I ECHOED, LOOKING back and forth between them—Xena with her creamy skin, almond eyes, and jet black hair, and Shenice with her cocoa skin, dark eyes, and micro braided hair.

"Distantly," Xena clarified.

"*Very* distantly," Shenice added.

"How do you know that? And what are the odds that—" I stopped abruptly, realizing what that meant. "So my job was all a set-up. It was fake."

"Sort of," Shenice said. "I really am a beautician. And you'll get paid for the time you put in."

"Is this even your shop?"

She nodded. "I was about to close permanently. If you hadn't noticed, there's not much business. But Xena gave me the money to stay open."

"I can't. I just can't anymore." I pointed a finger at Xena. "You're just as bad as Xavier, keeping me in the dark about everything. How am I supposed to follow the rules, or effect positive change, or do whatever the heck it is I'm supposed to do *if I don't know anything?*"

"Here," Xena said, setting up a folding chair for me. I collapsed into it. She hopped up on the washing machine, her legs dangling down the front.

Seeing her up there made me think about how small

and slight she was. How had she even managed to manhandle me like she had? I could have sworn my captor had the strength of a WWE fighter. Instead she had the appearance of a twelve-year-old girl.

To be fair, Xena wasn't human.

But she used to be, I assumed. I didn't know exactly how the whole angel thing worked because—getting back to my original point—no one told me anything!

"So you remember the story about your angel ancestor?" she asked.

I nodded. As if I could forget. He fell in love with a woman and she conceived a child, but she died in childbirth. He couldn't handle the grief and asked to be allowed back into heaven. He was kind of a teacher's pet up there, so his wish was granted, but at the cost of his descendants working as seekers. It was pretty messed up. Unforgivable, really.

But I'd seen the raw pain in his eyes, as real as if she'd died yesterday instead of centuries ago. So while it was unforgivable, it was understandable.

Given the last few days, I could definitely understand.

"The woman came from a large family," Xena continued. "I'm a descendant of her brother."

I furrowed my brow. "So that would make us..."

"Loosely related," Xena said. "It doesn't matter, but if you really want to hash it out, we could go on ancestry.com."

"I'm good, thanks." I leaned back in the chair and put my hands on my forehead. "Loosely related. Do I have any other angel relatives?"

"Not that I'm aware of," Xena said.

What she said confirmed my earlier theory that Xena had once been human. I wanted to ask her how she became an angel, but that would require asking about how she died, and that seemed a little too personal. And morbid.

And just weird.

She'd died. Yet she was sitting in front of me, breathing the same air I was.

It sort of reminded me of Cole.

Nope, not going there.

"So what does that mean, exactly? Why does it matter that we're related?"

"Most handlers have a connection to the seekers they're assigned to, which allows them to locate the seekers, but ours is much deeper. That's how I can find you—because we share blood."

"I asked you about that. You said you didn't understand how it worked."

She shrugged. "I don't. Not exactly. But that's the best I can figure. There aren't any other handlers and seekers who are related. And what I told you before is true."

I tried to remember everything she told me, which wasn't much. More specifically, I tried to remember the manner in which she told me those things. She hadn't lied, but she'd definitely been evasive and misleading.

"How does Shenice come into play?"

"She's another descendant."

I cocked my head at her. "But you're not an angel, right?"

She smiled. "I'm more human than you are."

My lips pressed into a thin line. I was sure she didn't mean any offense, but I was a little sensitive when it came to my seeker status. Although, could you blame me? It had basically ruined my life.

And her comment got me thinking—more human than me. Did that mean I wasn't 100% human? I'd never considered that. I was part angel, but weren't angels former humans? So how did that make me *less* human? Unless my ancestor was an original angel, in which case—

I was making my own head spin.

"I'm just another descendant," Shenice explained. "But I also come from a line of sensitives."

"You're a psychic?"

"*Sensitive*," Shenice corrected. "Psychic makes it sound like I'm one of those fools scamming people on TV."

"So you communicate with the dead." Huh. So that was real and not just some hokey pokey crap.

"My mother does. And my sister does. My dad and brother don't have any of it. It only seems to run in the females in my line. Anyway, I don't deal with the dead."

"She deals with angels," Xena said.

"How?" I asked. I'd never heard of anything like that before.

"I can see them. And sense when they're around, which is more often than you'd think."

"Why can't I see them? I'm a seeker. I have angel blood."

Xena shook her head. "It's not the same thing. Shenice's gift is really rare. She's the only one of her kind that we know of."

Shenice smiled as if Xena complemented her. Did she really consider it a gift? Being a seeker meant I felt like a freak, and there were more of me. If Shenice was really the only one of her kind, how did she not feel like an outcast?

"Your angel ancestor—"

"What's his name?" I interrupted Xena. "It would be easier if we just called him by his name."

"Areli."

"Was he ever human?"

"No," Xena said. "He's one of the originals, but you won't find him listed in any text. That was another part of his punishment—his very existence was stripped off the record."

"Why would that matter? Do angels care about that sort of thing?"

Xena shrugged. "Some do. He doesn't."

I was trying to get a feel for how the whole angel thing worked. The way Xena talked, it almost sounded like the angels were more like Greek Gods, interfering in humans' lives, rather than celestial beings.

"As I was saying," Xena said, her tone indicating she was annoyed to have been interrupted by my questions. I didn't care. She could be annoyed. "Areli arranged for Shenice to help me look after you since he can't."

"Then why did you leave?" I demanded of Shenice. "How can you protect me if you're not here? You both left at the same time!"

"I needed to visit my family and set up some precautions to keep them safe," Shenice explained. "Getting involved in your situation isn't without risk."

Guilt struck me for a moment but I shook it off. Just like everything else in my life, I hadn't asked for Shenice's help. While I was grateful for what she agreed to do for me, I wasn't the one who asked it of her. I wasn't responsible for endangering her family. I would never let anyone do that for my sake.

But it was probably too late for her to turn back now.

"Anyway." Xena dragged out the word. "Areli's already gotten himself in a lot of trouble for bringing back Cole. And he's still not recovered. Sharing his blood weakened him."

In other words, I'd better not get anyone else killed because Areli wouldn't be able to bring them back. Check. Got it. Wasn't planning on it.

But that gave me an idea.

"If he shared his blood with my mom, would that help her?"

Xena frowned and opened her mouth to reply, but I spoke again before she could. "I know he can't right now, but could it help? Maybe?"

She hesitated and hope blossomed again.

"No, I don't think so." Her lips pressed together in a thin line. Her hesitation was because she didn't want to disappoint me, not because she had good news. "She already has his blood, so all it would do is boost whatever healing agents are already at play. But the healing agents already aren't working."

The hope shriveled.

Xena and Shenice exchanged another look and I groaned. I knew what that meant.

"Lay it on me," I said.

"I couldn't find out anything about your mother's illness," Xena said. "It turns out Xavier is completely unique. There's no one else like him."

Wasn't that just the theme of the evening? I was surrounded by special snowflakes.

But you know what? I was glad Xavier was unique. The world was a better place for not having others like him.

"Good," I said. "I would hate to think there were Xavier clones running around."

Another look passed between the two women.

"What?" I asked. "What am I missing?"

"Xavier is the only one who can help your mom."

CHAPTER 19

I CLOSED MY EYES, LETTING Xena's words soak in.

"You have to be mistaken," I finally said. "There has to be *someone* who can help her."

Xena shook her head. "That's why I was gone. I talked to everyone I could think of. No one has ever seen anything like this before."

I curled my hands into fists. I wanted to cry. I wanted to laugh. But most of all I wanted to scream.

Getting revenge on Xavier had been at the top of my to do list for months. And now I was being told that wasn't possible because I needed him. He was my only hope for saving my mom.

What if I had somehow managed to find him? If given the opportunity tonight, I wouldn't have hesitated to unload a full clip of 9mm rounds into him. I might have killed him, which would have destroyed my mom's only chance of survival. Wouldn't that have been some twisted karma.

But that hadn't happened. Xavier was still out there. And now I was more determined than ever to find him, detain him, and force him to tell us how to help my mom.

"How do we find him?" I asked.

"We can't," Xena said. "If he doesn't want to be found, he can mask his presence."

"But you're like him. He can't hide from you, can he?"

Xena fixed her unwavering gaze on me.

When most people fibbed or lied by omission, they tended to avoid eye contact. Xena was the opposite. There was something she wasn't telling me. I didn't bother trying to get it out of her. It would do no good and I didn't have the energy.

"Okay, then," I said. "What about her?" I looked over at Shenice.

"If he's around, I should be able to see him whether he masks his presence or not," she said. "I'm not entirely sure. This is all new to me. But I do know I can't locate him, not like Xena can locate you. I don't have that power."

"There are more angels among us than you realize," Xena said. "But people can't see them."

"But people can see you. And Xavier." None of this made any sense to me.

"We're *fallen* angels. There's a difference. Angels no longer have a human essence so humans generally can't see them. It takes a really powerful angel, like Areli, to show himself to humans. Fallen angels take on a human essence, which allows them to be seen. We can still mask ourselves from humans if we want to, though."

That actually sounded like a handy skill to have. It was a built-in Cloak of Invisibility.

"Is that how you show up so abruptly?" I asked.

Xena gave me another bland stare. Nope, she wasn't answering that question. *Damn.* I really wanted to know how she did that.

"So what do we do now?" I asked. This conversation was actually making me feel a little better. It was horrible that Xavier could possibly be my mom's savior, but at least now I had some information to work with. We could come up with a plan instead of sitting back and watching my mother deteriorate. It had been killing me seeing it happen and not being able to do anything about it. So this felt good. Action was better than inaction.

"We'll have to wait for him to come to us," Xena said.

"You've got to be kidding me, right? *That's* the plan?" So much for action.

Xena crossed her arms, a grim expression on her face. "It's the best we've got."

Fudge-tastic.

THE NEXT MORNING XENA WAS waiting for me in the car when I came outside. I shook my head and rolled my eyes skyward. If she could show up anywhere like that, then why didn't she just show up at the park where we were meeting Cole?

Before I'd left the shop last night, Xena had me text Cole to make arrangements to meet him today. He'd called me almost immediately, but I'd let it go to voice mail. He probably only wanted more information, but I wasn't ready to talk to him, not even for that. After the call, he'd texted a short message saying he'd be there.

I didn't reply.

Bill had still been awake when I got home. As I had opened the front door, I'd heard his bedroom door closing. He'd waited up for me. No questions, no reprimands, just waited up to make sure I got home safely.

Cole was right—Bill was a good guy.

When I got in the car, Xena wordlessly handed me a cup from the local coffee shop. I put it to my lips—still hot. So hot I almost burned myself. But since it was hot chocolate and *not* coffee, I forgave her. But now I *really* wanted to know how she did it—that shop was miles from here.

Cole was sitting on the same bench in the same park in a deja vu moment of yesterday. Only this time, when his eyes locked on mine, he didn't look away. He watched me walk all the way over to him.

I couldn't do this. Not right now. Not today. Not until my mom was better. I fumbled in my pocket for the pair of dark sunglasses I'd stashed there. I slipped them on.

Was I hiding behind them? Yes. Yes, I was. But I didn't care if that made me a coward.

Sometimes cowards were the only survivors.

"Cole, Xena. Xena, Cole." There—introductions were done. I walked to a bench a few yards away and plopped down.

Cole's eyes were on me again. I crossed my eyes and looked away and in my peripheral vision, I saw Cole turn his attention to Xena.

Good. That was why we were here.

I swung my legs up onto the bench and rested my chin in my hands on the backrest. This really was a pretty park—lots of thick old trees, so big around I couldn't wrap my arms around them. Stone walking trails that led to the different play areas. A fenced in dog run over on the far side.

I'd always wanted a dog, but with my mom's odd hours and our apartment living, she'd said it wasn't a good idea. There was also all the moving—it would be hard to continually find apartments we could afford that allowed pets.

But I wasn't one to give up easily. When I was eight, I asked every day for a pet—a furry one. One I could pet and cuddle. On my ninth birthday, my mom got me a hamster. She was fluffy and golden in color, so I named her Golda. Every day I'd cut up carrots to give her as a treat, and I'd save the toilet paper rolls for her to play with in her cage. I was so happy and the best pet owner ever.

That lasted about a week. Eight days to be exact.

Golda died. She'd gotten wet tail, which is pretty common in hamsters. She'd probably already had it when she came home from the pet store.

I was heartbroken. I created a little coffin out of a shoe box and we buried her in the woods behind our apartment.

I wanted to make a little gravestone for her, but we moved before I was able to.

My mom said she'd get me another hamster, but in the move, the cage got left behind and neither one of us mentioned it again.

It was my first encounter with death. Even at the tender age of nine, I'd understood that the only way to escape the pain of losing someone you loved was to never have them at all.

Maybe it was time I remembered that.

I stood and gave a little wave as I walked out of the park.

I DROVE PAST THE HIGH school on my way to the hospital. It had only been a few days since I'd attended, but it felt like much, much longer than that. I guess I was technically skipping school, but I didn't care. I had more important things to worry about.

I circled around the hospital parking lot looking for a space and came up empty. *Damn.* There was a parking garage on the next street, but I'd have to pay for that and—*big surprise*—I was short on cash. Maybe the hospital validated. Or maybe I could feel around in the seat cushions for change. Either way, I was parking there and visiting my mom. What would they do? Hold me prisoner for not paying the two dollar parking fee? I'd like to see them try.

As I was driving up the ramp to the third floor of the garage, the gas light came on. *Great.* Now, *gas* was something I really was worried about paying for. I'd either have to borrow money from Bill or remind Shenice she promised to pay me for those few hours I worked.

I drove up and down the rows on the third floor and sighed. Were they throwing a party at the hospital or something? Why were there *so many* people here? I made my way back to the ramp to head up to the fourth floor.

Just as I started going up the ramp, I saw someone dressed in black out of the corner of my eye. He got my attention because he was dressed in a long black duster, kind of like Neo in *The Matrix*.

But it was the flash of red fabric that really got me.

I craned my neck, keeping one eye on the ramp so I didn't crash into the concrete wall.

He gave me a little wave and one side of his mouth quirked up in a sneer.

Xavier.

I hit the gas and careened up the rest of the ramp, barely keeping from rubbing against the concrete wall. Once on the fourth floor, I pulled into the first space I saw, thanking my lucky stars there was one right up front. It wasn't until I jumped out of the car that I noticed the handicap sign. What the hell? Who put a handicap spot on the fourth floor of a parking garage?

I didn't have time to move my car or there was no chance I'd catch him. I sprinted toward the stairs and flung the heavy metal door open. The putrid odor of urine slapped me in the face and I nearly gagged. Some of the local homeless must be using this as their bathroom. *Ugh.*

Taking the stairs two at a time, I tried to breathe through my mouth. I was nearly to the third floor door when I realized I'd left the gun in the car. *Dammit!*

Oh, well. It was probably better that way. I needed Xavier alive. At least I wouldn't have to worry about accidentally killing him if I took shots at him.

I burst onto the third floor, my eyes scanning the level. Nothing but rows and rows of cars. Except there— behind a large van on the other side. There he was!

"Hey!" I yelled, taking off again. I pumped my arms, breathing heavily. I was out of shape.

He spared me a glance before pushing through a metal door. It took me a good five seconds to reach it. I yanked on the handle, but the door was locked. I held onto it and leaned my weight back on my heels, but it wasn't budging. Now I wished I'd brought the gun so I could shoot the lock like they did in the movies. That probably didn't even work in real life, though.

I let out a scream of frustration. A couple walking by jumped and picked up their pace.

I stalked to the edge of the level and peered over the side, watching to see if he would emerge on the street. I could've run back to the stairs and gone down a level, but it was pointless. I wasn't going to catch up with him.

After about a minute, Xavier appeared and crossed the street just below me.

"Xavier!" I yelled. "Get your ass back up here!"

He stopped in the middle of traffic and looked up at me, then gave a little salute before carrying on.

I pounded my fists on the concrete wall and screamed.

It didn't make sense. A few days ago he chased me down on his motorcycle, nearly getting Xena and me—and innocent bystanders—killed. Today I actually *wanted* to see him and *he* was running away from *me*.

It didn't make one tiny iota of sense.

I returned to the stairs, trying to rub the stitch out of my side. Dang, I really was out of shape. I needed to start training or something. Yeah...I'd have to get right on that in all my free time.

Why would Xavier evade me? What made it all the more infuriating was he didn't even attempt to hurry. No, instead he *sauntered* out of there. It was like he was toying with me. He wanted me to see him but didn't want me to catch him.

Why, why, why? If I was the hair pulling sort, I would be bald by now. I couldn't figure him out. Why would he *want* me to see him?

Oh, Jesus.

Ignoring the stitch in my side, I ran down the stairs, losing my footing near the bottom and sliding down the last couple. If I hadn't been holding onto the hand rail, I would have eaten concrete.

Horns blared as I cut through traffic and one driver gave me the one-finger salute. Once in the hospital lobby, I pounded on the elevator button. *Hurry up, hurry up.*

When the door finally opened, I rushed inside and pressed the button for the fifth floor. It stopped on the second and an orderly pushed a patient in a wheelchair in, only the chair got stuck on the threshold of the elevator.

I took hold of the chair and tugged it the rest of the way in.

The orderly glared at me and I smiled sweetly. "You're welcome."

Luckily the elevator didn't make any more stops and when the doors opened on the fifth floor, I pushed past the wheelchair. I ran down the hallway, getting yelled at by several nurses, and skidded around the corner. Reaching my mom's room, I threw open the door and hurled myself into the doorway.

The nurse who was taking my mom's vitals looked up, startled. Unlike the orderly in the elevator, she smiled kindly. "Eager to see your mom?"

That and I was worried a psychotic fallen angel had done her in once and for all.

I nodded, pushing my hair out of my eyes and breathing heavily. As I sucked in air, I noticed something peculiar, something I hadn't smelled in quite a while.

But this particular scent would haunt me forever.

Cinnamon.

Xavier *had* been here.

Oh, no. Fear dug its claws into my heart.

I stepped closer to the bed, wanting to get a better look at her. "How is she?" I asked the nurse.

She shot me a sad look before removing the blood pressure cuff from my mom's arm. "Same. But no worse, so that's good, right?"

I attempted a smile for the nice nurse's sake, but I

think it came out more like a grimace.

Maybe the cinnamon was a coincidence. The smell wasn't as strong as it had been in the past. The important thing was my mom was...I was about to say, *okay,* but that wasn't right. The nurse was right in this instance—it was good she was no worse. Because if Xavier really had been here, she could be a lot, lot worse.

She could be dead.

"I'll leave you to your visit. Make sure you talk to her. Hearing loved ones' voices really does help patients in comas."

My heart convulsed at the "c" word. No one had used that term with me—they'd all just referred to her as sleeping. Trying to protect me, I guess. "Sleeping" made it sound safe and innocent. Coma made it sound so much scarier.

I perched on the edge of her bed. "Hi, Mom." The nurse gave me an encouraging smile and slipped out the door, pulling it closed behind her.

What did I talk about? Telling her about all the depressing things that were happening in my life didn't seem like the right thing to do, but I could hear her protest in my mind—*Ava, I always want to know what's going on with you, no matter good or bad.*

"Well, Mom, the stuff has really hit the fan this time. I don't even know where to begin. I'll start with Xena, our new handler. You haven't met her yet, have you?" I peered down at my mom as if she'd respond. "She said she wouldn't bother you until you're better, but with her, you never know. She's...interesting. I think you'd like her. She has a good heart, not like Xavier. But I'm still not sure exactly what to do with her...for her...you know what I mean."

I picked up her hand and held it in mine, running my fingers over her skin below the IV. It felt so thin, like tissue paper.

"Let's see. What else? My job that I didn't tell you

about. Let's just pretend you already knew. Guess what? It was a set-up. A fake! Our angel ancestor—turns out his name is Areli. He set everything up. Shenice—that's my boss—is a sensitive. Only instead of communicating with the dead, she can sense angels. Weird, right?"

I hesitated before saying this next part, then shrugged. Might as well since I was laying it all out.

"Xavier has been around. He tried to kill me. Or at least run me off the road. That counts, right? So the car Bill lent me is all messed up. But *shh*...don't tell him. He doesn't know yet, and I can't bear to break the news to him."

I smoothed her hair away from her face the way she liked. It was getting oily. I needed to ask the nurses about washing it for her. Or maybe I could bring some dry shampoo.

I took a deep breath. "Things with Cole are still bad, but I have to be honest, I can't care. It's not that I *don't* care. I just *can't*." I choked back a sob and paused, taking a moment to gather myself. My heart clenched and squeezed and bled inside me, spreading the hurt everywhere. Because I cared so much. *Too* much.

"I can't care right now. If I do, it'll break me. I've had to turn it off where he's concerned. It's just too much. I can't."

My chest felt lighter for a moment, then I felt bad unloading my troubles onto my comatose mother.

She was lying right up against the guard rail on my side, so I crossed to the other side of the bed, wanting to climb into bed with her and cuddle like we did when I was little. I didn't know if it was allowed, but screw hospital policy. If hearing my voice was supposed to help her, then wouldn't cuddling help, too? Wasn't touch therapy a *thing* now?

I lifted her arm to make room and something fell out of her hand.

It was a vial of blood with a bright red ribbon tied

around it.

CHAPTER 20

I STARED AT THE VIAL. *What...the...hell?*

Had one of the nurses drawn blood and then somehow forgotten to take it with her? I so badly wanted this to be the case.

But then there was the red ribbon in the exact shade Xavier always wore. And he'd been here.

"Damn it," I whispered.

What did this mean?

The nurse poked her head in, and I shoved my hand behind my back like a guilty kid.

"You still doing okay in here?" she asked.

I nodded, not trusting my voice. I'd never been a good liar. Though I was getting better. Now what did that say about me?

As soon as the nurse left, I hunted around for a plastic bag to put the vial in. Xavier wouldn't have gone through the trouble to leave it here if it weren't important, so I was taking it with me. But I didn't want to be carrying around a vial of blood. For one thing, just eww. Gross. What if it came open and splashed blood all over me? Also, it wasn't exactly normal for a teenage girl to be walking around with a vial of blood.

Not that I'd ever been the poster child for normal.

But still, I didn't want to call any attention to myself.

I stuffed the vial in a baggie I found under the sink and shoved it in my pocket. Then I kissed my mom good-bye.

"I'm not giving up on you," I whispered. "I promise I'll figure this out."

On the way to the car, I kept alert, scanning the area for any sign of Xavier. But of course he wasn't there. Why would he be? I was actually looking for him.

As soon as I was safely locked in the car, I called Xena. I'd finally remembered to get her number after she'd pseudo-kidnapped me.

"Where are you?" I asked.

"Still working with Cole."

Damn. That was not the answer I was looking for. Though I supposed that was good. It took me off the hook. And he really did need to learn how to manage the auras. Even with this *thing* between us, I still wanted him to be able to live as normal a life as possible.

Though he had hurt me, I didn't wish him any ill-will. I honestly wanted the best for him and not just in the I'm-saying-this-because-I'm-supposed-to way. I genuinely wanted him to be happy.

Now if he started parading a new girl around in front of me, I might change my stance. I hoped I'd be the bigger person and not claw her eyes out, but I couldn't guarantee that. And besides, I had a lot of pent-up aggression these days. I wouldn't mind having a reason to claw someone's eyes out.

"Okay, I need to talk to you about something," I told Xena. I didn't want to discuss it on the phone, though. "I'm on my way."

"We left the park. We're in his apartment."

"*What?* Why?"

"I was hungry. So we went through a drive-thru and came here. Plus it's cold outside."

I cut over through traffic to get in the left lane so I could make a U-turn.

As I drove the familiar route to the shop, my nerves multiplied like bunnies in heat. I hadn't been to his apartment since I stayed with him while he was sick. I'd been trying to give him space and keep things in neutral territory.

But we were in this together whether we liked it or not. Xavier killing him that night set into motion events that bound us together for life. To what extent, I still hadn't figured out.

I ran through the shop with a quick wave to Bill and took the steps to Cole's apartment two at a time. I put my hand on the doorknob prepared to let myself in, then I pulled my hand away like the knob had bitten me. I couldn't just walk in anymore.

So I knocked.

Cole answered the door and my breath was sucked from my lungs.

God, he was gorgeous. He didn't have any right to be so tall, dark, and handsome. Not while I was trying to detach myself from him.

But standing there in the doorway with his right forearm leaning against the door frame and his dark eyes blazing into me...it was like seeing him for the first time all over again.

It felt like a punch to the stomach, one that took my breath away and made it hard to stay upright.

"Is Xena here?" I asked.

He stepped back so I could enter. I stepped through the doorway, careful not to touch him as I passed. But I got close enough to catch a whiff of him—that clean scent, laced with a hint of peppermint from the mints he liked.

My heart pitter-pattered, remembering what it was like to kiss him, to taste that peppermint on his lips. To feel his lips on mine. To be wrapped up in him.

I took a shaky breath, pushing the memory out of my mind.

Xena sat primly on his couch, looking completely out

of place in this rundown apartment with her trendy hair and black clothing. In my worn jeans, hoodie, and pen-marked knock-off Toms, I fit right in.

I sat next to her. Cole took a spot on the other side of the room—which, given the size of the place, wasn't far away. He crossed his arms and leaned against the wall.

"I saw Xavier."

At the mention of Xavier, Cole stood at attention, his fists clenched at his sides. I realized he didn't know about the new must-keep-Xavier-alive policy. We'd have to inform him of that and quick. If Xavier showed himself—let's just say Cole was an excellent shot and he wouldn't hesitate.

"Where?" Xena asked, her eyebrows scrunched together.

"The hospital. To be more specific, in the parking garage. I chased him, but he got away. It was weird. It was like he wanted me to see him, but he didn't want me to catch him. But he's Xavier, so I thought nothing is weird where he's concerned and continued on to see my mom. Anyway, in her room, I found this." I stood up so I could pull the vial out of my pocket. It still had the red ribbon on it.

Xena took it from me and held it up to the light.

"Is that what I think it is?" Cole asked.

"If you think it's blood, then you'd be correct," Xena said. "But whose blood?"

"Exactly," I said. "And why would he leave it for me with no explanation? If he's trying to send a message, I'm not getting it. So what's the point?"

"I wonder..." Xena wrenched the stopper off the vial, then stuck her finger in. She sniffed it and put it to her tongue.

Turning away, I gagged.

Xena was supposed to be an angel, not a freaking vampire.

I noticed even Cole cringed and it took a lot to shake

him.

"It's not human blood," Xena said, putting the stopper back on the vial. "I'm pretty sure it's angel blood."

"How can you tell?" I asked.

"I just can."

Of course she could. Why wouldn't she be able to?

"Why would he leave us angel blood?" I mused aloud. It didn't make any sense. I felt like that was all I ever thought or said these days.

"I can ask around," Xena said. "Someone might know something."

"You might want to be careful who you talk to," Cole said. "Word might get around that you're asking, and I'm not sure we want everyone to know about this."

We...Cole's use of that word didn't escape my attention. Guess he also understood we were all in this— stuck together—for the time being.

Xena regarded Cole for a moment. "Good point."

I almost grumbled aloud. If I had said that, I probably would've gotten Xena's annoyed how-dare-you-correct-me stare.

Had Cole somehow managed to charm Xena in the short time they were together? He could be completely and utterly charming, but most times, especially when you were getting to know him and he didn't know or trust you yet, he was irritating. And a little bit of an asshole.

I'd hated him a little when I first met him. Oh, I'd still been attracted to him, but that only made me hate him more.

"But I'll probably only ask Areli," Xena clarified.

"Who's that?" Cole asked.

I realized he wasn't up to date on all the latest developments since he wasn't present for my faux kidnapping.

It would have been a lot better if he was. I would have loved to have seen Xena try to overpower Cole.

"That's my angel ancestor," I said. "The one who

brought you back to life."

Cole's eyes clouded over and I wanted to kick myself. Why did I bring that up? He would have known who I was talking about if I'd just left it at "angel ancestor." It wasn't like I had more than one.

I chose to ignore his dark look. I couldn't deal with the guilt right now, not on top of everything else. Even if I did deserve it.

I'd carry the guilt with me until the day I died—the day the Reapers were done with me.

I hadn't talked to Xena about the Reapers at all. I wondered how they fit into the hierarchy. That would be a question for another time.

"How did the lesson go?" I asked.

"Good," Xena said. "He's getting the hang of it. He's progressing much faster than I would have expected given his advanced age."

"Advanced age?" Cole repeated in a dry voice.

I snorted and my eyes drifted over to Cole to check his reaction, then I quickly looked at the ground.

We shared a sense of humor and I missed it. I missed laughing with him. Though there wasn't much to laugh about these days.

"You're rather old to just now be coming into your abilities," Xena explained. "But you're doing really well. You could probably try school tomorrow if you want."

Cole nodded. "I need to go. I already have too many absences. I guess it'll be a sink or swim kind of experiment."

"Since you're nineteen, maybe you won't see the freshmen's auras. That will help cut things down," I offered. "And if the auras get to be too much, just let them all in. It'll suck, but it will make you sick enough that your absence won't be questioned since they'll have seen how sick you are firsthand."

"Good point," Cole said. "Thanks."

I clasped my hands in front of me. "No problem."

"Welp," Xena said, and I jerked my neck around toward her. Did she just say *welp*? "I think I'm going to head out. Got lots of people to see, lots of questions to ask."

"I can drive you wherever you need to go," I offered. It was partly a selfish offer—I wanted to worm my way into going with her when she asked her "lots of questions," and also I just wanted an excuse to get the heck out of dodge.

The memories in this apartment were choking me.

"No, I'm good." Xena jumped up and practically flung herself out the door. "See you later!" she called on her way down the stairs.

She did that on purpose.

She *knew* things were stressed between Cole and me. If she thought she could leave us in this apartment and we could "seven minutes in heaven" our way out of this, she was dead wrong.

Before I could get up and leave through the door she left open, Cole walked over and shut it. Oh, frick. What did that mean?

He didn't look at me at first. His gaze was focused on the ground and several uncomfortable seconds passed. Should I just say my good-byes and re-open the door? He wouldn't have shut it if he hadn't wanted me to stay. But why would he want me to stay?

I should leave. That was the best course of action. We'd done well being together with Xena here. There was no need to push things.

Then he looked up and his eyes blasted me with all kinds of emotion—confusion, anger, hope, love.

I hadn't peeked at his aura since before he'd died and been brought back, but I couldn't resist now.

I was nearly blinded by a brilliant white light, whiter and purer than I'd ever seen before. My mouth fell open slightly as I basked in the magnificence of it. When the light touched me, I felt warm, loved, safe.

It reminded me of Areli's light.

I closed my eyes for a moment as tears filled them from the brightness—that and the pureness of what I felt in the light. When I opened my eyes again, I saw streaks of luminescent blue and red—tranquility, loyalty, strength, passion.

And love.

It was overwhelming.

I slammed my guards in place and wiped my eyes.

"Are you okay?" Cole asked.

"I'm fine," I said, sniffing and wiping away the last of the tears. "I looked at your aura and it was really bright."

"Brighter than before?" His expression was both curious and troubled. I wished I could explain about his aura, but that would have to be a question for Xena, if she'd even answer it.

"Yes. Much brighter. The brightest I've seen," I admitted. "But I've never seen another seeker's aura— well, other than mine, anyway—so I don't know if that's normal. It probably is."

"Your aura looks just like everyone else's," Cole said.

"Oh." I didn't know how to respond to that and was oddly disappointed. No matter how much I wanted to fit in and be normal, a part of me also wanted to stand out. It was a teenage conundrum.

The color and brightness of our auras was just another mystery that we didn't have an explanation for. These days, I was more shocked if we actually knew something instead of the other way around.

"Well, I'm glad you're doing well with putting your guards in place," I said. "I guess Xena was able to explain it to you better."

"Actually, no," Cole admitted. "She's never blocked auras herself. Apparently fallen angels can't see them."

"Oh, right." I should have known. Nothing had ever been confirmed, but I'd figured Xavier couldn't see auras. Otherwise, why would he need seekers?

"Yeah, she's a really sucky teacher. She basically just

stared at me and commanded me to block the auras. So I did what you said."

"What I said?" I echoed.

"Yeah, I imagined a door." He rubbed his neck, a sure sign he was embarrassed. God, he was cute when he did that. And there went his cheeks—turning a slight shade of pink. He rarely blushed, but when he did, it made my knees weak.

It was the vulnerability. Cole was never vulnerable, or at least, he didn't show it easily. So when he did, it just made me love him more.

"I'm glad it worked for you," I said.

"It's keeping it shut that's the problem. How do you do that? As soon as I stop thinking about it, the auras flood back in."

I considered. "It's kind of like on a computer, how programs run in the background. Eventually you learn to do that. It'll take practice, but the more you do it, the easier it will get. Soon it will be second nature."

"I hope so. I'm gonna go to school tomorrow, but I don't know how long I'll last."

"You've got to start somewhere."

"Yes," he said slowly, looking at me intently. "You do."

What exactly were we talking about here?

I didn't have time to figure it out. I stood, preparing to leave.

He closed the distance between us and cradled his hands around the back of my neck and head, tilting my face toward his. He stared at me for a split second, and my mouth opened a bit in shock. I stilled, becoming a statue.

He crushed his mouth to mine in a kiss that was urgent and gentle, intense and lazy, so many things—*everything*—all at once.

My body was rigid, but as his tongue passed over my lips, my body melded to his and I threw my arms around him, returning the kiss hungrily.

He pushed me backward until my back was against

the door and I jumped up, wrapping my legs around him. He laid me down on the couch and braced himself above me, the lengths of our bodies touching. The warmth and pressure felt so good, so familiar, *so right*.

His hand snaked under my shirt to caress my stomach, making its way up to my breast. His touch felt divine and I craved it, wrapping myself around him. My fingertips danced along his back.

Rational thought evaded me. All I could think was *this is Cole. I love him so much. Cole...Cole...Cole.*

His mouth moved to my throat. "Ava," he breathed.

It was the sound of my name that snapped me out of it. I pushed hard against his chest. "No, Cole. We can't do this."

He jumped off me like I'd shocked him and plastered himself against the wall on the other side of the room. I sat up and fixed my clothes.

"I want us to get back to the way we were before," he said.

"I'm not sure we can."

His hands fisted and his mouth pressed in a thin line. "Why not?"

I stood so I was closer to his eye level. "Look me in the eyes and tell me you don't resent me for deciding to make you a seeker."

I wanted so much for him to be able to do it, so much so I actually held my breath. I never wanted to be proved wrong so badly in my life.

He maintained eye contact for a few long seconds before dragging his gaze away.

I exhaled. *Damn*, I hated being right this time. I expected it, but it still felt like claws were raking across my heart.

"That's what I thought," I said quietly. I gathered up my things and left, closing the door quietly behind me.

CHAPTER 21

THE NEXT DAY, I WENT to school. You know, just to change things up. It was funny how in only a few days, something that once seemed so normal—school—had become foreign. All around me, people were going about their business on this ordinary weekday morning, not having a clue my world had become totally and utterly messed up beyond repair.

As I stood at my locker, trying to sort through my binders and textbooks and remember what was what, Kaley threw herself in my arms.

"Uh, hi," I said, hugging her back. Even if I wasn't overly fond of PDA, I was happy to see her.

"I missed you!" She pulled back. "Are you okay? How's your mom?"

"Yes and same."

Kaley had texted me when I missed school, and I'd been vague about my mom's situation. It wasn't that I didn't trust her, but she didn't know about the whole seeker thing and I didn't have the energy to come up with a viable story.

Being a seeker made having friends complicated.

Heck, who was I kidding? It made *life* complicated.

"Let me know if there's anything you need," Kaley said, sensing I didn't want to talk about it and leaving it at that.

"Thanks." I was a crappy friend—taking, taking, taking all the time. Kaley tutored me in math and always seemed to be getting my makeup work or checking up on me or something. But for some reason, she had latched on to me and I couldn't say I minded.

It might be smarter not to have friends, but it was lonely as hell.

In my first class, my teacher gave me a pitying look when she loaded me up with my make-up work. Dang...how much work did I miss? The stack of papers *did* look ominous, but it shouldn't take more than a few hours.

The same thing happened in my second class, only this teacher asked me about my mom. So that explained the pitying looks. There was only one explanation—the counselor must have talked to Bill.

On one hand, I was grateful they'd talked because it meant I didn't get harassed about my absences. On the other hand, that meant I had to endure the sympathetic looks from my teachers. I was kind of hoping to have a somewhat normal day and not have to worry about angels or auras or angels' blood.

But there was no escaping it.

At lunch, I poked at my pizza and mandatory fries that were served with every meal. Oh, and the ketchup—can't forget that since it counted as one of the required vegetables. Except weren't tomatoes technically fruit?

"Do you want me to help you get caught up in trig?" Kaley asked.

I shook my head. "I'm too overwhelmed to focus right now." Although I didn't see that changing anytime soon, so I probably should just suck it up and get started on the make-up work that had grown exponentially since this morning.

"That's understandable," Kaley said, pulling her trig textbook out of her backpack. "You've got a lot going on."

She didn't know the half of it.

Cole walked into the cafeteria and even from across the room, I could tell he wasn't doing so well. His face was pale and there was a glossy sheen to his skin, like he'd been sweating. He headed toward the food line, then stumbled a few steps, putting a hand up to his eyes. After that, he spun on his heel and hightailed it out of there.

I sighed. Poor Cole.

"I need to check on Cole," I told Kaley. She nodded like nothing was unusual, and I realized she didn't know about our split. I'd leave it that way for now. I especially didn't want to talk about that.

I went through the line and grabbed him a sandwich, a bag of chips, and a water. Then I headed toward the side door of the school. There was only one place he would be.

In the Rustinator.

As expected, I found him there, lying flat on his back across the front seats with his arm thrown over his face. He looked like hell. Coming back to school this soon was probably too big of a step.

I rapped my knuckles on the window.

He moved his arm and squinted up at me. When he realized it was me, he sat up and unlocked the doors. I circled around to the passenger seat and got in.

"How's it going?" I asked.

"Not well," he admitted.

"I figured." I offered the food. "Hungry?"

"Starved." He took the sandwich from me and tore open the wrapper. "Thanks. It wasn't so bad in class when there were only thirty people, but I couldn't handle the cafeteria. It was too much."

"I get it." I paused. I didn't really have much else to say. Even though I'd emotionally closed myself off from Cole, I still felt responsible for him—the *seeker* part of him. So regardless of how much it hurt or how numb it made me, I'd continue to support him while he got things straightened out.

But my work here was done. "I should get back," I

said, moving to open the door.

"Ava." His tone was pleading.

I paused.

"I'm sorry about yesterday," he said. "With everything that's going on with us, I shouldn't have come onto you like that."

I looked down at my hands. "I participated. It's okay."

But was it really? How could it be? The resentment he felt toward me had become a third party to our relationship, and while he seemed content to ignore it, I couldn't.

If I let myself, I could feel very, very hurt by his actions yesterday, but there was no point. I was hurting enough already. And I *had* participated, so the blame wasn't solely on his shoulders.

But the bottom line was we couldn't kiss and make up until our unresolved issues were taken care of.

"I just want things to get back to normal with us," he said. "With as fucked up as the rest of my life is, things were always good—*normal*—with you."

I looked at him incredulously. "You thought we—" I gestured back and forth between us "—were normal."

He ran a hand through his hair, a sure sign he was frustrated. "Well, yeah."

As much as I wished things were normal between us, they never were and they never would be.

"Cole, I'm a seeker. When we got together, we were on the run for your life because I set the Reapers after you. I don't think that's normal."

"Maybe normal isn't the right term. Stable, maybe?"

I leaned my head back against the headrest. "I can't be your normal. And I can't be your stable, either. Because of what I am, my life will always be in flux. I thought you realized that."

"I do," he said slowly. "But soon I'll have the aura thing under control."

Like that would be the end of the problems. That was

just the beginning. Looking over at him, I snorted.

He didn't find his statement amusing. He was totally serious.

Shit. He was in total denial. I didn't see that coming. He always faced problems head on, so this was throwing me.

"I don't think so," I said. "Becoming a seeker and seeing auras isn't like getting a cold or something. You don't recover from it. It's a new way of life. And it's a messed up way of life."

Cole opened his mouth to reply, but I didn't get to find out what he was going to say because my phone rang. I didn't recognize the number, but I answered it anyway, grateful for the temporary reprieve from this conversation.

"Is this Ms. Parks?"

"Um, yes. This is Ms. Parks." No one called me that. It made me squirm.

"This is Tidewater Hospital. You might want to come now if you can."

"Oh, shit." I didn't even cringe at my cursing while speaking to an adult. "Why? What's wrong?"

"Your mother had a string of seizures this morning, and the doctors are having trouble stabilizing her."

"I'm on my way."

My hands were shaking so bad I had to push the "end call" button several times before it took.

Cole started the ignition before I could say anything, and I automatically buckled my seat belt. He pulled out of the school parking lot so fast he probably left skid marks.

"What is it?" he asked.

"She's having seizures. They can't stabilize her."

"Call Xena," he said, running a red light. "She should be there, too."

"She's never met my mom," I said stupidly. "My mom wouldn't want to meet her like this."

But I dialed the number anyway and mechanically

told her to hurry.

"Call Bill, too," Cole instructed.

"Bill's on the contact list at the hospital. They would have called him when they called me."

"Good." Cole took his eyes off the road for a second to glance over at me. He reached for my hand. "Hey, it's going to be okay."

I didn't think so, but I appreciated the sentiment.

Cole dropped me off at the front door. Before I got out, I warned him to keep an eye out for Xavier. He nodded grimly, then pulled off to find a parking space. I headed directly to my mom's room.

Xena was waiting in the hall when I got there. "They wouldn't let me in," she said. She held out her hand and I took it.

I opened the door, expecting to find a slew of doctors and nurses poking and prodding at my mom. Instead, there was just one doctor—the one who admitted her—and the friendly nurse.

"She's stable," the doctor said. "But I have to warn you she's slipped several times this morning. We lost her once already."

Her skin matched the sheets, and there wasn't any sign of life other than the shallow movement of her chest.

She looked half dead already.

I choked back a sob. "Is there any permanent damage? Can she recover from this?"

The doctor pursed her lips. "I can't say until we do more tests. I have to be honest with you—I've never seen anything like this before."

"No one has," I whispered.

"Excuse me?" The doctor leaned forward so she could hear me better.

I shook my head. "Nothing."

The doctor signaled to the nurse, who straightened my mom's blanket one more time. Then she patted me on the arm and stepped out of the room.

"You know where the call button is?" The doctor pointed to an ominous red button. I doubted we'd need it. Not that my mom wouldn't run into trouble, but she was connected to so many monitors that if anything happened the nurses would probably be in here before we could take one step toward the button.

I nodded.

"I'll leave you alone, then," the doctor said. She exited, leaving the door partly ajar. Xena and I were left in silence, the only sounds the mechanical beeping and whirring of the machines.

After a moment, Xena walked over and firmly shut the door.

"I'm not leaving her," I said. "I'll sleep in the chair if I have to." If the nurses and doctors wanted me out, then they'd have to physically remove me. If this was it—if this was going to be her end—then I'd stay by her side the whole time.

There was a quiet knock on the door, and Xena went to answer it while I stood vigil over my mom.

Cole entered the room and walked over to stand to my left. He looked down at my mom and swallowed, then glanced at me. I could tell he didn't know what to do. Like should he comfort me? I crossed my arms over my chest, making the decision for him.

I didn't want his comfort. Not now. Too much sympathy and I would break.

"We need to find Xavier," he said, his eyes flashing. "This is bullshit. Why are we sitting around when we could be doing something?"

He voiced my sentiments exactly.

There was the Cole I knew and loved. I hated seeing him weakened by his seeker abilities. It wasn't in his nature to be down and out. He was a take-action kind of guy.

"Xavier is dangerous," Xena said, seeming annoyed that she needed to remind us of that, as if we could ever forget. "And besides that, unless he wants to be found, we won't find him."

"We have to try," Cole said. "We can't just let Ava's mom suffer if there's something we could do to help her."

"I showed the blood to Areli," Xena said, pulling it out of her pocket. She looked down at it with disdain. "It's not normal."

That word was being thrown around a lot today.

"What do you mean?" I asked. "Normal for what?"

"For angel blood." She pursed her lips. "His has...*evolved*."

Cole and I exchanged a look.

"What the hell does that mean?" Cole asked, once again voicing my thoughts.

We were interrupted by another knock. Xena went to answer the door again, and she opened it wide so I could see who it was.

Bill stood in the doorway, his shoulders hunched over. He twirled his worn baseball cap in his hands.

"Bill," I said. "Thanks for coming."

"Of course," he said, like it was a given.

But it wasn't. Less than two weeks ago, Bill hadn't been in my life. Not this way, anyway. He'd stepped in and filled a role I hadn't even known was missing from my life. I'd never be able to repay him.

"I'm Xena, a friend of Cole and Ava's." She held out her hand.

Bill took it and nodded. "What did the doctor say?" He shifted his grip on his hat, revealing a gift bag clutched in his hands.

Tied to it was a blood red ribbon.

My stomach clenched and knotted.

"What's that?" I asked, even though I knew what it was.

"This?" He held it up as if he'd forgotten he was holding it. "It was right outside the door."

I turned to Cole and he shook his head, anticipating

my question. "It wasn't there a minute ago. I would have noticed it."

Xavier had been here. While we were talking about needing to find him, he slipped in and out of the hospital without us even knowing. He'd literally been just feet away from us.

"Impossible," Xena said, shaking her head. "I should have realized..."

I shot her a sharp look, but I couldn't ask why she was so troubled. Not with Bill in the room.

"Do you want it?" Bill held out the bag to me.

Hell, no. I didn't want it, but there was no avoiding it.

I took it and pushed aside the tissue paper to peek inside. Then I blinked. *What the heck?*

"It's a syringe."

"That's it?" Cole asked. "No note? Nothing?"

I shook my head. "There's just—"

My mom convulsed on the bed and a machine started going haywire. I clutched at her hand. "Mom," I pleaded. "Please snap out of it."

I glanced over at the red button, but true to my prediction, several nurses burst through the door before I could reach for it.

Bill and Xena immediately moved out of the way for them, but they'd have to forcefully pry my hand from hers if they wanted me to move.

My mom's body stilled.

"Clear out," one of the nurses said, stepping up to the bed. "Everyone clear out."

The machine silenced, like nothing had even happened.

The nurse looked at the machine in disbelief, then down at my mom. "She seems the same. That machine did go off, correct? Did her condition change in the last minute?"

Behind the nurse, Xena caught my gaze and shook her head. I took her lead.

"No," I said. "There was no change."

"Huh. That's weird." The main nurse nodded to the other two and they exited. "This equipment must be faulty. I'm going to disconnect her from this one for now."

"What if something happens?" I asked.

"Don't worry," the nurse assured me. "I'm getting a replacement ASAP."

Once the nurse left, I turned to Xena.

"Why would he leave us a syringe?" I asked. I no longer cared that Bill was in the room. It was a rule that seekers weren't supposed to out ourselves to normal people. But come to think of it, that was Xavier's rule, so it might not even be a real rule.

Real or not, I didn't care. The matter at hand was too urgent.

And Bill was family.

Xena looked to the vial of blood in her hand, then to the syringe. I closed my eyes. Without speaking, she'd confirmed my hunch.

Xavier wanted us to inject my mom with his blood.

CHAPTER 22

"IT MAKES SENSE," I SAID, hating the hollowness of my voice. "Areli's blood saved Cole. Maybe Xavier's blood can save her."

Bill shifted uncomfortably. Cole and I exchanged a look.

"Bill, I'll explain everything to you later."

"Okay," he said, but he still looked uneasy. It couldn't be helped.

"It could be a trap," Cole said. "If he wanted to save her, why wouldn't he give us proper instructions?"

"Because he's Xavier," I said blandly. Cole didn't know him like I did. "Nothing is simple with him."

"But why now?" Cole insisted. "Why would he give us the cure now?"

I didn't know and at that moment, I didn't care.

"She's dying," I said quietly.

"The doctors—"

"The doctors won't say it, but I know it. She won't come back from this unless we do something."

I was willing to try anything at this point. Cole was right about one thing—we couldn't sit around if a possible solution presented itself.

And as much as I hated to take a risk based on Xavier's convoluted offering without knowing his motive, we were left with little choice.

She would die soon if we did nothing.

But if we gave her Xavier's blood, what then? What irreversible change were we thrusting upon her? It was the Cole situation all over again, and I had to make a life-altering decision for someone else. It wasn't any easier this time around.

Cole took my hand and squeezed. I looked away, wiping the tears from my eyes, but I didn't let go of his hand.

My mom's body twitched on the bed, making my heart lurch. Then she began spasming, her eyes moving wildly under her closed eyelids.

"Shit, shit, shit," I whispered. I held her shoulders down so she wouldn't injure herself.

"Do it," Xena said, forcefully. "We don't need the nurses in here for this. Come on." She gestured to Bill. "We'll stand guard." She pressed the vial of blood into my hand and then they left.

I stared in horror at the vial, then looked at the syringe. "I don't know how to do this."

My mom jerked, like her body was possessed. God, maybe it was.

The time was now. I needed to woman up and get this done. It couldn't be that hard, right? Just find a vein and shoot it in.

My fingers shook as I uncapped the vial, the liquid sloshing around inside.

It's just liquid, I told myself. *Not blood. Just liquid. Liquid medicine.*

I held out a shaking hand. "Give me the syringe."

Cole took one look at me and picked it up. "No. I'll do it. Find something to tie around her upper arm."

I hadn't even thought about that. Thank God Cole knew what he was doing.

I searched around for something to use, and my gaze landed on the ribbon tied on the gift bag. I quickly untied it and wrapped it around my mom's arm.

"Tighter," Cole said.

I pulled it taut and held one end of the ribbon with my mouth so I could put my finger on the knot to make it tight.

"Is this good?" I asked through clenched teeth.

Cole looked over from preparing the syringe. "Yeah. Now hold her arm. If she jerks while I'm doing this, I might miss."

I gripped her arm just above and below her elbow, holding it down on the bed. Cole tapped on the inside of her elbow, then leaned close to examine her veins.

"Damn, these are tiny," he muttered. I looked to where his fingers were pressed. I couldn't see *any* veins.

He ran his fingers over her veins again just as her legs began to twitch. He took his time, wanting to do it right, but it was taking too long.

"Cole, hurry."

He looked over at my mom and then at me, and I saw he wasn't as cool, calm, and collected as I'd first thought. Sweat beaded on his forehead and worry clouded his eyes.

"Okay," he said to himself. "Here goes."

He inserted the needle in her arm, then pressed on the plunger until the syringe was empty.

Her body jerked once more and then was still—still as death.

I STRIPPED THE RIBBON OFF her arm just as there was a commotion outside the room. With a final look at my mom, we rushed to the door, flinging it open.

Xena was lying on the floor and appeared to be passed out. Two nurses surrounded her.

Oh, no. Not Xena, too.

I knelt beside her and when her eyes flickered open, I sighed with relief. "Xena, what happened?"

"I...I..."

"Catch your breath," the nurse said, then turned to me. "She fainted, just like that." She snapped her fingers to emphasize the quickness of it.

"Right in the middle of talking to you, I started feeling woozy," Xena said to the nurse. "That's all I remember." She looked over at me and our eyes locked.

I sat back on my heels. Xena was faking. Sure enough, right behind her on a cart was the new piece of equipment for my mom. Xena had put on the theatrical show to stall them.

Cole shot me a dry look then crossed his arms and leaned against a wall, out of the way. Under other circumstances, this might be amusing. Xena was a rather sucky actress.

Shit. We'd better get her out of there before the nurses figured out she was faking. They *were* medical professionals after all.

"Can you sit up?" I asked.

"Yes, I think so." Xena pushed herself up and sat with her arms anchored behind her to hold herself up. She wore a dazed expression.

"I told you you needed to eat," I chided, then turned to the nurse. "She has a habit of not eating when she's stressed."

The nurse nodded knowingly. "That'll do it. We can check your blood sugar if you like, though, just to be on the safe side."

"No, she's right," Xena said. "I haven't eaten today. I just need food."

"Bill, can you get her something to eat and take her home?" I asked. I realized I was asking an impossible question—where the heck did Xena live? Did she even have a home, or did she flit from place to place, popping in whenever she felt like it? Where the heck did fallen angels reside? I'd obviously never seen Xavier's home.

Just another reminder that I knew next to nothing

about angels, fallen angels, *everything*.

"Sure," Bill said in his obliging way. I shot him an apologetic look, but he just shrugged. Maybe since my mom and I had moved in, he was starting to get over his aversion to females.

"That would be great," Xena said, allowing us to help her up.

I'd give it to her—she sold it, leaning on Bill all the way down the hallway to the elevator. I wondered if she'd actually make him get her something to eat. Though Bill came across as slow sometimes, he was a lot brighter than he let on. It was part of his charm. So he probably knew she was faking, but he wouldn't dare suggest it to her. He was a gentleman like that.

God bless him.

"Well," the nurse said brightly. "Lots of excitement around here today." She retrieved the equipment from the cart. "But hopefully no more due to equipment failure. I'll just hook this up." She went into my mom's room and Cole and I followed.

Now that the hallway diversion was over, apprehension set in. My mom looked the same as she had when I'd first arrived.

The nurse hummed a little as she set up the new equipment. It seemed like it was taking her an extra long time. When she was done, she turned to us. "Let me know if you need anything." She frowned at Cole. "Past visiting hours it's supposed to be family only."

"He *is* family," I said, daring the nurse to challenge me.

She shrugged and left.

I sat on the edge of the bed and held my mom's hand. "What do you think?" I asked Cole.

"I don't know." He stared down at her for a moment. "I don't know what to expect."

He sat, cradling his head in his hands. He hadn't said anything and probably never would, but that had to be hard for him. His mother was an addict, which was no doubt how he'd known how to administer the injection—from watching his own mother shoot up.

"Thank you," I said simply.

He picked his head up, his tired eyes meeting mine. "Of course."

AT THE FEEL OF SOMEONE'S hand stroking my hair, I jumped up, upending the chair I'd been sleeping in.

My mom put her hands up to quiet me. "It's just me."

"Mom..." I didn't know what to say—I wasn't sure if I'd ever get to speak to her again. But here she was, lucid and her eyes clearer than they'd been in weeks. There was even a slight pink tint to her cheeks.

I threw myself at her, wrapping my arms around her and sobbing. "I thought you were going to die."

"Shh...it's okay. I'm here. I'm not going anywhere...at least not today." She held me, her frail arms embracing me with the power that only mothers had.

After a moment, I collected myself and eased off her. Dang, it wasn't smart to hurl myself at her like that, not while she was still weak.

"I can't believe you're awake." After we'd given her Xavier's blood, nothing changed for hours, and I'd been afraid we'd been wrong about Xavier's gift. That he'd just been toying with us yet again.

She frowned. "How long was I out?"

"A few days," I said. It felt like so much longer.

"I heard you," she said. "I heard you talking to me. Telling me everything that's been going on."

I blinked. "You remember what I said?"

She nodded. "You should have told me the new handler contacted you."

I cast my eyes downward. "I didn't want to worry you."

"I'm your mom. It's my job to worry." She sounded forlorn and I felt guilty, like I'd been robbing her of something she considered her natural right. But I wouldn't change my actions. For starters, she'd been flirting with death. And anyway, everything I'd been dealing with in the past year, especially the last few months, had stripped me of whatever childhood I'd had left. My eighteenth birthday was still a few months away, but I'd been shouldering adult-sized problems for a while now.

"Not right now it isn't," I insisted. "Right now your only job is to get better. Leave everything else to me."

She sighed, looking away. We both knew that was the best course of action, even if she wouldn't admit it out loud.

"Should we let the nurses know you're awake?" I asked.

"In a minute," she said. "I want to spend a few more minutes with just us before they start poking and prodding."

"I wish we could tell them that nothing they're doing is making a difference," I said. "Maybe then they'd leave you alone." I'd thought about this before, but despite the costs of hospitalization and the fact that the doctors couldn't do anything to cure her, the hospital was the best place for her, at least while she was unconscious. She still needed care, like nourishment and fluids.

She shook her head. "You know we can't."

"Yeah." I paused and rubbed my hands over my face. I didn't want to say this next part, but she deserved to know. "You didn't miraculously get better. Xavier sent us a vial of his blood and a syringe."

"You injected me with Xavier's blood?" Her voice was flat, her tone disbelieving.

"Yes," I whispered. "We didn't know what else to do."

She closed her eyes and exhaled a long slow breath. "Okay," she said slowly. I wondered if she'd ever be able to come to terms with it. I didn't know if I would.

"How do you feel?" I asked.

"Better than I have in weeks."

CHAPTER 23

THE NEXT DAY, WE—MEANING BILL, Cole, Xena, my mom and I—all sat around Bill's dining room table in a dysfunctional family meeting. My mom had checked herself out of the hospital yesterday afternoon against doctor's orders. No doubt the doctor had been expecting to draw up a death certificate any day now, and she was flabbergasted by my mom's miraculous recovery, calling it a miracle.

We weren't about to enlighten her.

"So you're an angel," Bill said, pointing at Xena.

"*Fallen* angel," she corrected.

Bill leaned back in his chair and shook his head, looking very much like he'd just stepped into an alternate reality and was having a hard time coming to grips with it. In a way, it was an alternate reality.

He'd actually taken things in stride, not really questioning us a whole lot. Who ever would have thought the grizzled old mechanic would be so open minded? Bill defied stereotypes, and I was truly coming to love him for it. I couldn't imagine my life without him. He made me wonder what it would have been like to grow up with a father.

"We're sorry for deceiving you," my mom said, folding her hands neatly in front of her. She sat at the head of the table, looking positively radiant and in control. You'd think she'd just come back from a stay at a spa instead of the hospital. The change over the last few hours was unreal.

"No, I understand," Bill said. "It's a lot to lay on a person. But I always suspected you two were different somehow."

My mom and I looked at one another with the same shocked expression. Not that we'd ever asked, but no one had ever told us anything like that before. Was Bill the only one who sensed it?

"How do you mean?" I asked.

He shrugged. "There's just something different. I can't explain it."

That was not helpful.

I glanced across the table at Cole, who'd been silent throughout the meeting. His eyes were trained on a marble he'd been rolling back and forth on the table. We three women hadn't consulted him before we'd spilled the beans to Bill. For the first time it occurred to me he might not want this secret shared. He hadn't had enough time to come to terms with it himself.

But there I was—making decisions for him again. This one affected all of us, though.

"I should go." Xena stood.

"Wait a minute." Bill's eyes shifted to his hands he held clasped in front of him. "Could you tell me about my daughter? If she's an angel?" The hope laced in his voice was soul-crushing.

Xena hesitated, her expression conflicted. "There are a lot of angels," she said finally. "I don't know them all."

Bill nodded, looking away.

I wished we could have given that to him—knowledge that his daughter was at peace. He was proof that parents would never truly get over the death of a child. He'd learned to live with it, but it weighed on him constantly.

Bill hadn't asked about Jill's mother, though, which

made me wonder again what had happened to her. He'd never even told us her name.

"Cole and Ava, would you mind stepping out on the porch with me for a few minutes?" Xena asked. Her tone implied it was a command rather than a request.

Cole scraped his chair back and left the room, not saying a word. Moments later I heard the front door open. *Guess he's complying.*

Something was up with him. He'd left the hospital shortly after injecting my mom with Xavier's blood, so I hadn't talked to him about it yet.

Xena gave me a pointed look that said *I'm waiting*.

"Coming," I muttered. I grabbed my coat on the way out the door.

Cole leaned against the railing, his arms crossed and bare against the chilly air. He didn't look at Xena and me when we came out. I wanted to go to him and wrap my arms around him to protect him from the cold. There was so much more going on I couldn't protect him from, though, no matter how much I wanted to.

My breath caught in my chest. My feelings for Cole were complicated. Despite my vow to keep my distance, I couldn't stop caring about him. It snuck up on me at random times, penetrating my defenses.

"I have an assignment for you," Xena said before the door had fully closed behind her.

"Excuse me?" I asked, cocking my head. Did she say what I thought she did?

"An assignment. It's time."

My nostrils flared as I took time to process her words. It felt like a betrayal. I'd never forgotten that Xena was my handler, but I thought we were on the same team. I didn't expect it to come to this.

I looked at Cole, but there was no reaction from him. He hadn't moved, and his gaze was still fixated on the floor.

Damn. Now I was really worried. The old Cole would

have reacted. Maybe told Xena to go to hell or something like that. Even Cole's inaction usually had a purpose. But now? This was pure apathy.

I looked back at Xena, and she had the same expression on her face she'd had inside—she wasn't giving us a request. It was a command.

I squared my shoulders and looked her right in the eye. "No."

She blinked. "No? What do you mean, no?"

"Just what I said. *No.*"

"You don't have a choice," she said.

"I think I do," I retorted. "I don't care what you do to me. I won't do it."

"You don't understand—"

"No, *you* don't understand!" I yelled, pointing my finger at her. "Bill is a broken man. You saw the look on his face when he asked about his daughter. I can't—I *won't*—put anyone else through that. It's not right." I whispered that last part.

Xena pursed her lips. "You're not seeing the big picture."

"No shit!" I exploded. "You've never shown me the big picture."

She narrowed her eyes at me before turning to Cole. "What about you?"

Damn. I hadn't realized both of us were included here, but why else would she want both of us outside?

Cole couldn't take on an assignment. He hadn't mastered blocking auras yet. I hadn't even begun to show him how to determine if the white ones were fated.

Besides that, I was pretty damn sure he was vehemently opposed to it. But that was his call to make.

He finally looked up and in his eyes I saw a void. Then he shrugged. "I'm with her." He jerked his head in my direction.

Good. At least we were putting up a united front. But damn, I really needed to talk to him to see if I could get him to snap out of it.

Xena sighed, and for the first time, she looked weary, like she'd witnessed centuries of hardship. Who knew? Maybe she had. Though she didn't look a day over fifteen, she could have been alive since the days when the world was still considered flat. Or was "existed" the better word? I didn't know what the right term was for angels because I didn't know if they were alive in the same sense as humans.

"The world is in trouble," she said and I snorted. Any moron who'd ever watched the evening news could tell you that. Natural disasters, man-made disasters, hate crimes...the list went on and on. It was enough to throw anyone into a deep depression, which was why my mom and I had a no news policy.

"You wanted me to tell you, so I'm telling you," Xena snapped, crossing her arms and giving me the evil eye.

"Sorry," I muttered. She had a point, so I clamped my mouth shut, vowing to keep my snarky comments—and snorts—to myself.

I stole a glance at Cole. He could normally be counted on for a smart ass comment or two, but he was still lost in his own mind.

"Years ago, souls became angels by chance," Xena explained. "If people with white auras passed on when their souls were fated, they would become angels. There were no seekers. As time passed, humanity changed, became more...*evil* for lack of a better word. Previously, the balance had always been on the side of good, but for the first time, good was losing ground to bad."

"When did this happen?" I asked. "Humans have always been evil. Look at Nero and Genghis Khan." I'd always paid attention in history class. Before I'd realized college wasn't in the cards for me, I'd even considered studying it there. So I knew enough to wonder when exactly humans became so evil. History was filled with stories of horror, like the French Revolution and Attila the

Hun's ruthlessness. It seemed to me it was in our DNA.

"I don't know the exact dates," Xena said. "When you've been around as long as I have, you stop paying attention to time. Anyway, angels are the embodiment of good and their purpose is to balance out the bad in the world. As the population grew, fewer and fewer souls were being transformed into angels. Right around the time this problem was being deliberated, Areli asked to be let back into heaven, which presented a solution."

"Seekers," I said.

Xena nodded. "Seekers. There were—and still are, actually—two factions of thought on this. Some angels were against it, arguing that if humans wanted to damn themselves we should let them, let nature follow its course. Others wanted to tip the scales and that's the faction that won out."

"What happens to pure souls that aren't fated when they pass?" I asked.

"They continue on to heaven with everyone else."

"So *everyone* goes to heaven?"

"No, not right away at least. If a soul hasn't performed enough good—meaning the aura doesn't land on the plus side of things—then the soul is sent back to Earth."

"Like reincarnation."

Xena grimaced. "Sort of."

"So is there a hell?"

She shook her head. "Not as most imagine it. Earth is probably the closest thing to hell."

I laughed out loud at that. How could I not? Oh, the irony of it all.

"If people knew that, then they'd commit suicide to be done with it."

"Suicides rarely make it into heaven," Xena said. "Anyway, more and more souls weren't making it into heaven, which is why the world population has exploded. In addition to all the new souls, existing ones are re-entering the world at an alarming rate. But back to seekers. They were put into place so souls could be reaped right at the point they are most likely to become angels."

"How many seekers are there?" I asked. "Do they descend from anyone else's line besides Areli?"

"A few." Xena looked right at my eyes as she said that, and I knew I wasn't going to get any more out of her on that subject. She didn't even address my second question.

"So what's happening with Xavier then? You said his blood has changed."

"Angels are the embodiment of good. When fallen angels stay on Earth too long, they start to take on human characteristics. In Xavier's case, he's losing his goodness and becoming evil."

"I'd say he lost his goodness a while ago."

Xena nodded. "Yes, most likely. He flew under the radar for quite a while." She paused. "I need the names in four days."

I did a double take. "I said no."

"But I explained everything." Xena's brow furrowed. She couldn't understand why my finally having some answers didn't make everything okay.

And I didn't have time to explain it to her. If she couldn't grasp on her own why I wasn't okay with sentencing people to death, then nothing I could say would make a difference.

It wasn't my place to play God.

"It doesn't matter," I said. "It's not right and I'm not doing it."

"You *have* to."

I shook my head. "No, I don't. Kill me if you want. Torture me first if you must, but I'm not doing it. You will never get another name from me."

XENA STOOD THERE ON THE front porch stuttering long after I'd gone inside and closed the door and Cole had raced off in the Rustinator. She was at a loss.

But I didn't care. I was, too.

I thought Xena was on my side. But anyone who wanted me to provide the names of pure souls for reaping wasn't on my side. She might care about me, but her loyalty lay elsewhere. It was time I remembered that.

I smelled the sweet scent of bacon frying, so I followed my nose to the kitchen. My mom stood at the stove, pushing the strips around in a cast iron skillet.

She looked over her shoulder at me and smiled. "Breakfast for dinner. When's the last time we did that?"

"I can't remember," I whispered. I stood, staring at her for a few moments before I took a seat at the kitchen table, resting my forehead in my hands. It was difficult to reconcile my mom's new pep with the woman who'd been on her deathbed just yesterday.

"Tired?" she asked.

I nodded. It was late—past nine—and I hadn't slept much the night before as I held vigil at my mom's bedside.

"I'm wide awake." She took the bacon out of the pan and placed it on a plate lined with a paper towel. "I don't know when I'll be able to sleep. It's like I got all the sleep I needed while I was...*asleep.*"

She hadn't been sleeping—she'd been in a coma. I had finally come to terms with it. And as hard as she tried, she couldn't protect me with semantics.

"Xena gave me an assignment," I said.

My mom's back stiffened, but she didn't turn around. "What did you tell her?"

"I told her no."

"Good girl," she whispered, then cleared her throat. "Good."

"I don't know what's going to happen now," I said. "I don't know if Xena will try to force me to do it. I didn't think she was like Xavier, but now I'm not so sure. I guess I don't know her as well as I thought."

"Once upon a time, I thought I knew Xavier. I don't

know Xena at all. But no matter how nice she seems, you can never forget you're a pawn to them. A tool."

I needed that reminder. Xena was only on my team when it was convenient for her.

But what about her pledge to Areli that she would protect me? What would take priority—her request for the name of a white aura or my safety? I desperately wanted to believe she wouldn't hurt me, but I wasn't going to let my guard down.

CHAPTER 24

As I PULLED INTO THE garage parking lot the next day after school, I saw Cole drop a cigarette butt at his feet and stomp on it. Without waiting for me to park, he shoved his hands in his pockets and went inside.

I backed into my usual space and took a deep breath. When I walked into Cole's bay, he was elbow deep in a Toyota's engine. He didn't acknowledge my presence.

"Since when do you smoke?" I asked.

"I don't," he muttered.

I shot him my best how-stupid-do-you-think-I-am look. "That's not what it looked like out there."

He threw a wrench into a metal toolbox, making a loud clang. "I don't need you judging me."

"I'm not judging you." Okay, maybe I was, just a little.

"That's not what it sounds like."

Touché.

I dug my toe into the concrete floor. "I'm just worried about you."

Cole gripped the edge of the car and put his head down between his arms. His biceps flexed as he squeezed tighter.

I hesitantly stepped closer, putting my hand on his shoulder. He straightened and when he looked at me, his eyes were filled with raw pain and anger.

"It seems that no matter what I do, I'm fucked," he said miserably.

I said nothing. Not because I didn't want to—I wanted to comfort him, but I wouldn't spout false promises, either.

He sighed and got back to work on the car. "Child Protective Services called. They opened a case against my mother."

"Really? When did that happen?" I kept my questions neutral. Cole's mother was a piece-of-work and one of the contributing factors to Cole making so many mistakes. She was also the reason why Cole was eager to attain guardianship over his brother.

So wouldn't it be good that the authorities were getting involved? It was about freaking time. They were too late to help Cole, but maybe they could help Kyle.

"They called yesterday to interview me and ask questions about the situation. And every damn answer I gave made her look bad. They're using me against myself."

"I don't understand."

"If Kyle ends up in foster care, it's over. Once the state takes control, it's going to be nearly impossible for me to gain custody of him."

"Wouldn't they be happy he has a family member to take him in? That's one less kid in the system."

"Not if the family member is a high school dropout with a record."

"You're not giving yourself enough credit," I said gently. "Besides, you're not a dropout anymore. You're back in school. In just a few months you'll have your diploma." I didn't say anything about his having a record. I'd known he had been involved in some bad stuff, but this was news to me.

Cole shot me a stony look and got back to work. That meant the discussion was closed. I sighed. I wished he had opened up to me yesterday, but at least now I knew what had caused his apathy yesterday. He'd finally hit his limit.

"Has Xena contacted you since last night?" I asked.

"No," he said. "But I saw her. She was outside the school first thing this morning and then across the street this afternoon."

"But she didn't say anything to you?"

He shook his head. "No, she just kind of watched. I'm surprised you didn't see her."

"That sounds creepy," I muttered. "What the heck is she up to?"

That question was on my mind as I left the shop. I wished I could have stayed to try to cheer Cole up, but Shenice had texted me this morning, saying she wanted me to come into work. Talk about a surprise. I figured once the cat was out of the bag about my job being a set-up, it was over.

I made it to Nice Beauty in record time and Shenice was sitting in the barber's chair, flipping through a magazine. The shop was empty.

She smiled when I walked through the door. "Hey, honey. How've you been?"

I exhaled as I set my backpack down. "That depends. Wouldn't your BFF Xena tell you?" I cringed at my snarky comment. I guessed I wasn't quite over being lied to.

Shenice didn't seem bothered by my disrespect. "Xena keeps me informed about what's going on, but that's not what I asked. I asked how you've been."

"I've been better," I said. "But all things considered, today I'm good."

My mom was home, and we'd passed the forty-eight hour mark and she was showing no signs of a relapse. Xena hadn't bothered me or Cole about our supposed assignments.

So yeah, today was a good day, better than I'd had in a while.

Shenice held out an envelope and I took it. "What's this?" I asked.

"Your paycheck."

I grinned and ripped open the envelope. It wasn't much, but it was the first paycheck I'd ever gotten. It was a drop in the bucket of what we owed Bill—not to mention the hospital bills—but it was a start.

"And I feel bad about lying to you," Shenice said. "I wanted to tell you the truth, but Xena seemed to think you were better off not knowing."

"Did she say why?" I asked.

"You know her. She doesn't explain anything."

I snorted. "That's the truth."

It troubled me I'd been so wrong about Xena. My gut was telling me she was good, but her actions were questionable. Just like everything else, though, there were shades of gray. Where on the spectrum did Xena fall?

If her spying on us this morning was any indication, she wasn't going anywhere soon, so time would tell.

"Anyway, I want to make it up to you," Shenice said. "I'm going to do your hair, your nails, everything. Just relax and let me pamper you."

"I thought you wanted me to work," I said. Free services at the salon sounded great, but I needed the job more than a manicure.

"I do, but not today," she said firmly and I sighed with relief. "Now get in this chair."

I hesitated for a moment, then gleefully complied with her request.

She ran her hands through my hair, then inspected the ends. She tsk-ed. "Split ends all over the place. When was the last time you had a trim?"

I guiltily ducked my head. "I don't remember."

Shenice sighed. "It's a shame you don't take care of your hair. It's so pretty. Now, what do you want? Maybe some layers?"

I bit my lip. "Doesn't that require, like, maintenance? I don't like spending a lot of time fixing my hair."

"You just have to blow it dry, but I'll tell you what. I'll trim it up and frame it around your face. Then I'll put in some highlights. How's that?"

"Sounds good."

We moved to the sink and she washed my hair, scrubbing my scalp. I almost moaned. It felt so good. Shenice's hands were magic.

"What's it like being a sensitive?" I asked.

Shenice cocked her head to the side, considering. "I don't know, really. I've always been a sensitive, so it's normal for me. Angels aren't like ghosts. My mom and sister sometimes have to hide from them. Once the ghosts find out they can see them, they get bombarded. 'Tell my wife this, tell my father that.' Ghosts are needy."

I hadn't considered that. I was at the beck and call of my handler, but I knew who that was. Well, usually. The past few months were an anomaly. It would be weird to be ambushed while you were just trying to go about your business.

Shenice turned the hot water on full blast and doused my head, rinsing all the product out. "Is the temperature good?"

"It feels heavenly," I said, then frowned. "Wait, how do ghosts fit with angels and all that?"

"Ghosts are souls that have been delayed in either going to heaven or being reintroduced into the world."

She wrapped my hair up in a towel and we moved to the barber's chair. She combed through it and started snipping. Locks of my hair fell to the ground, looking like cobwebs against the white linoleum.

"I used to wish I was different," Shenice said while she worked. "Different than I am, I mean. Because I already was *different*. Obviously, I wasn't like the other folks in my neighborhood. And even in my own family I was different. At first my parents couldn't figure out what was 'wrong' with me." She used air quotes around the word "wrong." "I saw things, but I wasn't seeing the same things my mom was. I had a rough time for a while. It wasn't until Areli visited that I understood my gift."

"He told me he wasn't supposed to visit me," I said, feeling somewhat betrayed and definitely jealous. It would have been so much easier coming to terms with everything if he'd been around to explain it. I still had so many questions. I wouldn't mind him coming back to see me, except I suspected that if he ever did come back, the reason wouldn't be a good one.

"I think that's true. He's forbidden from visiting his descendants. But I'm not his descendant. I'm the woman's descendant. He checks on all of us from time to time." She paused. "I think he knows what he did to his own descendants was wrong. But some wrongs can't be undone. And he knows that, too."

I thought of Cole. Truer words were never spoken.

I CAME HOME TO THE smell of dinner. Inhaling deeply, I grinned. It'd been over a week now—eight days—since my mom got out of the hospital, and each day I breathed a little easier.

In the last week, she'd been cooking up a storm—made-from-scratch meals every night, baked goods, and chocolate you-name-it. Cake, brownies, cookies. Even chocolate swirl cheesecake. Good thing for us our seeker blood gave us fast metabolisms. Poor Bill had already had to take his belt out a notch, but I don't think he minded.

He was waiting at the kitchen table, which was set for the three of us. We never ate in the dining room, instead eating at the smaller kitchen table. I liked it. It was cozy.

What an odd little family we'd turned into.

"Hey!" my mom exclaimed. "Look at your hair."

I touched it self-consciously. "Do you like it?"

"It's fantastic. It suits you."

I beamed, pleased she'd noticed and that she liked it.

"Here," my mom said, setting a plate at my usual seat. "Chicken, squash casserole, and mashed potatoes."

"Any muffins?" I asked hopefully, sliding into my seat. She made those from scratch, too, and they were mouthwatering. As if the oven understood me, its timer sounded.

"Blueberry muffins, coming up!" She slipped mitts over her hands and turned to open the oven.

"How did the trig test go?" Bill asked, shoveling a heap of potatoes into his mouth.

I grimaced. "Not so good. I won't know my grade until tomorrow or the next day, but I'm pretty sure I bombed it. Math and I don't mix."

"Don't worry," he said. "You'll get caught up."

"I hope so," I grumbled. I talked a big game, but deep down I wanted to do well. If not for college applications, then for my own personal satisfaction. At this rate, though, I was going to have to retake trig, which was irritating. Despite all my absences, I'd managed to keep all my grades up except for this one. Poor Kaley was beside herself. As my tutor, it was a personal affront to her that I was earning failing grades.

"Any sign of Xena?" my mom asked, keeping her voice light, but I could tell there was anxiety there.

I contemplated not telling her about Xena hanging around the school and the beauty shop. She was always there. Watching. Waiting. But for what I didn't know. And with her freaky teleportation ability—that's what I was still calling it because I didn't know how else to describe it— she could be whizzing to all sorts of locations, practically keeping an eye on me and Cole simultaneously.

"Sort of," I said. "She's still around, but she hasn't approached me. It's totally weird."

She didn't say anything and continued taking the muffins out of the pan.

I was still pissed at Xena, but I sort of missed her as well. I took her silence as an indicator she'd accepted my stance on seeking. What else could it mean?

Was she facing any repercussions because of it? Or

did she find another seeker whose morals weren't as stringent as mine? But if that was the case, then why was she still hanging around? Was it because she had been formally assigned to me? Except I didn't know how that worked. It seemed that every little bit I learned just multiplied into even more questions.

I looked up from my plate just as my mom turned to bring the basket of muffins to the table. My eyes met hers and I reached out for the basket.

Then everything turned to slow motion.

Her eyes rolled to the back of her head and she dropped to her knees. The basket hit the floor and muffins rolled everywhere.

"Mom!" I stood up so fast I knocked my chair over.

She collapsed the rest of the way, her body sprawled on the kitchen floor in unnatural angles.

Bill reached her before I did and he gathered her in his arms. "She's not breathing," he said.

He rolled her onto her back and leaned down to give her mouth-to-mouth. After pinching her nose shut and breathing air into her mouth, he started chest compressions.

I knelt on the ground next to them and clutched her hand, praying to a God I wasn't sure I believed in.

"Call 911," Bill said after he gave her another bout of air.

I looked at him stupidly for a moment before rushing to grab my phone out of my backpack by the front door. Before my shaking fingers could press the digits, the front door burst open and Xena walked in.

"She needs this," Xena said, holding up the vial of blood and a syringe. The sight of it brought me out of my stupor.

I dropped my phone. "Hurry."

We rushed into the kitchen, and I searched for something to tie around my mom's arm, like I'd done for Cole at the hospital. My gaze fell on an apron and I grabbed it. The straps would work.

Bill continued the CPR while I wrapped the apron strap around her arm and Xena prepped the syringe. I didn't have time to make a decent knot, so I help the strap in place and moved out of the way so Xena could get closer.

She examined her arm for just a few seconds before expertly inserting the needle, like she'd done it a thousand times.

Xena leaned back, intently watching my mom. A few seconds passed, and then her chest slowly rose and fell.

CHAPTER 25

WHILE BILL AND I GOT my mom settled in bed, Xena must have called Cole because he was just coming in the front door when I came downstairs.

As he shut the door behind him, he looked up at me and our eyes locked. I slowed my steps, stopping completely as *something* passed between us. We were in Limbo Land. I'd never stopped caring about him and I wanted to be with him, but not if he had resentment toward me for the way I'd saved him. And I didn't think he was ready to let that go yet. Maybe someday, but not today.

In the last week, I hadn't seen him other than in passing at school. I'd put him out of my mind—self-preservation at its best. So being in his presence felt odd. Uncomfortable, even. It was funny how quickly things changed.

I didn't like it.

"How is she?" he asked, concern in his eyes. At least that part hadn't changed.

"Okay, I think." Every time I blinked, I saw the basket hit the floor and the muffins she'd lovingly made rolling under the table.

"No hospital this time?"

I shook my head. As long as we could get fluids and

nourishment in her, what was the point? The only thing admitting her to the hospital would do was leave us with more bills we couldn't pay. Doctors couldn't help her.

Numbness set in as the events of the evening hit me. I sat down on the steps and rested my head in my hands. I should have known the last week was too good to be true. Nothing in these past few months had been as simple as that.

"How about you?" Cole asked, tucking his hands in his pockets in a way that signaled he didn't know what to do with them. "How are you?"

Once upon a time, he would have gathered me in his arms and that would have been enough to take some of the pain away.

"Not good," I said. "This sucks."

"Yeah."

There wasn't much else either of us could say. We were trapped in a pattern of one step forward, two steps back. Every time I thought my mom was getting better, *wham!* Two steps back. She hadn't been getting better this whole time. She'd been getting much, much worse.

"Any news about your mom and Kyle?"

"No. You know government. They move slow."

"Well, that's something, at least."

He shrugged. "I guess so." He didn't seem too optimistic, nor did he offer any more information, so I let it go. One problem at a time. Besides, there was absolutely nothing I could do.

I stood and we went into the kitchen. Bill was cleaning up the mess from dinner. I looked around, but there was no petite fallen angel in sight.

"Where's Xena?"

"I don't know," Bill replied. "She wasn't here when I came downstairs." I'd stayed with my mom ten minutes after Bill left, making sure she was comfortable. She still hadn't woken up, but I didn't think she was in a full-on coma this time, for whatever my non-medical opinion was worth.

It was so frustrating. The past week I'd gotten my mom back, and she'd even said she was going to apply for jobs next week.

And now Xena had done her disappearing act again. Apparently she thought it was okay to waltz in here, stab my mom with a needle, and flit out.

I grabbed my phone and called her, but it went straight to voicemail. I disconnected without leaving a message.

"Screw that," I muttered. I stalked to the front door and grabbed my coat off the hook. "Bill, I'm going to find her."

"I'll come with you," Cole said, coming up behind me and opening the front door. "Where do you think she went?"

"No clue," I said angrily. "But we'll find her."

"I'll drive."

I climbed into the passenger seat of the Rustinator as I'd done so many times before. I should have insisted on driving or at least taking my car because the heat in Cole's car took forever to get going, but I was a stress ball of emotions. It was probably better I didn't get behind the wheel.

My hands shook as I sat in the passenger seat, so I crossed my arms. "As usual, she's not telling us everything."

Cole snorted. "Did she ever?"

"No," I said darkly. "Go by the salon. That's the only place I can think where she'd be."

I might have seemed confident I'd be able to find her, but in reality I didn't even know where to look. But I had to do *something*. If I sat around the house waiting for my mom to wake up, I'd go crazy.

Cole pulled to a stop at a red light, and in the silence, I heard the slight click of the back door opening and closing.

Gotcha!

Actually, it was the other way around. We hadn't found her—she found us.

I whirled around. "What the hell, Xena?" I said just as Cole let out a stream of expletives.

Cole hadn't witnessed Xena's trick yet and had laughed at me when I'd explained it to him. A juvenile part of me wanted to tell him *I told you so.* But I bit my tongue where that was concerned.

"How did you happen to be right outside with Xavier's blood just as my mom collapsed?" I asked.

"I promised Areli I would look out for you. Your being mad at me doesn't change that."

The way she said it made it sound like I was merely pitching a hissy fit over something trivial instead of refusing to sentence innocent people to death. I could respect that she'd stayed true to her word she'd given Areli. Without her, my mom wouldn't be alive right now.

But I was still pissed. And I still wasn't seeking. The sooner we could get that issue settled between us, the sooner we could focus on more important things.

Like Xavier.

"Fine," I said. "Did you tell the powers that be that the Reapers won't be getting any more names from me?"

"About that," Xena said. "I think you should reconsider."

She had to be freaking kidding me. I'd made myself perfectly clear, and there was nothing she could say that would change my mind.

"No. No way, no how. It's not happening."

Cole pulled into an empty parking lot and put the car in park so he could turn and be part of the conversation. At least, I hoped that's what he was doing. Last time, he'd been like a zombie.

"You don't know the mistake you're making," she said, her voice carrying more emotion than usual.

"I would if you'd tell me," I said through gritted teeth.

I wanted to grab her by her shoulders and shake some sense into her. Keeping secrets didn't benefit anyone. When would she get that through her thick head? Xena was one of the most stubborn, set-in-her-ways people I'd ever met.

That was probably due to her being only God knew how old.

She sighed, looking down at her fidgeting hands. "We're already running low on blood."

I stilled, letting her words reverberate in my mind. Then I closed my eyes and put my hand over them as the poignancy of what this meant hit me.

How had I not put two and two together? I could only blame it on my emotional state.

My mom needed Xavier's blood to survive. There wasn't a one-time cure. What he'd done to her was chronic, and she'd need continuous injections to stay healthy.

That was the only explanation. And it was horrible. He'd damned her in the worst possible way, linking her to him for the rest of her life.

Her life depended on Xavier.

Cole squeezed my hand and I looked up, meeting his eyes, which were stricken. He'd figured it out, too.

"When did you know she'd need his blood again?" I asked. Had she always known?

"I suspected it immediately after you gave it to her the first time," she said. "Xavier contacted me that night and confirmed it."

But she hadn't told me. No, instead she'd gone along—business as usual—giving me and Cole an assignment. My stomach lurched as I put the time table together in my mind.

"Who did my assignment come from?" I asked quietly.

Crossing her arms and looking out the window, Xena didn't answer.

"Who...did...my...assignment...come...from?"

"You already know the answer to that question or else you wouldn't be asking me like that," Xena muttered.

"What the hell?" Cole exploded. He'd finally reached his boiling point, and I was selfishly glad. I didn't want to fight this battle alone. "That's seriously fucked up if you think I'm going to give a name to Xavier. You do realize *he killed me*, right?"

"It's the only way he'd agree to help Ava's mom," Xena said wearily. "I tried to reason with him, but you can guess how that went. He only asked for one name, but I thought it might be better to have both of you search just in case one of you came up short. If we got two, then we'd have one in the hole."

One in the hole. This wasn't a freaking game. That "one in the hole" was someone's life. A parent's child. A parent like Bill.

Xena was once human, but somewhere along the way, she'd lost her humanity. But I hadn't lost mine. Not yet, anyway.

I felt sick to my stomach. Bile rose in my throat, and I flung open the car door before I lost it. I fell out into the cold and sucked in the chilly air in huge gulps.

He'd done it. Xavier had won. He had leverage over me that I would never be willing to compromise on.

I sank down to my knees as warm, salty tears flowed down my face.

Cole knelt in front of me and wiped the tears with his thumb. I clung to him as I cried. We stayed that way— kneeling on the pavement with his arms wrapped around me—for at least ten minutes. Then once I had it all out, I pulled away.

Immediately, I felt the loss of his warmth in more ways than one.

Xena had gotten out of the car and was leaning against it with her arms crossed. I couldn't read her expression, but I didn't care how she felt or thought. She was a handler, in the same class as Xavier. How many seekers' lives had handlers waltzed in and out of, not caring about the decimation in their wake? I'd let myself forget that Xena played for the other team, but never again.

"How many doses do we have left?" I asked.

"Two," she said.

I did the math. Unless I gave Xavier a name, in three weeks my mom would be dead.

WHEN I CAME OUTSIDE THE next morning, Cole was leaning against my car with a thermal mug in his hands. I took a deep breath and walked down the porch stairs to meet him. He handed me the mug.

"Thanks," I said, wrapping my hands around it. I flipped the lid open. Hot chocolate, my favorite. I inhaled deeply.

"I'll take a look at the transmission in your car this afternoon," he said. His hands were shoved in his pockets, and he kicked at the frost on the grass.

That was his way of bridging the divide between us. Cole always was a man of action.

"Thanks," I said again. Since I'd been driving Bill's car, I'd forgotten all about ours. Bill had had it towed to his shop when we moved in with him. At some point, I was also going to have to deal with the damage to Bill's car.

"What are you going to do?" I didn't need to ask what he was referring to. It was all I'd been thinking about since last night.

"I don't know."

But I did know. I'd do whatever it took to save my mom. Last night when I'd come home, I'd sat beside her, holding her hand. She'd woken up, but only for a few minutes. She'd been groggy and disoriented.

But alive. And I wanted to keep her that way.

So it looked like I'd be seeking. But not at school. What if Kaley's aura turned white? Would I be willing to sacrifice her to give my mom a few more weeks? Then who would be next? Where would it stop? I wasn't naive enough to think it would end with one name. No, Xavier would milk this for as long as he could. He had the permanent upper hand.

"I'll go with you," Cole said.

He knew me so well. He knew exactly what I was going to do.

I shook my head. "No. This is between me and Xavier. I won't put you through that."

Also, I didn't want him to watch me preying on people. Strangers, because in my warped logic seeking strangers wasn't as bad an offense. My lowest point was always when I found a white aura, knowing I was about to sentence that person to death. He didn't need to see that.

I didn't want him to witness my aura as it became darker and darker until finally my soul was evil. I saw no other way this could end.

He sighed. "That might be best. I don't know if I could do it anyway. I'm still not great at reading auras." He sounded miserable. But I was content to let him take his time honing that skill. He couldn't seek if he couldn't read the auras.

"It's not a skill I'm proud of," I said. "Thanks for the hot chocolate." I stepped away to get in my car.

It didn't take long to get to school and park, but I took my time getting out of the car and walking into the building. All day, I went through the motions, but it was pointless. My stomach was in knots and I couldn't concentrate.

But I stayed until the final bell. I couldn't start seeking until school was out anyway.

I lingered in my car for a bit before setting off to a Target about thirty miles away. I was bound to run into teenagers there, if even only the employees. There was also a row of fast food restaurants I could check out.

I gripped the steering wheel and stared at the big bulls-eye sign, reluctant to get started. I'd vowed never to do this again. And now not only would I have to do it again, I'd have to repeat this at least once a month for the rest of my mom's life. If I failed just one time, then it was game over for her. I didn't expect Xavier to be forgiving.

I opened the car door and swung my feet out. I stood on shaky legs, holding onto the car's frame for support.

I could do this. I had to do this.

The real question was if I'd be able to live with myself afterward.

Immediately upon entering the store I spied a group of girls in the clothing section, so I walked over and positioned myself nearby, pretending to examine a pair of skinny jeans hanging on a rack. Slowly, I lowered my guards.

The auras hit me hard and I winced. It'd been a while since I looked at them. Shades of pink and purple swirled together, typical for teenage girls. The tallest girl's aura was pale with shimmers of white. Sometime in the future, her aura might end up pure, but not today.

She'd gotten lucky.

I circled around the store, my worn knock-off Uggs slapping on the linoleum. The right sole nearly had a hole in the bottom, but we hadn't had money for new things in a while.

The store was nearly empty. I traipsed through the grocery section in a last ditch effort, but I came up empty.

My final stop was the line of cashiers. Nothing there either, except one aura that was a shade away from being pure black.

Looking at the guy, I shuddered. Even if I hadn't been able to see his aura, he still would have given me the creeps. He had that *look* about him—the kind that made me wonder if he skinned neighborhood cats in his garage.

His gaze landed on me and he narrowed his eyes,

curling his lip slightly, as if he knew what I was thinking about him. I hurried out of the store.

I sat in my car again, staring at the row of fast food restaurants. A car full of teenage guys pulled up, and they pushed and shoved one another good-naturedly on their way into the building. The distance was too great for me to check their auras from here.

I wondered if that would make it easier—not having to see them up close. Probably not. And besides, I'd be unlikely to get the person's name if I was far away.

It was the name that made it personal.

It was the death that made it unbearable.

What was bothering me even more than that, though, was I didn't know what Xavier's plan was. There was no way he was requesting names to add to the flock of angels that would balance the good/evil ratio. What were his motives? What was I contributing to?

And if I knew the answers to these questions, would I be able to go through with it? At least in a normal seeking situation, the souls would most likely become angels. I could see the good—*the purpose*—in that, even if I didn't agree with the means.

This wasn't happening today—I couldn't do it. I had three more weeks. I'd try again tomorrow.

CHAPTER 26

ON THE DRIVE HOME, I called Bill to check on my mom.
Apparently she was up and as perky as ever. She'd wanted
to borrow a car to go job hunting.

I shook my head. She and I needed to have a talk. Did
she even remember what happened last night? There was
no way she could get a job. Because yeah, I'm sure her boss
wouldn't mind Xena busting in there once a week to stab
her with a needle and inject her with blood. It was gross
under normal circumstances, but in a restaurant? Ick.

Sighing, I backed into my normal space at Bill's. I
really needed to woman up and tell him about the car.
Chances were he'd already noticed it and didn't say
anything. Bill was a good guy like that.

My mom was in the kitchen, baking. Rows of cooling
chocolate chip and oatmeal cookies were lined up on the
counter.

Xena sat at the table with a plate of cookies and a glass
of milk. I had mixed feelings about that. We still weren't
on chummy let's-share-an-after-school-snack terms.

And even though she'd saved my mom's life, I
irrationally still wanted to keep Xena away from her.

"Where were you?" my mom asked, coming to me and
putting her hands on my shoulders.

I shifted my eyes to Xena, who looked away guiltily. At least she had the grace to feel bad for lying to my mom.

"Target," I said.

My mom crossed her arms. "Why?"

"Just...because," I answered lamely.

"She knows," Xena said quietly. Or maybe that was what she felt bad for—telling my mom without me. We couldn't keep the truth from her forever, but I'd wanted to be the one to tell her. Or at least be present.

"Mom, I'm going to fix this," I promised. "I'll find a name and we'll get you the medicine you need." I couldn't keep referring to it as Xavier's blood. The thought of it running through my mom's veins ripped at my heart.

She nodded numbly, her eyes not quite focusing. The oven buzzer sounded and she mechanically pulled the cookie tray out of the oven.

"I need a moment," she said, leaving the room.

I stared at the bowl full of raw cookie dough, then stalked over to the oven to turn it off.

"I really wish you would have waited," I told Xena, putting the bowl of cookie dough in the refrigerator and angrily slamming the door.

"She needed to know before we meet Xavier."

"*Excuse me?*"

She shrugged. "He wanted to talk to you, so I bargained with him." She pulled a vial of blood out of her pocket and set it on the table. "This will get her through another month."

I exhaled, my eyes trained on the red liquid. After a moment, Xena got up and put it in the refrigerator with the other one.

"Thanks," I said begrudgingly. I didn't want to see Xavier, but I was grateful Xena had used the situation to our advantage. "Why does he want to meet?"

"I told him you were reluctant to seek."

Reluctant? More like morally opposed. More like it made my skin crawl. More like I'd rather feed *Xavier* to the Reapers.

But that certainly wasn't an option.

"So what?" I said. "Does he want to convince me or something? Because I've already decided to do it. We all know I have no choice."

"There's always a choice."

"Letting my mom die is *not* a choice." I paused, wondering if I should ask Xena about Xavier's intent for the souls. It would be easier not to know. But I couldn't go into this with my eyes closed. "Why does Xavier want the names?"

Xena's eyes stayed trained on the cookies in front of her, and she systemically pulverized the crumbs between her fingers until they were nothing but dust. "He's been rogue ever since he left you. And it's unclear what he did with the last name your mom gave him. The teacher."

My hands shook. "What do you mean?"

When I hadn't been able to fulfill my assignment, my mom had turned in a name instead. I'd never forget the expression on my mom's face as she sat with a glass of wine and the news article reporting the death laid out in front of her. Though I hadn't been the one to provide the teacher's name, her death was my fault.

She'd had three children—children who would now grow up without their mother.

"Just what I said. No one knows what happened to the soul. The woman died, but..." Xena trailed off.

"I still don't get it. How can no one know? Her soul has got to be *somewhere*, right? Either an angel or a ghost or in heaven."

"It's unaccounted for," she said. "That's all I know."

I sat back for a moment, staring at her. For once, I believed she didn't know more than what she was telling me. I didn't know what to think about all of this. How could a soul just vanish?

Xena pursed her lips for a moment. "Xavier wants to see Cole, too."

Not good. Not good at all. I didn't want Cole anywhere near Xavier, but I couldn't make that call.

"You'll have to ask him. I don't make decisions for him."

I bit my cuticle. What was the point of meeting Xavier anyway? There was no reason to talk to him. He'd given us the medicine already. Until I had a name, he wasn't going to give us more.

"I can tell what you're thinking," Xena said. "That vial is only half of the arrangement. At the meeting, he'll give you another one."

Dang. Once again, he'd left me no option. He was good at that. That was the trouble when your enemy had known you your entire life.

"All right," I grumbled.

"But Cole has to come, too. That's part of the deal."

I put my palms on the counter and leaned on them. "If you tell him the situation, he'll agree to come," I said quietly. I didn't want to force him into anything, and telling him what was at stake was basically doing that. But again, what choice did I have?

"I'll call him."

I took several deep breaths, inhaling the sweet smell of freshly baked cookies. The scent reminded me of Areli, who'd smelled like sugar. In English, we'd studied Greek drama and at the end, there was sometimes a deus est machina, which basically meant something came down from the sky to save the day.

I kind of thought it meant the playwright had written himself into a corner and didn't know how to get out of it.

But Areli had been a literal deus est machina. Selfishly, I wanted another one of those. Needed one.

I was backed into a corner with no visible way out.

I FOUND MY MOM IN her bedroom sitting on her bed with

her arms wrapped around her knees. Though she still had streaks of gray hair, she'd never looked younger—she looked like a scared little kid.

I sat on the edge of the bed, realizing not for the first time how much our roles had become reversed. One of the first days after we'd moved here, my mom had come into my room and sat on my bed just like I was doing now. I'd been so angry at her I could barely stand to look at her.

What a little bitch I'd been.

"Are you okay?" I asked.

"Sorry." She pushed her hair away from her face. "It's a shock, that's all. I'd finally come to terms with Xavier's blood flowing through my veins."

I cringed as she said that. I still hadn't been able to accept it, so I tried not to think about it at all.

"He's evil," she said simply. "And now I have some of that inside me. It's that evilness that's keeping me alive."

"Don't think of it like that," I said empathetically. But I was such a hypocrite. If I were in her position, I'd be fixated on the same thing. Heck, I kind of already was.

"It's funny. For years I did his bidding, sometimes even conning myself into believing I was acting for the greater good. Angels are good, right? I was helping to bring good into the world. But now when I look back, I see what a fool I've been. Xavier kept getting worse and worse, and I ignored it because I was afraid of causing trouble. But especially now, I find it hard to believe that Xavier is acting for the greater good."

"I know," I murmured. She'd hit upon my biggest concern. Xena said seekers were enabled to help balance the scales of good and evil. Xavier couldn't be on the side of good, not if he'd gone rogue. Not if there were missing souls.

"I don't know if I even want to know the truth." Her voice was quiet, and she traced the pattern on the quilt with her fingertip. "I'm a coward."

"You're not," I said firmly. "You did what you had to

all those years to keep me safe."

And now I was going to do what I had to do to keep her safe, which included not letting her know about Xavier's rogue status.

"I guess." Her voice hitched and tears filed her eyes. She looked away for a moment, wiping the tears from her cheeks. Then she smiled and let out a little defeated laugh.

A hole formed in my heart.

Parents were supposed to be superhuman, able to fix every problem, every ache, every sorrow. They were supposed to be perfect—no mistakes allowed. It was an unfair expectation, but there it was.

Seeing my mom so vulnerable made me see her for what she was—a human being who tried to do the best she could. It pained me to acknowledge that sometimes her best fell short.

MY MOM SILENTLY BOXED UP the cookies as Xena slipped her coat on.

"I called Cole," she said. "We're all set for tomorrow morning."

I closed my eyes. That was soon. Xavier always was impatient. But it was better this way. Knots and butterflies had already formed in my stomach, and they would only multiply until it was over.

Ha...what a joke. It would never be over.

"He said he'll pick you up tomorrow at nine," Xena said.

I nodded and she let herself out, the click of the front door sounding somehow ominous.

I sank down into a chair at the kitchen table. My gaze landed on the ceramic salt and pepper shakers that had a permanent home in the center of the table. The pepper shaker was a yellow and orange chicken and the salt shaker was a light blue egg, which made no sense. Weren't only robins' eggs blue? I ran my finger along the side of it, pushing it into the groove carved out between the chicken's wings.

My mom noticed me playing with them. "Jill got those for Bill one Christmas at her school's little Christmas store."

And he'd not only kept them but used them daily. I wondered if it was a painful reminder for him or if the memory brought him joy. They were ugly, but I bet he'd made her feel like it was the best gift in the world. Bill had probably been a great dad.

It was like the time I got my mom a gift from the convenience store up the street. I was only seven and I'd squirreled away loose change for months, taking a quarter here, a dime there out of my mom's wallet. In retrospect, I realized this was stealing, but seven-year-old me had no other way to get money. Anyway, once I had what I thought was enough, I slipped out of the house while the babysitter was preoccupied with *The Price is Right*. I ran as fast as I could to the store, petrified the babysitter would notice I was missing but also full of exhilaration. I bought her the prettiest jewelry set I could find, which also happened to be pink, plastic, and covered with glittery hearts.

She wore it every day for a month until it finally broke, exclaiming every morning how the jewelry completed her outfit and made her feel pretty. I'd beamed, so proud of myself for making her happy.

But I'd never be on the other side of things.

"I'm never having kids." The words slipped out and at my mom's startled expression, I clarified, "This ends with me."

"That's what I said, too," she said, sitting across from me. I was proof that she hadn't stayed true to her word, but I couldn't imagine anything that would make me change my mind.

"What happened?"

"You. *You* happened." She sighed. "You weren't planned, which I'm sure you've figured out by now. I partied a lot when I was in my early twenties. I was irresponsible. It was how I coped with the seeker stuff. By the time I realized I was pregnant, your father was long gone. He was just a fling that lasted a couple weeks."

"Did you try to find him?"

"Not really. He'd skipped town already and this was before social media, so people were harder to track down."

My mom never talked about my father, and I'd stopped asking long ago. I'd figured he wasn't important since he hadn't bothered to stick around. I didn't realize he didn't even know I existed. He wasn't even listed on my birth certificate. All I knew about him was that his name was Michael.

"Anyway, it didn't matter." She took a deep breath. "I'd decided I couldn't take any more. And I wasn't going to bring a child into this. So I got good and drunk one night and slit my wrists."

I gaped at her. Xavier had mentioned my mom had an "indiscretion" shortly before I was born, but I didn't know anything about it. My gaze immediately dropped down to her wrists, which were only partially exposed. Faintly, I could make out pale white lines I'd never noticed before. Unless you were looking for them, you'd never find them. She must have cut really deep for there to be scars. Seeker healing abilities rarely left them.

"Reapers intervened and saved me. And you. It was then I realized I couldn't escape, so I decided I would protect my baby and give her the best life I could. That's why I went along with Xavier all these years. I'd have to do it anyway, so I might as well cooperate and make things more pleasant for my daughter. I didn't want you growing up thinking you were surrounded by evil."

"But I was," I whispered.

"When Xavier was around, yes. I couldn't help that."

"So you hid it."

Her expression was stricken. "Yes."

I reached across to squeeze her hand. "I'm not judging you."

"I don't think I'd blame you if you did."

"Did you judge your mom?"

She didn't talk much about my grandma. All I knew was that she'd died shortly after my mom graduated high school.

My mom leaned back now. "Yes," she whispered. "I did judge her. After I turned eighteen, she figured her job was done. She stopped seeking and didn't care about the consequences. So the Reapers released her."

I didn't ask what "released" was a euphemism for. Grandma was dead. That was all I needed to know.

CHAPTER 27

MY MOM AND I STOOD at the front door waiting for Cole. I wore a cross body purse underneath my coat with Bill's gun tucked inside.

It weighed on me.

Last night, I'd tossed and turned in bed trying to decide whether to bring it, finally running out to my car in the middle of the night to retrieve it and hide it before my mom saw. It felt like eons had passed since I'd last practiced with Cole at the range, but hopefully my aim would be true if I needed to use it.

Shooting Xavier would give my mom a death sentence, but I didn't trust him. I'd defend myself and my family by any means necessary.

My mom twirled her hair around her finger and with the other hand she fiddled with the zipper on her coat, making a continuous *zip, zip, zip* sound that put me on edge.

I put my hand on her arm, stopping the sound. "Everything will be okay."

She gave me a tight smile, then looked away, resuming fiddling with the zipper. *Zip, zip, zip.* So much for my pep talk. I wasn't feeling too peppy either, though.

I glanced at the clock. Cole was five minutes late,

which was totally unlike him. I was starting to get worried when he pulled up. We ran out to the car.

"Sorry," Cole said as soon as I opened the door. "The car wouldn't start."

I arched an eyebrow and smirked at him as I buckled my seatbelt. His admitting something negative about the Rustinator was the silver lining in this mess.

"Don't even say it," he muttered.

"Say what?" I innocently batted my eyes.

I didn't know what he was talking about. I'd never had the first disparaging thought about the Rustinator.

Snort.

Then the moment passed and I stared out the window and my stomach rearranged itself, the knots coiling and tightening.

"Is there a game plan?" Cole asked.

"Try to keep myself from ripping his eyes from his sockets," I said dryly. If only it were that simple.

I'd really like to shoot him full of holes and then bottle his blood as it drained out of him. Morbid? Perhaps. The only thing stopping me was the fact that blood didn't keep.

"Besides that." Cole's fingers tapped on the steering wheel.

"I don't know because I don't know what he wants." I stretched my hands out on my knees, rubbing my damp palms on my jeans. "He has no reason to see me until I get him a name, which I don't have yet."

I pressed a hand to my stomach, trying to stop it from rolling. I'd taken one bite of cereal this morning before pushing it away. Now that one bite was threatening to come up again.

I was about to come face-to-face with the man who had ruined not only my life, but numerous others, including my mom's and Cole's.

He needed to die. And if he couldn't die in the traditional sense, he needed to be neutralized.

Too bad neither of those could happen. Xavier had

taunted me once saying I couldn't win against him. I hated to give him the satisfaction of knowing he was right.

Heck, I hated everything about him being right. Everything about this situation sucked.

"Where's Xena?" my mom asked from the backseat. If I'd been thinking clearly, I would have wondered the same thing.

"Meeting us there," Cole replied.

We were meeting in the same park where I'd tried to train Cole. It was likely to be deserted at this time of day. We didn't want any innocent bystanders. Just in case.

I ran my shaking hand over the purse, feeling the hard outline of the gun.

Even though the parking lot was empty when we pulled in, I was still on high alert. No cars didn't mean there were no fallen angels present.

Sure enough, Xena appeared seemingly out of thin air by the back passenger door. She waited patiently for Cole to unlock it so she could open it.

"What, no letting yourself in this time?" Cole asked as Xena slid into the backseat.

"It has come to my attention that some people may find it rude," she said stiffly, then muttered, "It's *efficient.*"

I exchanged a look with Cole and rolled my eyes. He chuckled, giving me a little grin. Then he reached over and squeezed my hand.

And didn't let go.

I gripped his hand, relishing the feel of his skin on mine. My heart flipped and then flopped before setting into a steady rhythm that was faster than normal.

Life could suck so much sometimes. As Xena alluded to, life could be considered hell on Earth. Having someone who understood made it bearable, enjoyable even. I had my mom and Bill. And I could have Cole, but I didn't because...suddenly I couldn't come up with a reason that was worth a damn.

What am I doing?

The walls I'd put up between us cracked and I was no longer sure pushing him away was the best course of action, no matter what issues we had between us.

"Xavier should be here soon," Xena said. "We're a little early."

"Do you know what he wants to talk to us about?" My mom's voice wavered slightly, another sign she was nervous. She had every right to be. In fact, after what he'd done to her, she'd be stupid not to be. The only way it could get worse was if he killed her.

He'd done that to Cole once. With a bullet, though, not his powers. For the first time, I wondered why Xavier had used the gun. Why hadn't he simply used his powers? Maybe he couldn't. Otherwise why would he carry around a gun? Maybe he could only hurt those with angel blood. Like me and my mom.

And now Cole.

Shit, shit, shit.

"No," Xena said. "But we'll keep it short and sweet. If he doesn't get to the point, then we'll get out of here."

So she too recognized Xavier's tendency to pontificate. I swore he liked to hear himself talk. I definitely didn't miss that. Xena was nearly the opposite— she didn't say enough sometimes.

"I'm getting out," my mom said. "I don't like just sitting here. I want to be able to see all around me."

"Good point," Xena said with a grimace. Then she blew on her hands and reached over the seat to hold them in front of the heat vent for a few seconds before following my mom.

Cole and I also got out of the car and we met in front of it. I started to follow my mom and Xena, but he grabbed my hand, holding me back.

I looked at him questioningly.

"Ava, I'm done."

My heartbeat slowed until I swore it stopped, and my breath was sucked from my lungs. A whimper involuntarily slipped out of my mouth.

He pulled me closer. "No, no, not like that. I mean, I'm done resenting you. I'm done with this bad blood between us." He ran his hand over his head, pulling off his beanie. His hair stuck up at all angles.

It was freaking adorable. And instead of taking my breath away, the sight of him returned it.

"There are so few good people in my life," he said. "I don't want to lose one of them over how she saved my life. I mean, you *saved my life*. Isn't that enough? What more do I want?"

"I..." I didn't know what to say. My chest felt so full I thought it would burst.

I went up on my toes and threw my arms around him, burying my face in his neck. He wrapped his arms around me, pulling me close.

"Can you forgive me?" he murmured.

I nodded. "Yes. You're not the one who needs forgiving. I'm the one—"

"No," he said firmly, moving me away from his body so he could look in my eyes. "No. You did the only thing you could do at the time. Did it suck? Yes. But it was the best option."

I blinked away the tears that were forming in my eyes.

He reached for my hand and as he did, I caught the glint of metal under his open coat. Cole was armed.

So was I. While talking to Cole, I'd somehow nearly forgotten about the gun tucked safely away in my purse. I unzipped it, reached in, and wrapped my hand around the hilt so I'd be able to get to it easily if I needed to.

I hoped to God I didn't. If I did, well, I didn't want to think about the consequences of that.

"Come on," Cole said. "We should wait with Xena and your mom."

We crossed through the park to Xena and my mom who were standing next to the row of benches. Cole and I didn't sit, either. The nervous energy in the air was thick, coming off each of us in waves.

I glanced at Xena, who swallowed and looked away. What reason did she have to be nervous? Sure, she cared about us in her own way, but this wasn't her fight. No matter the outcome, she'd eventually walk away to continue her life.

Did fallen angels live their lives like humans did? Did they have homes, hobbies, and loved ones? I didn't know.

In the woods on the far side of the park, I saw movement. I squinted against the glaring sun, but I couldn't make out who or what it was.

Moments later, Xavier emerged. He wore his trademark black and his lips were wrapped around a cigar. He strolled toward us like he hadn't a care in the world.

He might not. What the hell did I know? I never pretended to understand Xavier. And I was still clueless as to what his end game was. What was he working toward? And *why* did he want white auras?

Perhaps the more important question was whether or not I could live with myself if I knew the truth.

I would do anything to save my mom. Or Cole or Bill for that matter. But something I'd been ignoring was the question of whether one life was worth the cost of who-knew-how-many others. Why should someone's child have to die so someone else could live?

Was I really calculating the value of my mom's life compared to another?

It was a punch to the stomach. Wrapping my arm around my belly, I felt sick, choking back bile.

But I couldn't ignore the implications of what Xavier wanted me to do anymore. I thought I could give him a name, but now, seeing him face to face again after all this time, I knew I couldn't.

Oh, God. What was I going to do?

Xavier stopped ten feet away from our group. He leisurely finished his cigar, the stench of smoke and the usual cinnamon wafting toward us. I gagged.

He dropped his cigar on the ground and crushed it under his black leather boot. I wondered how he'd gotten here and if his motorcycle was stowed away somewhere.

His black eyes looked us over, his gaze landing on each of us in turn. None of us said anything. Cole's fists clenched at his sides and anger radiated from him.

A sinister smile appeared on Xavier's face as he looked at my mom. "Mary, you're looking well."

My lip curled and my nostrils flared.

"And Cole, I must say," Xavier stroked his goatee, "you have a lot more color than the last time I saw you."

Son of a—

I lunged toward him. Cole wrapped his arms around my waist, holding me back.

"Don't you dare talk to them!" I snarled. "Don't even look at them, you piece of shit!"

He laughed. "You haven't changed at all, Ava. I would have thought you'd have learned by now."

Dammit. I'd lost my composure the minute he opened his mouth, just like he'd known I would. He'd baited me.

But he was wrong. I *had* changed. Just not the way he thought I should.

"What do you want, Xavier?" my mom asked.

"To finalize the arrangement with Ava, of course," he said. "I'm old fashioned that way. I want a handshake to seal the deal."

"You owe us a vial of blood," Xena spoke up. "That was our deal."

In my rage at seeing Xavier, I'd forgotten all about that part. Thank goodness Xena still had her wits about her.

Xavier reached inside his jacket and pulled out a vial. Xena stepped forward to take it. She then pulled the cap off and sniffed it. With a satisfied nod, she sealed it and tucked it away in her pocket.

Xavier smiled broadly, stretching his arms out. "You

see? I'm a man of my word. Now let's see if Ava is as honorable as I am."

"Honor?" I said, my voice filled with venom. "You think what you do is honorable?"

My mom put her hand up to silence me. "What are you going to do with the names Ava gives you?"

"The same thing I've always done."

"Bullshit," Xena spat. "You're no longer a handler."

Xavier looked at her contemptuously. "I had such high hopes for you. But you're a disgrace of my line."

Cole and I looked at one another, surprise mirrored in our eyes.

"What?" I asked when I finally found my voice.

Xavier's eyebrows raised and his lips stretched wide. "Xena didn't tell you? She's my great-great granddaughter."

CHAPTER 28

"No," I whispered, turning to Xena. Her expression showed so many things—despair, hatred, sorrow.

But most of all, guilt.

She lifted her chin up a notch under my scrutiny.

"I trusted you." I always knew Xena wasn't giving me the full story, but I never imagined this.

"I never lied to you," Xena said.

Technically, she was right. But I'd never felt more betrayed.

"No, but you sure as hell should have told us that," Cole said. "What the fuck?"

"Why do you think I didn't?" Xena retorted, meeting his angry stare with one of her own. "*This* is why."

Cole growled and ran his hands through his hair, pacing in a prowl.

"You said *we* were related," I said numbly. I'd brought the gun with the intent of defending my family. Xena had been included. The stupidity of that thought struck me hard.

"We are. I'm a descendant of both Xavier and Areli's lover's family." Xena's eyes were pleading, but I cast mine to the ground. I couldn't look at her.

"You never answered the question," my mom said to

Xavier, not distracted by the bombshell he'd just dropped. "What are you doing with the white auras?"

Her insistence made me wonder if Xena had already told her about Xavier going rogue. I hoped not.

Xavier simply grinned. "That's really none of your concern. I'll give you my blood in exchange for names. That's all you need to know." He looked over at me. "And just to show you how generous I am, I'll give you another month to train your boyfriend. He doesn't need to provide a name right now."

I stilled and beside me Cole stiffened. He had to provide names, too? Xena had given both of us assignments, but I had thought Cole's assignment was just a back-up in case I didn't come through.

I glanced over at him. His hands were fisted at his sides and his jaw worked as he narrowed his eyes at Xavier.

My first thought was a selfish one. I'd just gotten him back and now this was enough to drive a wedge between us.

"Tell me why you want the auras." My mom's voice was more forceful and demanding than it had ever been. She stared him down, looking fierce. She was usually so gentle and mild-mannered. I didn't know she had it in her.

Xavier chuckled. Then he reached into his jacket to pull out another cigar. He didn't have the decency to answer her, not even with a snide comment.

Dammit! I wanted to kill Xavier. To pull the gun out of my purse and fill him full of holes. Judging by the expressions of everyone surrounding me, I'd have to get in line.

But I still didn't know if that would be enough to kill him. Xena had never clarified that point.

I didn't get it. What was Xavier's motivation? Why had he wanted to meet with us? What did he want? Maybe if I understood that, I could figure out how to reason with him. Or thwart him or something. He couldn't just be one of those villains whose sole purpose was to wreak havoc and take over the world. At one point, Xavier was a true angel. He'd had goodness in him. All it took was one look into his black eyes to know he'd lost all of that. But this made me even more convinced he had some sort of purpose. *Something* had to have caused the change in him.

But I didn't get to give it any more thought.

Before I knew what was happening, my mom strode over to me and reached into my purse, pulling out the gun.

She aimed it at Xavier, switching off the safety. "Go to hell."

"No!" I yelled, reaching for her, but she pushed me aside, holding firm.

She squeezed the trigger, sending a bullet into Xavier's chest. Cole wrapped his arms around me, pulling me away from the shooting.

The shot barely affected Xavier. If not for the damage to his jacket, you wouldn't have even known he'd been hit.

"Help me," I desperately pleaded to Cole. "We have to stop her."

He shook his head. "It's too dangerous."

The second shot hit his shoulder, pushing him a step back.

"Mom, stop!" I struggled against Cole, but he didn't budge.

My mom moved forward, pulling off two more shots, the first of which went wide. The second of the two hit him in the collar bone.

Xavier's expression slowly turned from shock to anger.

"Shit, shit, shit," I whispered.

But my mom didn't stop. She stepped closer and kept firing. Watching in horror, I lost track of how many shots.

Xavier let out a roar and she raised the gun slightly.

"Screw you," she whispered, then pulled the trigger one last time, hitting him in the face in an explosion of blood.

Xavier crumpled to the ground and didn't move.

"Oh my God," I said. Cole finally let me go and I dashed toward Xavier, but Xena grabbed me before I could get there.

"No," she said firmly. "We need to leave."

"We need to make sure he's alive!" I shrieked. "We can't let him die."

"Yes, we can." My mom calmly reset the safety on the gun and let it hang at her side. "He can rot in hell."

I gaped at her. How could she have done that? She *knew* what was at stake, and yet she'd done it anyway.

Sirens sounded in the distance.

"Let's go," Xena said, tugging on my arm again.

We ran to the car. Once inside, I peered through the window, watching for signs of movement.

But everything was still.

THE CAR WAS SILENT ON the way back to Bill's. I stared straight ahead, the events I'd just witnessed replaying in my mind.

Finally, Xena spoke. "He won't die," she said quietly.

In the rearview mirror, I saw my mom cross her arms and look out the window. I expected her to be in shock, but she seemed perfectly in control.

She'd known what she was doing. Xavier would never help her now. She'd sacrificed herself to save me from being beholden to him.

But in freeing me, she'd signed her own death sentence.

Once at Bill's, my mom went straight up to her room, closing the door behind her with a resounding click.

Xena, Cole, and I congregated in the living room. Cole wrapped his arms around me, but I was numb inside. The tears wouldn't come.

Because I was pissed.

"How could she do that?" I asked angrily.

"She knew what she was doing," Xena said.

"Did you know?" I accused. I wanted someone to blame, someone other than her to hold responsible. Because how could she knowingly do this? We'd just talked about how her mom had given up.

And now she'd essentially done the same thing.

Gone was the mature Ava who'd carried more than her share these past few months. In her place was the immature, scared Ava—the little girl who wanted her mom.

I wanted her to take care of me. I wanted her to make everything okay again. But most of all, I wanted her to love me enough to stay.

Because that was what this felt like to me—abandonment. She was peacing out on life and all that came with it, including me.

Xena shook her head. "I'm as surprised as you."

"But she didn't even kill him," I said. "So what was the point?" That was the kicker. Nothing was gained. One step forward, two steps back.

"You know why she did it," Cole said quietly.

I looked up at him, staring into his dark brown eyes. In them, I saw the truth. And I hated it. My emotions were all over the place. I was angry, full of despair, and worst of all, a little relieved.

I didn't have to seek for Xavier anymore and a small part of me was overjoyed. Admitting that made me sick to my stomach. What kind of a daughter was I?

A human one said a small voice in my mind. It sounded suspiciously like Areli.

I shrugged it off. There were no explanations or excuses that could make any part of this okay. Unless Areli was going to pull another deus est machina, but that was unlikely. Two miracles in one lifetime was a little much to ask. Much less two in the span of several months.

"I was going to save her." I sank onto the couch and rested my head in my hands.

"She didn't want to be saved."

I looked up at Xena with a scathing stare. "Why are you here?" I spat at her. "Shouldn't you be tending to your great-grandfather or whatever the hell he is to you?"

"Ava." Cole's tone held a warning, but when I looked at him, he couldn't hold my gaze. He knew as well as I did that what Xena did was wrong. She should have told us.

She couldn't be trusted. I was a fool to ever think otherwise.

"Get out," I said.

Xena opened her mouth to speak, then closed it. She left without a word.

Maybe I was lashing out at the wrong person, but I didn't care. She'd set up the meeting, so she was at least partially to blame.

But Xena's words echoed in my mind long after she'd left, long after Bill had come home, long after my mom refused to come out of her room.

I couldn't deny the truth in them.

She didn't want to be saved.

COLE STAYED THE NIGHT, AND Bill whisked him away to have a stern talking with him man-to-man before he was allowed in my room. If not for the circumstances, it would have been funny—Bill puffing up his chest and Cole turning bright red. It was nice to have a father figure, though it was a little weird that Bill was a father figure for *both* of us.

Bill needn't have worried, though. Romance was definitely not in the air tonight.

Even Cole's strong arms around me couldn't stop the whirring of my mind. Long after his breathing had grown steady beside me and his limbs became limp, I lay awake.

He and I hadn't talked much about what happened. Well, we'd told Bill everything, but only the facts. Neither one of us was ready to get into the important stuff—like how we felt about it or what it meant. We were both shell-shocked, silently watching the evening news to see if the incident was reported. How long had Xavier been down? Long enough for paramedics to get to him? I didn't care other than how it would affect my family. I didn't want the "crime" to be traced back to Bill since it was his gun or Cole since he drove us in the Rustinator.

Calling it a "crime" though was far-fetched. It was closer to justice and it even fell miles short of that.

I could only assume Xavier survived. Maybe he was there when the paramedics arrived. Maybe he had somehow hauled his bloody, broken body away before they could get there.

Either way, I hoped his healing powers wouldn't be enough to fix his mutilated face. I hoped he would bear the scars my mother inflicted for the rest of his miserable existence.

We certainly bore more than our share.

Finally around four a.m., I slipped out of bed, quietly closing the door behind me so I wouldn't wake Cole. I wrapped my arms around myself, immediately feeling his absence. Perhaps I should have stayed in bed, reveling in the feel of Cole's body against mine. This day sure had taken unexpected turns.

I stumbled into the kitchen. My mom sat at the table cradling a mug in her hands. Her back was toward me, and I debated scurrying away before she realized I was there. But she looked over her shoulder at me. Her eyes were bloodshot. She'd been crying the tears I couldn't muster.

I stood across from her. "How could you?" My tone was biting, causing her to flinch, but I didn't care. "You know what this means."

I couldn't bring myself to say the words—*that you'll die.* My gaze strayed to the refrigerator where we had ten doses of medicine.

Ten doses, ten weeks to live.

"You'll be okay."

"You don't know that," I retorted. "You sure as hell can't make any promises because you won't be around to keep them!"

She slammed her mug down on the table.

"*Ava!*" She said my name like I was a toddler who'd gotten caught sneaking cookies, not a surly teenager who'd said one of the worst, most hurtful things I could think of.

I sank down into the chair. "How could you?" This time, my tone was pleading. I needed to understand.

"Would you really have given Xavier a name?" she asked.

I stuck my chin out. "Yes."

"Every month for the rest of my life?"

"You know I would."

She leaned back in her chair. "That's why I had to do it. Because I know you. And I know what it would cost you to do that. And my life isn't worth it."

"Yes, it is!" A sob escaped my throat as my anger faded away to despair and frustration.

She shook her head. "We don't even know what he's doing with the names, but it's not good. I know that much at least. Could you live with contributing to whatever he's doing?"

My chin quivered and I opened my mouth to tell her I could, to tell her I could and would do whatever it took to save her.

But the words wouldn't come out.

She reached across the table to squeeze my hand. "I didn't want you to be forced to make that choice. I wouldn't be able to bear watching what it would do to your soul and knowing I could have stopped it before it began. And it's just not right. I'm one person."

The same argument could be said for me, that *I* was

one person. How many names did she give Xavier over the years in order to keep me safe?

But I didn't ask this. I'd already said too many hurtful things.

"Are you hungry?" she asked. "Can I make you some tea?"

The answer to both questions was no, but looking at her tear-filled eyes, I didn't have the heart to deny her the privilege of doing something for me, which she desperately seemed to need to do.

So I nodded. "Breakfast sounds great."

She released my hand and as she turned away to walk to the refrigerator, I wiped the tears out of my eyes so I was ready with a smile when she faced me.

I let her take care of me, even though I so badly wanted to fix everything for her, to ensure she'd be able to take care of me for as long as she wanted to.

But life didn't work that way.

So instead, I'd soak up everything I could in the next ten weeks.

Hopefully it would be enough to last a lifetime.

COLE SAT ON THE EDGE of the bed, resting his elbows on his knees. He was bleary-eyed, shirtless, and more handsome than he had any right to be.

I shut the door behind me and leaned against it.

"You talked to your mom." He picked at the ever-present motor oil stuck under his nails. It used to gross me out when I'd see that on men's hands. Now my two very favorite guys in the world sported it, so the sight of it was comforting. A constant.

"Yeah."

He looked up at me and his eyes met mine. No words were needed. He simply opened his arms and I walked into them, sinking down onto the bed with him.

"You've got me and Bill," he said. "You'll get through this."

I nodded mutely, clinging to him. I appreciated that he didn't say it would be okay. Because it wouldn't. But I guessed you sometimes had to learn to live with that.

The clock on the wall caught my eye. Almost seven a.m.

"Are you going to school?" I asked.

"I have to," he replied. "I'm out of days. How about you?"

"My mom wants me to. She wants everything to continue on like normal."

Normal...I was really beginning to hate that word.

I allowed myself a few more moments of Cole's comfort before reluctantly pulling away. I picked up my phone from the nightstand to check for messages as I always did in the morning. There was a voice mail from Xena.

My finger hovered over the delete button.

"What is it?" Cole asked.

"A message from Xena."

"You should listen to it."

As much as I wanted nothing to do with her, he was right.

I hit play.

"Ava, I know you don't want to hear from me right now, but there's something you need to know. No one except us knows that Cole is a seeker. Well, us and Xavier. For his sake, try to keep it that way. As long as no one knows...you know what that means. He can live a normal life."

There was a pause in the message and elation filled me. *Finally.* Something was going to be okay. Sure, Cole would see auras for the rest of his life, but that was a small thing. Soon blocking them would be second nature.

I closed my eyes. *I didn't mess up his life after all.*

I'd almost forgotten I was still holding the phone to

my face when I heard Xena's voice again.

"Considering everything that's happened, I've been removed from your case. You'll get a new handler soon. I'll try to delay it as long as I can, but no promises."

My fingers shook as I ended the call.

"What's going on?" Cole asked, alarm in his voice.

"Nothing," I said as smoothly as I could manage. "She's just checking in."

Cole's brow furrowed. He wasn't buying my lie.

"I need to shower," I said quickly, turning my back on him and exiting the room.

I locked myself in the bathroom, putting my fist up to my mouth to keep from screaming. *One step forward, two steps back.*

What were the odds a new handler would be as chill as Xena about certain things? Like keeping Cole's status as a seeker a secret?

Probably not too good.

I wasn't about to let another person I cared about be forced to suffer because of me. It was too late for me to save my mom, but I wouldn't fail here. Cole would have a normal life if I had anything to do with it. He'd be able to take in his brother, which was what he'd been working toward for the last year. I owed him that, at least.

So I would have to keep that handler away from Cole.

Which meant I'd have to keep Cole away from me.

EPILOGUE

IT WAS COLE'S GRADUATION DAY, but I didn't sit in the school stadium to watch him walk across the stage in a stupid-looking hat. Instead I stood knee-deep in the ocean, clutching an urn full of ashes.

Clutching my mom.

A sob escaped my mouth and the salty wind mixed with the salt of my tears.

I hadn't cried at the service. There was only a handful of people there—Bill, Cole, Shenice, Kaley, and a few co-workers from the last job she'd had.

It was nothing like the funerals of the kids I'd had a part in killing. They'd been overflowing with people and raw grief.

My mom's had been short, somber, and to the point. She hadn't wanted anything elaborate. In fact, she hadn't wanted anything at all, but I think she was worried I wouldn't get closure without a service.

Closure was holding the last physical reminder of my mom's time on Earth in my hands.

The water lapped at my knees. Though it was June, the temperature was low and it didn't take long for my teeth to chatter.

If I looked over my right shoulder, I knew I'd see Shenice hovering near the dunes. I'd said I wanted to do this alone, but Shenice refused to comply with my wishes. She kept her distance but was close enough I knew she was there if I needed her.

I kind of liked that. My mom never met Shenice, but she would have liked her.

I pulled the lid off the urn and some particles of dust got caught up in the breeze, flying out over the ocean. I wanted to reach out and retrieve them.

But deep down, I knew those cinders and the ashes I held in my hands weren't my mom. Her soul was already gone. I hoped she'd made it into heaven, but I doubted it.

Seekers didn't deserve heaven.

Perhaps her soul would find peace in its next life. I was still fuzzy on how all of that worked.

I reached into the urn and my fingers mixed with the ashes of a mother who'd had the odds stacked against her but who'd done her best.

I was her legacy now.

I let the ashes fly into the wind. They landed in the water, the ebb and flow of the ocean accepting them into its tide.

My tears dried as I watched every little piece disappear for good.

Then I turned and walked purposefully toward Shenice. She waited for me.

"I want to find other seekers," I said without preamble.

"Why?" she wanted to know.

Because I still needed to know the truth, because I needed a mission to keep me going, because I was alone.

Or I would be soon.

I'd tried to start pulling away from Cole, but I was finding it difficult to keep my promise to myself, to protect him from the life of a seeker. I was weak. Every day I'd tell myself *just one more day. I'll give myself just one more day with him.* I'd never find the strength to set him free unless I physically removed myself from his life.

And now that my mom was gone, I had no reason to stick around. I'd miss Bill, but Cole needed him more than I did. He could help Cole with his brother.

"Will you help me?" I asked.

She sighed. "What makes you think I'll be able to find them? You and Cole look just like every other human I've ever seen."

"You might not be able to pick out seekers," I said, "but you can identify fallen angels, which means you can find the handlers. They'll lead us to the seekers."

My new handler still hadn't shown, but once or twice I'd caught a glimpse of Xena hovering in the distance. I guessed she was staying true to her word and delaying my new handler's arrival.

I should be grateful to her for that. But mainly, I was still angry. Angry and still tired of the lies and deception.

Shenice's mouth twisted and she crossed her arms. "It seems to me you're looking for trouble."

Maybe. Maybe not.

"Will you help me?" I asked again, not deterred.

"After you're eighteen and done with school," she said.

"Promise?"

She nodded. "Yes."

I regarded her for a moment, determining if she'd stay true to her word. When I was satisfied, I nodded back and turned to stare at the ocean. Shenice didn't know, but I was scheduled to take the GED test next month. And she must not have looked at my employment documents too closely or she'd know I had an early birthday and would turn eighteen in three short weeks.

I might be looking for trouble, but I liked to think I was finishing what my mom started when she stood up to Xavier.

Nothing in this world was infallible, not even Xavier. I would find his weakness and use it against him.

And when he ceased to exist, he would go out knowing

I was the one who ended him.

Thank you for reading *Retribution*! I hope you enjoyed it. If you did, please help other readers find this book by telling your friends and leaving a review on Amazon, Goodreads, or your favorite book retailer. Word of mouth and reviews help authors more than you know!

ACKNOWLEDGEMENTS

Writing is a solitary endeavor, but no author does it alone.

A special thank you to my biggest champion, my husband. Sometimes I think you believe in my dreams more than I do.

To my children—you inspire me every day. Your pride in me and my books warms my heart.

A special thank you to my editor, Judy Roth. You are a wonder woman.

To my writer friends—Marnee, Terri, the Dreamweavers, the NAC, #TeamSarah, and countless others that I'm forgetting—your friendship means so much to me. There are no words.

ABOUT THE AUTHOR

 Jessica lives in Virginia with her college-sweetheart husband, two rambunctious sons, and two rowdy but lovable rescue dogs. Since her house is overflowing with testosterone, it's a good thing she has a healthy appreciation for Marvel movies, Nerf guns, and football.

To learn more about Jessica, visit her website jessicaruddick.com. Connect with her on Twitter at @JessicaMRuddick or on Facebook at facebook.com/AuthorJessicaRuddick.

Other Books by Jessica Ruddick

Birthright: The Legacy Series, Book One
Letting Go (Love on Campus #1)
Wanting More (Love on Campus #2)

CPSIA information can be obtained
at www.ICGtesting.com
Printed in the USA
LVOW07s1404300717
543157LV00001B/50/P